Joseph Tome... ...s of Strangford Lough, Coun... ...welve became apprenticed t... ...le. He won a scholarship to The Tech in Belfast to finish his apprenticeship, and it was around this time that he began to develop his interest in writing and acting.

A distinguished career as an actor was to follow, with appearances in such films as *Odd Man Out* (part of which is set in Belfast's Crown Bar), but he is probably best remembered for his performances as Bobby Greer in *The McCooeys*, the radio serial he wrote for the BBC for seven years.

Amongst his works for the theatre are the comedies *Right Again Barnum* and *Mugs and Money*, both inspired by the actress Min Milligan (whose daughter he was to marry!), *Is the Priest at Home?*, *The End House*, and *All Souls Night*, now regarded as an Ulster classic.

Red is the Port Light was his first novel, published in 1948. His second novel, *The Apprentice* (1953), was reissued by The Blackstaff Press in 1983.

A tragic car crash in 1955 all but ended his acting career and severely curtailed his writing output. He now lives in County Louth, with his wife. They have two daughters, Frances and Roma, both distinguished actresses, and four grandchildren.

RED IS THE
PORT LIGHT

RED IS THE PORT LIGHT

Joseph Tomelty

THE
BLACKSTAFF
PRESS

First published in 1948 by Jonathan Cape Limited
This Blackstaff Press edition is a photolithographic facsimile
of the first edition printed at the Alden Press and is
unabridged with the exception of the preliminary pages.

First paperback edition published in 1983
by The Blackstaff Press
3 Galway Park, Dundonald, Belfast BT16 0AN
with the assistance of
The Arts Council of Northern Ireland

British Library Cataloguing in Publication Data

Tomelty, Joseph
Red is the port light.
I. Title
823'.914[F]   PR6039.O347

ISBN 0–85640–299–0

To

H. L. MORROW

FOREWORD

Thirty-six years ago Joe Tomelty wrote a short story called 'Dancing Dog'. Before me here I have a copy of the periodical in which the story appeared, the issue for September 1947 of *The Irish Bookman*, which was then being produced under the management of Father Senan Moynihan and the editorship of J.J. (Seamus) Campbell – both now gone from us. Another reason why I recall the date of publication so exactly is that it coincided with the first time I ever encountered the author.

That encounter took place on the platform of Amiens Street Station, as it was then called, and David Kennedy of Queen's University was also of the party, and while Campbell went off to do some work with Senan, Tomelty, Kennedy and myself did the town. That was a day to remember. In Webb's on the quays, now one of the last resorts left to bookmen in Dublin, I discovered a first edition of Joseph Campbell's *The Mountainy Singer* and a copy of Patrick MacGill's great comic novel *Lanty Hanlon*. Joe Tomelty I also discovered, and his knowledge, wisdom, piety and the fear of God; and, above all, his non-stop all-embracing good humour. Indeed in parts of two continents I have somewhat dishonestly acquired a mild reputation as a humorous man simply by retelling some of the stories I heard from Joe Tomelty on that memorable day, even to the story of the lady who was announced as being about to sing, at a concert in St Mary's Hall, 'The Bonnie Bonnie Banks of Loch Lomond'.

But about that other story, the one that was printed in 1947. It clicks into place in my mind with one of my favourite Chekhov stories: the one about the travelling salesman with the performing dog and sow and goose (was it a goose?). The Russian master tells you what happened almost as the dog saw it. The Tomelty story is told by a man who has been in the travelling show business, and told about another showman who was out on his own for having a way with dogs: the only man, it was claimed, who ever taught a dog to smoke a cigar. The circus people call the trainer Voogoo, a mispronunciation of Voodoo, and the narrator discovers, in a pub in Barrow-in-Furness, that the dog, called Corona, because of the cigars, has also been trained to buy a round of drinks:

When Voogoo shouted at the barmaid to bring three gills of bitter I wondered who the third drink was for. But when we sat down in the snug, Voogoo took a little enamel dish from his pocket, emptied the gill of beer into it and gave it to Corona. Corona scoffed it off in about three licks. When I had stood my round, Voogoo took a half-dollar from his pocket and gave it to the dog. The dog took the coin between his little toes and jumped onto the counter, giving three loud bow-wows.

For three more beers, of course, for those were the days when a halfcrown meant money and not, as now, a mocking memory.

Now in that story, 'Dancing Dog', Joe Tomelty was not, as you might too readily think, giving us another shaggy dog story. No, he was giving us the benefit of his knowledge of the odd corners of life and his sympathy for the people who inoffensively inhabit them; and that same knowledge and sympathy infuse, in varying degrees, his stage plays and his novels, *The Apprentice* and *Red is the Port Light*.

The cover on the recent and most successful new edition of *The Apprentice* (published by The Blackstaff Press) is a reproduction of a fine painting by Gerard Dillon. It shows four house-painters having a break from their work in a room suitably denuded for their attentions, and is a most careful arrangement of colour and exact form and, on behalf of Gerard Dillon, displays affectionate memory. For before he became that sort of painter, he had tried his hand at the other sort of painting. As had Joe Tomelty before he took to the stage and

2

the screen, and the writing of plays and novels; and the apprentice of that novel is a Belfast boy, in the years between the Kaiser war and the Hitler war, leaving school at the age of fourteen to serve his time to the painting trade. We follow him through the five years until he comes perilously and painfully to the threshold of manhood and, God help him, few young fellows were ever less cut-out to be heroes and, right from the start, he seems to need all the sympathy that we or the novelist can afford him.

To begin with, there is the schoolmaster who grudgingly writes him a sort of reference and roars at him to wash his hands before he touches the paper it is written on:

'Fourteen years of age,' said the master, 'and two hands higher than a duck. The Corporation had better watch out or you might sue them for bumping your bottom on the pavement.' He laughed, but closed his mouth suddenly as his false teeth dropped.

Then, since the boy has a bad halt in his speech, the master advises him also to take refuge in the thought that Napoleon was a crowl of a man. And so casts him out on the world; an orphan who lives under the tyranny of an aunt who passes her own misery on to him. Like most of us the boy has his dreams, and his ideas on everything from God to girls, and he survives because of them and because of a few good friends, inside and outside the trade: a group of real Belfast people, Orange and Green, beautifully drawn by a writer who knows and understands them. Not all beautiful, though, and I cannot resist quoting the description of the prefect of the confraternity who is one of the many plagues that afflict the young fellow:

He was a smallish man with a bald head; his eyes looked as though he was always crying, his nose was crooked and his chin shot down like the tongue of a boot. When he laughed, his upper lip almost disappeared, and his long chin reached up to the point of his crooked nose. He had a peculiar way of walking, as if he used the sides of his feet. He attended all the Gaelic classes and could speak Irish; he was never known to curse or drink; and was in all the sodalities and confraternities connected with the church. Every Saturday he collected for the black babies, and every Sunday for the white babies. Sally Blair's father had called him a 'religious informer'. It was said that he was in everything connected with the church except the crib at Christmas.

Yet the poor fellow's sudden death takes a tear from us and he becomes absorbed in Tomelty's universal sympathy, as wide as the world and Wanderaway. It is at its most embracing in the novel which is here before us and which is well able to speak for itself. But since it happens to be one of my favourite contemporary Irish novels, I cannot resist the vanity of linking my name with its most welcome reappearance.

Just as a simple matter of technical skill it would be difficult to surpass the precision and economy of the opening chapters. Perhaps the skilled playwright is at work here, conscious that no commodity may be more recklessly wasted than words. Within the turning of a few pages we know Stephen Durnan, who doesn't know where he came from, and his sad, sin-haunted mother, and we see the little houses of the Ards and every detail of the landscape – and the sea. That vision of the Ards was something of a revelation to me when I first read the novel, a vision strengthened and expanded by the reading of Sam Hanna Bell's *December Bride*.

We are perturbed, too, by an uneasy irony, the fragment of the old ballad of Rambleaway, which I prefer as one word, the harbourmaster's throwaway lines about the fine, free life of the sailor, spoken to a man who is bound by galling bonds: and sad Stephen, the homeless, is moved beyond measure by the hope of home that his innocent eye sees in the glow of the portlight. For if we should feel at any moment inclined to argue that Fate too relentlessly impels the young sailor, then we should reflect that innocence and the world about it are capable, all too capable, of making odd couplings.

But the great triumph of the novel is the creation of Robert and Susan and their odd home, the *Summer Breeze*, and the one-legged seagull that Susan has spoiled: and their faith and love. It was away beyond happiness to meet them again on this rereading. They have a lesson for the North and Ireland and the whole sad world. Let me quote Robert, for he is worth listening to over and over again:

'Susie never mentioned religion to me since the day and hour we were married. She taught me prayers, the only ones she knew. You know, Stephen, at sea people don't feel the same about religion as they do on land. On the land they never seem to find God, so they must fight about Him all the time. But at sea you can see Him everywhere, in the water, in the moon, in the stars, and you can hear Him in the wind . . . He's always there, like a strong but silent friend.'

Benedict Kiely
September 1983

CHAPTER ONE

STEPHEN DURNAN had just come into the church porch, and was about to dip his fingers in the water font when Sandy Killops, the gravedigger, caught his arm.

'My brother Jacob says she's short handed, if you'd care for the job,' he whispered loudly.

Durnan withdrew his fingers from the water and, mechanically touching his forehead and chest, looked at the gravedigger with a questioning expression. The gravedigger peered into Durnan's face. 'The *Glendry*. She's discharging coal at the quay right now. The lamp trimmer's left her. His wife took bad,' he whispered.

Durnan remembered the steamer at the quay, but he made no answer to the gravedigger. He touched the water with his fingers again, crossed himself and came into the church, pausing, before he walked to the front seat, to glance at the handful of people who had come to see his mother buried.

He knelt down, and for a time the shivering reflections of the altar candles on the brass breastplate of the coffin made his head spin. Then the vestry door opened with a squeal and the priest crossed the altar steps and motioned to Durnan that he was ready for the burial.

They carried the coffin along the gravel path and lowered it into the soft, squelchy, clay grave.

Durnan was dazed, but the slaps of the spades on the wet red clay brought him back, and the sucking sounds went through him like cold smacks.

His mother's funeral, her coffin covered, the clay bleeding its brown blood over the breastplate, flattening itself on the coffin lid, until the thudding stopped and, as the grave was filled, each spadeful kissed until all melted together.

The gravedigger scraped the last of the clay from the bank,

the wiregrass holding it as the tattered hair of a woman might hold a comb.

'I can get no more from it,' he said, resting his spade against the next tombstone. He lit his pipe. 'I hope you didn't mind me making mention of the job, and you on such an errand,' he said to Durnan.

'My brother Jacob said it would suit you.' Turning, the gravedigger motioned his brother towards him.

'I've just been telling Stephen here about the job.'

'Have you now?' said the small fat man. 'I would have waited until he was leaving the chapel yard. But now that it's done it's as well now, I suppose, as any time.'

'Let the two of you walk home together, and you can tell him about it,' the gravedigger said, cleaning his spade with a pointed stone.

Jacob groaned as he bent to clean the clay from his button boots. He was the harbourmaster, a small barrel of a man. Tossing over his shoulders the wisp of grass he had used for cleaning his boots, he said to Durnan, 'If you are walking towards the town, I'll be company for you.'

Durnan reached a crumpled ten shilling note to the grave-digger. The gravedigger spat on it, and fumbled beneath his bag apron for his trouser pocket.

'My brother Andy is a bit loose in the mouth. He couldn't keep his own wind,' said Jacob as they passed out through the chapel gates. 'I wasn't going to mention the job to you until later. But you must know that Andy's ignorant. He's at the right job, the gravedigging. His true vocation. But would the job suit you?'

'What job?'

'Lamp trimmer on the *Glendry*. Wilson, the mate, asked me if I knew of anyone, so I thought of you. Don't think it un-christian of me to suggest it. I felt that you might want to forget your mother's death, and I know the remedy is get back to sea at once.' The harbourmaster paused for breath.

'You're right, maybe, Jacob,' Durnan said.

'I know a thing or two, not like that oaf we left in the graveyard. You wouldn't think the same man fathered us both at all.'

'What's the *Glendry* like, Jacob?'

'She belongs to Polton Brothers of Cardiff. A bit pushed. But
sure, what firm nowadays don't push their ships hell for leather?'

'Is she a good sea boat?'

The harbourmaster unbuttoned his waistcoat. Wiping his
face with his hand he went on: 'I would think she isn't the best
of a sea boat. A bit too long in the hatch for my taste. But she'd
do for a time until you'd get a bird's-eye view of the Liverpool
docks. Couldn't you jump her for a deep sea berth if the notion
took you?'

'Yes, I suppose you're right.'

'I know you're the same turn as myself. When I was your age,
Stephen, there was no hanging about for me. Up and away to
sea every time.' The harbourmaster puffed his jaws at this.

'Yes, that's true,' Durnan said quietly.

'True,' exclaimed the harbourmaster, 'you could swear on any
bible you like, authorized or otherwise. I had a Dutch woman in
Bordeaux when I was seventeen. Not, mind you, that that's
anything to have on your tombstone. But it shows you I wasn't
letting the moss grow about my feet.'

Durnan lit a cigarette, and the old man bent his head, breathing
loudly. They walked slowly towards the town. The harbourmaster pushed a handkerchief under his shirt and wiped his
sweating chest. Durnan could hear his wheezing breath, hoars-
ing its repetitions. 'I know you're like myself. You have no
ties. No women to greet after you. You're not a fireside hugger,
nor a dry land sailor either. Amn't I right?' Half way up Jack's
Brae, Durnan felt the old man grip his arm. 'Don't walk so fast,
Stephen.' He tapped his naked chest. 'It's asthma. God above,
but it'll lay me low one of these days.' Regaining his breath,
Durnan took his arm as they climbed slowly up the hill.

The old man paused again, and pointed across the fields to the
town. The fields slid gently down, and the rows of hawthorn

9

seemed to peg them lest they should slide into the sea. 'There she is,' said the harbourmaster, pointing towards the quay.

Durnan stood up on the ditch, for the latticed view of the ship through the hedge did not satisfy him. Her long black funnel with its white letter P looked about to fall, so acute was its rake to her bow.

'When is she leaving?'

'About twelve, or thereabouts, tomorrow. They should have her cleared by then, and it's as near high water as makes no difference,' said the harbourmaster.

Again they walked on. The soft slaps of the spades smoothing the clay kept pulsing in Durnan's mind.

'Come into Jane's and we'll have a half'un,' said the old man as they entered the village street.

A bell tinged as he opened the door, and Jane Whorry, the owner of the pub, came down the long hall, her flat awkward feet shuffling along in her loose slippers.

'Good afternoon, men,' she said.

'Two half'uns from the black bottle, Jane,' said the harbourmaster.

'No, no, Jane; it's on me,' Durnan added quickly.

'Pay no heed to this fella. It's on me,' said the old man.

When Jane poured the whisky, she started swabbing the counter in front of the men with a damp cloth.

'You've see the last of your mother, Stephen,' she said.

'I have.'

'In a way, you won't miss her. I mean you were never that often at home. I never see you but I don't think of the song "Ramble Away".'

A smile came as she sang in a squealy voice, shaking her head to keep time:

> Ramble away, ramble away,
> Are you the young man
> They call Ramble Away?

A whistling kettle in the kitchen made her excuse herself, but not before she had refilled the drinks.

'Am I to tell the mate you'll join her?' the harbourmaster asked.

'Where is she going to?'

'I dunno. Likely Aberdeen, Whitehaven or maybe Maryport.'

'Yes . . . I'll . . . Yes, I'll join her.'

'Fetch your bag and stores aboard in the morning, and I'll away now, and tell the mate.'

'Have another drink before you go?' said Durnan.

'Not now, maybe tomorrow. Enough's as good as a feast, the old man said, making for the door.

Jane returned. 'You'll have a drink on me, Stephen?' she said.

'No, thanks, Jane, I've had enough.'

'Nonsense, man. Your mother was a good grocery customer of mine, and you must have a drink on account of what day it is.'

'Did she owe you any money, Jane?'

'What your mother owed me, son, won't keep her from God's sunshine.'

'How much was it?'

'Away out of this man, and not bother me.'

'But, Jane, you know I'm an odd fella and I'd like to pay it. That's how I feel. . . .'

'Well, if I must tell you, it is a shilling. A silver shilling that never reared anybody. She owed it to me for salt. She was saving a few dozen herrings for the winter, and she was without her purse the day she got it.'

Durnan paid the shilling, and Jane poured its value of whisky into his glass. 'Now, I've got my own way, after all,' she laughed.

The door opened and the postman entered. Taking three letters from his bag, he let the bag fall to the floor.

Durnan glanced at the letters in front of him. One of them was to Captain F. Norton, *S.S. Glendry*, Portaferry. Suddenly he remembered the raking funnel and its white P. Polton of Cardiff; that was the firm he had heard Norton was with.

'What are you drinking?' asked the postman.

'Nothing, thank you all the same.'

He must get home; if he stayed the schoolmaster and the gravedigger would come in, and he might get drunk.

As he made to go the postman caught his arm.

'I was passing your way,' said the postman, 'and your goat was in agony to be milked. I couldn't see anyone about the cottage, so I milked her to the ground.'

'You did the wise thing,' said Durnan. He had forgotten about the goat with the fuss of the funeral, but he wondered why Susan King had not milked her.

'Tell me,' said the postman, 'if it isn't a nosey question on my part. You wouldn't think of selling her? My youngest is mad for a goat.'

This was the first reminder of the empty cottage; a lonely goat crying to be milked. Now he was going back to sea again; but he could not leave the goat at large.

'You can have the goat,' he told the postman.

'How much?'

'Nothing, only be good to her.'

'But dammit, man, you must take something; even it's only a glass of whisky.'

'No, nothing.'

'Not even a packet of fags?'

Durnan shook his head. Now and then his eyes went to the letter addressed to Captain Norton.

'Holy God, man, you must have something. . . .'

'No, nothing. I'm going back to sea tomorrow and . . .'

'When can I get her?'

'Any time between this and tomorrow forenoon.'

The bell tinged again. Durnan came out and walked along the shore road to his cottage.

CHAPTER TWO

ON one side of the road the little houses rested shoulder to shoulder. They were barn shaped, and sparrows and blue tits flitted about the moss margins on the slates.

There were straws and streaks of droppings about the eaves, marking where the sandmartins had nested earlier in the year. Durnan's eyes caught the crooked windows, and he glanced at the old women stretching their heads coaxingly to the light, stitching rapidly the flowers on the linen handkerchiefs that brought them their bread; stitching with their mouths mumping, eager to finish a cloth before darkness came.

Passing the house of a bachelor he could see, on the flat window sills, newly tarred bladders, pieces of burnt cork and sail needles with slanting eyes that gaped like the mouths of goldfish.

The white road was swept dry by the October wind and its face was crisp. In the opening where the small slip started, he saw empty limpet shells and lifeless starfish. On the other side of the road was the wall that kept the sea from washing over the doorsteps of the villages, and beyond it was the sea. Behind him, he could hear the steamer's winch grumble as it lifted the iron tubs of coal and crashed them into the carts that were backed close to its side.

The row of houses finished with a gable resting against a mass of stones that reached to its chimney; it was the end of the main street of Portaferry.

Now he was on the open road, with the sea on one side and the rough red banks on the other. He kept looking out to sea until he rounded the bend. Then he turned his head to the banks. These banks were lifeless. Never once, in all the years he had passed them on his way to school, had he ever seen a bird, a mouse, a rat or a rabbit about them. They looked as if some great cloud had vomited them from the sky.

Some day, he thought, the water licking and seeping under the muddy road would topple them into the sea. This had always been one of his nightmares; these banks crashing down on top of him. Even now as he turned into the loanen that led to his home, he shuddered.

His feet squelched the soft mud of the loanen face; and he bent now and then to tear the bracken that clung to his knees. It was wise of Robert King to 'advise them to carry his mother's coffin through the field to the road, for they never could have kept their feet in the loanen.

Near the gable of the cottage he saw the hoof tracks of the goat, flooded with blue milk.

Inside the cottage the fire sizzled, and grey beards of sap bubbled from the logs that Susan King had built under the kettle.

He entered the small room that ran from the kitchen. Susan had not yet stripped the bed of its death clothes. The broad creases where the coffin head had rested were marked strongly on the white pillow. On the table was the saucer of salt that they had placed on her chest. A dead fly lay in the middle of it, one of its wings catching the light, making it translucent like a scale from a herring. He opened the window and with a sigh the salt was scattered into the hedge. Then he peeled the shiny sheets from the bed; they felt icy cold, making him feel there was life in them, for they seemed to want to fold themselves. It was strange now to look at the grey tick with the whiteness gone from it, as if snow had melted.

He made some tea and stretched himself on the sofa, listening to the hissing of the logs. It was not loud, this hissing. It was restful. Almost a soft nervous sighing, like the tune of the grasshopper. Slowly his mind became active again, and he thought of his new job.

He would have to pack his bag and get some food, but there did not seem to be any urgency about it. It would give him a break to get away from the cottage, until it was free from the death atmosphere. Susan King could clean it out for him, and he could come back to it in a month's time for a good rest. The

Glendry was only a coaster; a couple of shirts, a few pairs of socks, dungarees and a suit for knocking about in, were all the clothes he needed.

What odds if Norton was the skipper? He had told the truth regarding Norton, so let him do his worst. No, Norton was not worth thinking about.

He felt his eyes closing, and the hissing of the logs was uppermost in his mind again. If his mother were alive, she would spoon this sap into an egg cup and drink it for her asthma.

But she was dead, her flesh cold as the white sheets he pulled from the bed. He was not sorry she was dead.

It had been a strange association. That's what it was, an association. There was no other word for it.

She had ceased to mean anything to him since he was thirteen, and the years before that made him unhappy to think about them.

She had never told him anything about himself, and now he was sorry, not because death had wrapped her in a brown shroud, but because she had left his life gaping, empty, unhappy. His soul had stored nothing but the ash tree that scratched the gable wall of the cottage, the stream that wrinkled to the sea, the brown banks and the huge stone that the heron cried from.

These things fed his longing in the moments when he lay in his bunk and closed his eyes; moments when other sailors would say they were thinking of their homes. He felt there might be a streak of madness in him. The madness that comes from the loneliness of the soul, for why should he recall to his mind such things? Why should the hoarse cursing groan of a heron have music for him?

There were no other ties. It seemed as if he were the child of another parent, and that someone, the moment he was born, had laid him in the bed of the woman he knew as his mother.

When he had watched the goat giving birth to her kid he had thought, as he looked at the string that curved from the goat to the kid, that this tie had been absent when he was born. As if he had not come out of her body at all. Strange, that that should happen on the day that Baxter, a schoolfellow, had shouted loudly in the playground, 'Durnan's a by-blow, a by-blow.'

He had hurried home to ask, 'What's a by-blow, Mother?' He remembered her eyes bulging, frightening him, and the glassy needles of spit that clung to her parting lips, and the gnarled blue-veined hand that swept the needles away.

'What's a by-blow, Mother?' he had repeated.

She dropped her head, and her hand fell, almost spilling the jug of buttermilk on the table, and she told him in an angry voice to fetch the goat to the hill for a mouthful of clover.

He knew he had said something wrong. It exploded in his mind, when at the mountain foot the kid came from the goat.

He had asked the teacher in the school, 'What's a by-blow, Sir?'

The teacher laughed suddenly and said a by-blow was a poffer.

'And what's a poffer, sir?'

'A poffer is an elephant's trunk stuffed with soldiers' buttons and served with mustard.' He remembered the teacher laughing until his false teeth dropped. Then he said, 'If I get you asking questions like that again, I'll cut the skin of you with the cane.'

Then one day he was sheltering from the rain in the red banks, when a priest bent in and said, 'It's a heavy shower, son, but it'll soon blow by.'

Looking into the sky, he watched the rain-ragged clouds drift towards Slieve Donard, and again the priest said, 'It's blowing by, son, it's blowing by.'

The words had twisted into a little rhyme in his head: blowing by, blowing by, blow by, blow by, by-blow, by-blow.

'Father, what is a by-blow?'

'A by-blow, son, is . . . What age are you?'

'Thirteen, father.'

'A by-blow, son, is a phrase, a dialect phrase for a child born out of wedlock. It is common in Northern Ireland speech, and, indeed, you'll hear it used in parts of England and Scotland.'

'What is wedlock, father?'

'Now, now, son, the shower has blown over. Go home like a good little man and do your homework and don't hamper your young mind with questions such as that. Ask the names of trees and birds and flowers, but not nasty things.'

Then in the school when the master had told him to shift the roll books, when he opened one, he read:

> Robert Blake, father's occupation, baker.
> James Jordan, father's occupation, thresher.
> Richard Killen, father's occupation, sailor.
> Stephen Durnan, father's occupation, ————

There was just a stroke of the pen. From then he knew. From then started his unhappiness. What was it? Was it his undeveloped soul longing for something to cling to? Was it broken, without pattern? This searching for a framework of things. A picture, even a likeness in a shell-clustered frame.

She should have told him, instead of repeating it, night after night, to God, through her whistly prayers. On her knees on the cold flags of the kitchen floor, she had asked God to forgive her this awful sin.

He was the sin that sent her rosary beads moving through her gnarled fingers.

Now she was dead, and her sin lived on in him. Was she now before God telling Him of how she had fallen? Did God look down from His heaven at him, as he threw the heaving lines over the bows of the ships he sailed in? Did God say: there is sin throwing that line?

Who was he, mother, my father? Was he big? Was he wee? Was he a drunkard? Was he a thief? Was he a wandering tinker or tramp? Was he stupid or clever? But never a word, always the moving lips and the travelling rosary beads.

How did it happen? Were you a servant maid? Did you sleep

with him? Did he promise you marriage? But never a word. Just the wide eyes glazed with tears, and the poker in her hand, prodding little squares from the burning logs.

He recalled the long voyage from Iceland when his ship was reported missing, and how he came back home and put fifty pounds in her lap as she sat by the fire toasting bread. He remembered how her face had reddened and the look of simplicity in her eyes, and again as she fingered the money he asked her, now, mother, who was he? Did he jilt you? Were you just a woman he met, a pick up?

Throwing the money on the table, she cried out, 'Why must you question me? I've fallen just as another. I'm crying to God in His great mercy to forgive me. Be a son and comfort me, not throw the red shame of sin into my face. I'm no street walker, nor no whore, I fell once. God in His almighty heart forgive me. . . .'

Again, just a week ago, as she lay on her death bed, in a voice soft with coaxing he had asked her. But she had lain with her frosted forehead pale, and her waxy fingers moving as if to rub the brass Christ from the cross she held, and praying loud, her voice groaning in her throat, until it softly stuttered the sigh of death.

But she was dead and the dead should rest. God, he knew, filled her life, filled the space and perhaps the yearning for the man whose child she bore.

CHAPTER THREE

'ARE you within at all?'
The voice startled him, and he got to his feet.
'I'm here, Susan,' he said.
'What fondness have you for the gloom of the evening, and death barely left the house, or have you no lamp oil?' asked Susan

King, as she hobbled to the fire. Bending she poked the logs to encourage a blaze.

'The postman's child is without. He says he's come for your goat.'

'All right, Susan, tell him he can have tether and stake as well.'

He heard her call out to the boy, and the goat cried as the boy led her away.

'She was friendly old thing, and a splendid milker,' Susan said, coming into the kitchen again. Crossing to the table, she cleaned the funnel of the lamp and lit the wick.

'That's much better,' she said. 'How you can sit alone in the dark, God, alone, knows.'

Durnan made no answer.

'I've come up for my white sheets, and my crucifix for a happy death. Maybe, soon, I'll have call for them myself.' He watched her eyes narrow as the light burst from the growing wick.

'You have parted with the goat. You're surely not going to part with the cottage?'

'No, Susan, but I'm off to sea again in the morning. Joining the *Glendry*.'

'And what are you for doing about the cottage?'

'I want to keep it. Maybe you would come and light an odd fire in it for me, to bay the damp?'

'I will to be sure. I'll do more. I'll come and live in it for a month if you'll let me?'

'Why a month, Susan?'

'Because the *Summer Breeze* needs caulking. The timbers of her are so far apart as to let daylight in. And if Robert lets it go another winter without attending to it, we'll be flooded out with the rain.'

In his mind he could see the black hulk of the *Summer Breeze*. Susan and her husband, Robert, had spent their days on this sixty-ton ketch ever since they were married. He remembered the morning they beached her. The steam roller was working on the shore road, and with ropes they towed the *Summer Breeze* up

19

the beach and let her rest, far above the high water mark. Now she served Susan and Robert as a dwelling in their old age.

'Come and stay in the cottage as long as you like, Susan.'

'Thanks, and God bless you. I'll tell Robert as soon as I go on board.'

It amused Durnan to hear Susan talk about going aboard and coming ashore. He knew Robert had always insisted on this.

'Have you a change of inside clothing and you for sea so soon?' she asked.

He told her he had.

'Because, I can lend you an inside shirt of Robert's. Patched like roof thatch, it is, but it's clean.'

'Thank you, Susan. I'll be all right. Likely the *Glendry* will be going to Whitehaven. . . .'

'Then go to Primmer's and say Susan King of the *Summer Breeze* sent you. Ask for Miss Primmer, and she'll treat you like a prince.'

Moving into the room, she returned with the sheets and crucifix. 'These are mine,' she said, kissing the crucifix and pushing the sheets under her arm.

'It's getting on, and I want to be on board afore the black night comes. Stephen, do you think you'll be content here, tonight?'

'Why shouldn't I be, Susan?'

'Well now, please yourself. But it wouldn't be my liking. You come aboard the *Summer Breeze* if you care, and we'd rig you a bed.'

'No, Susan, I'll be all right, here.'

'Where will you leave the key?'

'I'll put it under the lucky stone at the gable, and you can get it when you want it.'

Turning from the door she said, 'Write a note, Stephen, and let me know when you're coming home, and I'll have things ready for you.'

When she had gone, he pulled the tin trunk from under the bed. When he opened it, there was a strong smell of peppermint.

In this trunk, his mother had kept all the things she treasured. As a boy, she would never let him near it. If he had ever been close to it, she would shout, 'Come away from there, boy, and quit your plundering.'

The words she used stabbed into his mind. He always thought of the word 'plundering' as hard and cruel.

If only she had been like Mrs. Reilly, how different his life might have been. Harry Reilly was his school chum, and when Harry was ill, he went to see him. Mrs. Reilly had shown him to the bedroom saying, 'My wee man is sick,' and when she entered the room, said, 'Stephen Durnan has come to see you, pulse of my heart.'

Sniffing the peppermint recalled the night he had left the cottage on his first trip to sea. It was Jacob, the harbourmaster, that had told his mother about the job of cook in the *West Mungo*.

'It'll make a man of you,' she had said. 'Jacob tells me, the skipper's a Highland man, easy to please. Surely to God, you can fry a bit of steak, or a couple of sausages, and boil an egg or make a taste of porridge, or stew.'

How dark the stairway was when he went to see the skipper How kind the skipper was. Patting his head and saying he had a son something like him, but his son was at college. And the skipper shook his hand saying he was willing to take him to sea, in the hope that one day he would be skipper of the liner *Montrose*.

From this tin trunk, that night, she had taken the paper-backed prayer book, telling him to read it; but there was nothing in the prayer book that soothed him.

There were no tears from her. Mrs. Reilly had shaken his hand and through her tears said, 'Pulse of my heart, will your mother not be lonely for her poor Stephen?'

He remembered, too, when they landed in Greece, the sailors coming on board and washing themselves in front of him, making him feel sick. All through that night they talked and

21

drank wine; one wondering if he had got a packet, another talking about the judy he was with. . . .

He kept looking through the porthole at the blue sky that never seemed to darken. The heron crying, the ash tree scraping its branches, and the stream were jumbled in his mind. He had cried that night, and Thomas the Welsh fireman kept shouting that the cook wanted a woman. But, Hagen, the Norwegian, had pushed Thomas away, saying in broken English, 'Go eassy for the kid, Tomas. He iss sick for home. I know he iss sick for home.'

Bending to the trunk again, he took out some postcards, looking at what was written on them before throwing them in the fire. Among the scraps of paper were prescriptions for curing asthma. He thought among this mass of papers there might be a faded letter referring to his father. But there was nothing and the withered peppermint leaves broke in his hand as his nails touched the bottom of the trunk.

He found an old exercise book, and turning its brown pages he saw her crooked figures, marking how much she had got for the winkles she gathered on the beach at Granagh. He smiled as he turned the pages, for here and there were drawings of steamers, some loaded, others light. On all their funnels were the letters SD., for in those days he imagined himself as a shipowner. He had chosen grand names for his ships, the names of Irish presidents. The *President Parnell*, the *President Healy*, the *President Cosgrove*; and the names he had for his deep-sea boats were: the *Irish Republic*, the *Irish Hero*, the *Irish Volunteer*.

He crumpled the exercise book and let it fall into the fire, watching the flames lick and twist it into black flakes. Suddenly he felt sad at having burned a link with his boyhood. Why was there this longing for the past? It seemed a life unlived that he craved, almost as if his soul made him taste something; something that was within him, that lay dormant, and he knew not how to bring it into action or make it bloom consciously.

This, whatever it was, had stifled his life. There seemed no relief. And yet he was happiest when he was sailing in spite of the monotony of lighthouses, endless jokes about women, lice, bugs, rats. . . .

His mother's awful litanies. Don't kick football, boy. Where am I to get money for boots? No money for books. There are too many scholars. No candle to bed, boy; you'll burn the house. . . .

And now she is dead. Gone to meet God, after twisting his soul. Frightened of hell, where she'd burn because of her bastard. Terrible to think of the mess humanity could get itself into. Put a robin redbreast in a cage and he won't sing. Plant a flower where the wind is strong and it won't grow; yet the human soul lived on. Put it where you like, whip it, torture it, crush it, bend it, starve it; do anything you like with it, then tell it, God created it to burn in hell for all eternity, because it did the things He made it do.

CHAPTER FOUR

IN Jane Whorry's grocery store Durnan bought his provisions and an empty sugar sack, which he stuffed with straw and chaff until he felt it ready for sleeping on. Then he came down the wide street that led to the quay. Approaching the *Glendry*, he knew she was old. Her sling anchors told him so. Never had he seen such a huge head on so small a steamer, nor so long a hatch.

She had one tall mast rising from her bow, and a sturdy samson post jammed against her bridgehead. The distance between the mast and the samson post was immense, almost like the distance between two street lamps.

He threw his bag over the rail to the foc's'le head, and climbed on board, making his way to the foc's'le. The foc's'le was dark, and near the stove a coloured fireman was sewing a button on a shirt. The fireman looked up, not so much at Durnan's entrance, but annoyed at the disappearance of the light from the doorway.

'Is the mate about?' Durnan asked.

The fireman was sucking a thread, his thick lips trying to point it. Durnan waited, looking at the nerve that puffed in the fireman's forehead.

'Is the mate about?' he repeated.

'I think he was go after,' said the fireman in tongue-twisted English. Drawing his chair nearer the door, the fireman continued sewing. Durnan kept staring at the greasy head. It reminded him of the fat of well-cooked roast beef.

The foc's'le was gloomy. Looking at the coloured man, Durnan felt it hard to believe that white men lived in it at all. There was a strong smell of tar, and the floor was sea sodden. The port-holes were smeared, staining the little light they borrowed with a tawny translucence. There were two rows of bunks running with the curve of the bow, and small rails on the outside of them, shaped like cases for holding milk bottles.

Durnan knew that, small as she was, the *Glendry* was no coast hugger, for all around him there was evidence that she wandered deep sea. The newspaper that served as a table cloth was French, and the tin of condensed milk was Spanish, and when the fireman took out cigarettes, Durnan could see they were Portuguese.

'Where did you come from, before this coal trip?' he asked the fireman.

'We come to Liverpool from Lisbon, with general, and before that, we come from Iceland with salted codfish.' Picking at his teeth with the needle the fireman continued, 'Once I get to Liverpool, I say goodbye and bugger you to this ship.'

'Why?'

'I jus wanna chuck her, that's all.'

A small, dark-haired man entered.

'Diss is the mate, now,' said the fireman.

'My name's Wilson. Are you the new hand?'

Durnan said he was and they shook hands.

'What was your last berth?' the mate asked.

'The *Kronvad*, Norwegian, deep sea.'

'What was wrong?'

'Had to come home to bury my mother.'

'Sorry to hear it,' said the mate, and turning he pointed out a bunk to Durnan, 'That's your doss, and locker number four is yours for your stores.'

'Where are we bound for?' asked Durnan.

The mate shook his head, 'Dunno, the orders haven't come yet. Maybe you'll lend a hand with the hatches as soon as you can.'

Durnan made ready his bed, packed his stores and pulling on a pair of overalls came outside. He helped to spread the hatches over her long hold, covered them with a wet slimy tarpaulin, making it fast over the sides of the hold by hammering wooden wedges tight. Then the two derricks were lowered and tied firmly in the mouths of their rests.

She was ready for sea. The coloured fireman had gone ashore for a final drink. The mate was in the wheelhouse. Looking up at him, Durnan thought it odd that the skipper wasn't there. As yet he had not asked who or what was the skipper's name. But what did it matter, he had nothing to fear.

'You'll stand by, aft,' he heard the mate shout. A bell went and the ship trembled.

'My name is Fenner,' said the young sailor standing at the capstan.

'My name's Durnan. You haven't been long at sea,' he added. 'Your paw is too soft.'

'Three weeks,' the young sailor laughed.

There was a softness in Fenner's eyes, a sad kindness about his face. Durnan immediately liked him.

'Is she a good sea boat?'

'I hardly know what you mean,' Fenner said. 'Three weeks at sea doesn't give one much of an idea of things.'

A telegram boy was riding down the quay. The mate called to the harbourmaster to read the telegram. He read, 'Proceed Barholm load potatoes for Bordeaux.'

The whistle tooted three times, and the fireman came running down the quay, holding a loaf in one hand, and his trousers up with the other. His grey sweat rag covered his mouth.

They swung her head away from the quay, and as the bell went for full speed ahead, she jumped slightly. Durnan waved to the harbourmaster, as she moved from the quay.

Leaning his arms on the capstan, Durnan fixed his eyes on the cottage as they sailed past it. Directly beneath it was the black hulk of the *Summer Breeze*, with its scarf of white smoke skimming its bowsprit. It was disappearing, looking like a huge boulder that was sinking into the beach; further up, the ash tree looked no bigger than a hawthorn.

Fenner was coiling a rope. 'Is Barholm far away?' he asked.

'No, just about forty miles down the coast. We should be there early in the morning. You've never been there?'

'No,' Fenner said. 'What's it like?'

'It's a small place, inside Strangford Lough. Tricky bar if the wind is boisterous.'

'I'm going forrit, to make a cup of tea. I'll put your name in the pot if it's O.K.,' Fenner said.

'Thanks, I don't mind.'

Fenner covered the capstan and went towards the foc's'le. Durnan turned his head, looking at the village. The mountains they were now passing were shutting it from the landscape. The sky was blue, with white patches of cloud, tipped at the bottoms with dying sunlight. The *Glendry* lifted her massive head and crashed it into the sea. The wind was rising.

Durnan lit the foc's'le lamp. It seemed to him that it should never have been put out. Fenner made tea and, as he cut the bread, Durnan saw his hands were spotlessly clean. His finger nails were pointed; there was a softness and suppleness about his hands that made them look like a young girl's.

After tea, they smoked. Then Fenner took a concertina from his bunk and started to play. He played a tune that Durnan had been taught at school, a tune called 'My Singing Bird'.

The coloured fireman entered the foc's'le bruising an Oxo between his finger and thumb. Laughing down at Fenner, he said, 'Play somezing for Joe Fish. Play, Ta la la, boom de lay.'

Fenner told him that some other time he would. Then, closing his eyes, Fenner played a hymn that Durnan had heard often in the churches at Bayonne and St. Malo.

The notes were weird, reminding Durnan of a shrill pipe that might play mysteriously from the sea. They were almost frightening.

'Will you for Christ's sake stop that snake charmer's music? Is it not enough to be sailing in a bloody coffin without being reminded of it?' called a drunken voice from the other side of the foc's'le.

Fenner stopped playing, apologizing to the sailor. In the silence Durnan seemed to hear the weird notes, as if Fenner hadn't ceased to play. The mate entered, and Durnan knew it was time he was seeing to the lights. Outside, the blue had gone from the sky, and the white patches of clouds were dissolving into a grey cloak. Durnan slid the headlight up the mast, and let the starboard light slide into its socket. Then he crossed to the port side.

The port light always fascinated him. It had the warmth of a homely fire in its red glow. He could kneel on the deck, polishing its glass, peering into its red heart. It was to him the symbol of home, of a real home, with a wife, with children. Sliding it into its clasp he stared at its reflection as it danced on the water.

'Our watch now. You and I are together,' he heard Fenner say, as he approached.

A handful of spray flung over Durnan's face, leaving its salty tang on his lips.

They climbed to the wheelhouse. 'What's that light in front of us?' Fenner asked.

'That's St. John's point.'

Looking down at the compass, Durnan gave the wheel a slight turn.

'What time do we get to Barholm?' Fenner asked.

27

'About four or five a.m.'

There was a silence. Fenner started humming.

'What was the name of that hymn you were playing, tonight?'

'That,' said Fenner, tossing his head.

'I've heard it before. In the Chapel at Bayonne, and St. Malo,' Durnan said.

'It's Gregorian, "Orbis Factor"', Fenner said, after a pause. Durnan looked at him wonderingly.

'Did you like it?'

'Yes, I like that kind of music. Somehow it's sad . . . I mean it makes you feel that there is a God somewhere. . . .'

'I suppose it does,' Fenner said softly.

Fenner was rubbing his hands. 'It's emotional, if you like.' Then he mumbled some words that Durnan couldn't make out.

'Are you musical?'

'I used to play the organ in the church at home,' Fenner continued, 'but I lost my faith . . .' Again his voice faded into mumblings.

'You don't believe in God, is that it?'

'I don't know. Sometimes I do, and sometimes I don't. If I could believe, I daresay I'd be happy. If I could disbelieve, I'd be happy too. It's the in between. One day believing, and the next, well . . .'

'Why don't you talk to a priest about it?'

'I have. He told me to say: I believe, Lord. Help thou my unbelief.'

A bell rang, and Fenner went to the speaking tube in the corner.

'We've just passed St. John's light, and all's well,' he spoke down it.

'That was the skipper,' he said. 'He should be sober by this.'

'Was he drunk?' Durnan asked, looking down to the compass.

'He's never anything else.'

'Is his name Norton?'

'It is. Do you know him?'

28

'Yes, much better than I like to. And he knows me.'

'I believe he has a secret sorrow, and that's why he's so fond of the bottle. He hasn't been sober since I joined the ship.'

'What secret sorrow has he?'

'I heard the mate say that he was a deep sea man but lost his ticket.'

'Yes, he did.' Durnan wondered if he should tell Fenner the whole story.

'He'll sober up before we berth,' Fenner said.

'Why?'

'I believe Barholm's his home town.'

'Yes, yes, you're right.' There was a silence. Durnan felt now that it might not be so easy to face Norton. He knew that far back in his mind there was an uneasiness starting. But he knew he had told the truth that day at the inquiry, so what was there to be afraid of? They had asked him if Norton was drunk in charge of the ship, and he had told them that he was. It had been a simple statement. Norton was incapable of handling the ship, she rammed a tanker . . . He knew there were sailors who said he was an informer, but that didn't worry him.

But if Norton got angry with him again, it was only a short journey from Barholm to Portaferry.

CHAPTER FIVE

WHEN Fenner wakened him, the *Glendry* was in Strangford Lough. Fenner had the table set and was making tea. After breakfast, Durnan came outside.

They were quite close to land and he could see the workers in the fields. The pilot was on board, and Fenner took him a cup of tea.

They stripped the long hatch of the steamer and raised the derricks in the air. Durnan kept looking up at the wheelhouse, but there was no sign of the skipper. The pilot saluted him. He was a sandy-haired man with one bulging eye.

Durnan had been troubled in his sleep about Norton. Still, he convinced himself he had committed no wrong in telling the truth at the inquiry. Sometimes he felt the truth could be horrible, and he knew there was something to be said for the sailors calling him an informer. But, on the other hand, if Norton had not been drunk that day, he would never had rammed the tanker and the eighteen lives might have been saved.

They were abreast of the quay when he heard Norton's voice. He was calling on Fenner to get the gangway ashore. Fenner tugged at the gangway, then called on Durnan to lend a hand. But Durnan pretended not to hear. Peering from the stokehole door, Durnan saw Norton going down the gangway with a parcel under his arm. The small bandy legs, the heavy body and the ragged hair showing under the back of his hat.

Coming to the foc's'le, Durnan found Fenner watching the dockers heaving three bales of hay on board.

'What's the hay for, Durnan?'

'To spread on the floor of the hatch, so as the coal dust won't dirty the potato bags.'

'You weren't annoyed with me for not lending a hand with the gangway?' Durnan asked, after a pause.

'I wasn't. But I felt it rather odd when you ignored my call.'

'I didn't want to see Norton.'

'Why?'

Briefly, he told Fenner the story.

'So as a result, he lost his deep sea ticket,' Fenner said.

'That's right. And yet in spite of its being the truth, I feel guilty about something.'

'Why should you? If you were giving evidence at a murder trial, no one would call you an informer, so what . . .?'

Durnan felt pleased with Fenner's attitude. It was sensible and sane. It had never occurred to him that it was much the same as

30

giving evidence at a murder trial. He felt suddenly relieved, making up his mind to face Norton as if he had never met him before.

'Durnan, would you stand by and check the cargo for an hour or so?' he heard the mate say. 'And keep an eye on how they stow the cargo. They're a careless set of bastards here. We don't want the cargo listing at all.'

Turning to Fenner the mate said, 'This trip is to the continent, so you'd better get extra stores. You'd maybe tell him, Durnan, what he should get.'

Durnan suggested to Fenner that they might grub together, and Fenner was agreeable. And on a small bit of paper he wrote down the following list:

> Eight loaves,
> Three tins bully beef,
> Four tins condensed milk,
> Two lb. of cheese,
> Two lb. of bacon,
> 1 lb. soap,
> Two packets washing powder,
> 1 lb. of tea,
> $\frac{1}{4}$ stone of sugar,
> Beecham's pills.

Fenner laughed loudly, saying he'd need one of the motor lorries on the quay to carry them. And as he walked up the quay, Durnan called after him, to tell him to bring some eggs and a spool of white thread.

On the quay, the dockers were stamping their feet and slapping their hands against their shoulders, for there was a bite in the wind that blew up the lough.

'What the hell is keeping them, below? You'd think they was laying a bloody carpet, instead of spreading a bale of hay,' said a docker with a chest that looked as red as a carrot. There were four motor lorries waiting, all loaded with potatoes. Then the signal came from the hold, and the dockers each grabbed a bag. In quick procession they climbed the gangway, tumbling their bags on to the shute that carried them into the hold.

Durnan took pleasure in watching the dockers. Their faces became powdered with the brown potato dust. Their eyes, curiously alive, made their faces look as though they were masked, and their shirts curled at their trouser tops, like tyres.

At eleven o'clock their wives brought them tea, in jugs and cans, and bread with eggs between the slices.

The rhythm went on, five tons, ten tons, twenty tons, fifty tons; each man, like an ant with a grub in its mouth, tearing up the gangway, dumping his bag into the wide belly of the *Glendry*.

The mate looked at them in the hold. 'Keep her trim, boys,' he shouted.

Durnan did not care whether she listed or not. He wanted away. Coasting to him was drudgery, dirty slavery. Something might turn up in Bordeaux. The mate relieved him, and Fenner came on board with the stores. They packed them, and Durnan boiled potatoes, and made a hash by champing them together with the bully beef.

The coloured fireman sat at the head of the table eating a boiled onion. 'Maybe, we get a night here,' he said. Durnan told him they'd be ready for sea at four o'clock. The fireman laughed, 'Dis iss the skipper's home port, he like a night in bed wif his wife. Tat's why we get a night here. He like to feel her body. . . .'

The fireman laughed loudly. Glancing at Fenner, Durnan saw that he wasn't amused at the fireman's joke. Instead, he looked disapprovingly under his brow. Durnan knew, then, Fenner had a clean mouth and he liked him the more.

Fenner took his concertina from under his pillow, and again the fireman asked him to play 'Ta la la, boom de lay'. This time Fenner played it, and the fireman went whooping round the table in a wild dance. His merriment was interrupted by the mate.

32

'You'd better come and cover the hatch,' he said. 'They can only get three fifty into it, that means a deck cargo of ten ton, for the complement's three sixty.' He was upset and angry. A docker had followed him in protesting: 'Listen, mate, our men here are as good as you'll get anywhere. . . .'

'How the hell is it, we could get three seventy into her in Strangford?' the mate shouted.

'They must have been lucky bags . . .' the docker insisted.

'What does it mean?' Fenner asked, after the mate had left.

'It means that we'll have to carry ten tons on top of the hold,' Durnan told him.

'Is that dangerous?'

'It could be, but come on and we'll cover her up.'

Again they spread the hatches, jumping on them when they refused to sit, where a potato bag jutted up. They battened the tarpaulin, and the dockers started to build the potatoes in an angle to the samson post.

A docker came into the foc's'le with a bag; dumping it on the floor he said, 'This is with the merchant's compliments.'

The fireman followed the docker out, asking if he might get a bag for the engineers. Fenner was playing the concertina again.

It became cold. The wind had strengthened, and it curled a ridge of brown dust on the foc's'le floor. Durnan went ashore for cigarettes. Returning to the ship, he paused at the head of the quay and looked down at her. Her clumsy stern rose out of the water. Everything about her was black. Her funnel, her body, her lifeboats, all were dead black, frosted in places with the salt sea.

She was ugly. There was nothing personal about her. Her crew did not seem to belong in her. They were all, like Joe Fish, the coloured fireman, slipping about quietly, making up their minds to get out of her as quickly as another berth offered itself.

Even her skipper, too, was forced to sail in her because of his misfortune. She was a whore, a sea whore. The men that sailed her regarded her as a convenience. Coming down the quay he saw the dockers pull the shute away. She was loaded. Chockful of bagged potatoes, and ready for her long tramp to France.

CHAPTER SIX

'WELL, boys, have a breather. She's ready. I told the skipper I'd give him a whistle. So there's no need to pull out immediately. Stretch yourselves for an hour if you feel like it,' the mate said.

Joe Fish wanted Fenner ashore for a drink, but he declined.

'Take yourself ashore, you black bugger, and buy yourself something to eat; answer you better, than a dose of black porter,' the mate said good naturedly. But the black man stabbed the air with his upturned fingers, and left the foc's'le laughing.

'A splash of sea at the bar,' the mate said.

'The wind's rising higher. It'll stay up,' Durnan said.

'We'll get shelter if we hug the coast. She's an ugly devil in dirty weather. You couldn't keep her straight,' said the mate.

'Why is she so black?' Fenner asked.

'Because she belongs to Polton Brothers of Cardiff. They wouldn't give you as much paint as would paint a yard door. The lousiest and meanest ship-owners in Britain. . . .'

Looking down the lough at the bar, the mate said quietly, 'There's a lively bit of weather out there.' Standing at the door, he said, 'Maybe, Durnan, Fenner and you might have another looksee at the hatch, just in case. . . .'

Durnan was never troubled with the thoughts of bad weather. He never knew what it was to be frightened of the sea. Other sailors had cried. One he had seen grip a table until the blood oozed from under his finger-nails. But, to Durnan, the sea was

34

there, just as the sky was. If it were rough, it would soon calm again. He never knew fear at sea.

Fenner and he went round the hatch, giving an extra tap to each wedge. Looking at the ten tons of potatoes built against the samson post, Durnan knew there would be little of them there by the time they reached France.

'Why is he so particular about the hatch?' Fenner said.

'He thinks we're in for a dirty night.'

'And are we?'

'I don't think so. She'll be a bit lively, but beyond that . . .'

Fenner was looking down the lough. Durnan knew he was watching the waves rise up at the ridge of rocks that jutted from Rock Angus light. Dark shadows, they looked, rising quickly, like clowns tumbling.

'What are those dark shadows?' Fenner asked.

'Breakers at the rocks. Nothing to worry about. We'll be all right if we cross it before dark.'

The wind was getting louder. It bellied the derrick ropes, and shivered the wires that held the samson post.

It fingered the brown dust, and sent it trembling into the nooks and corners of the decks. Looking towards the long street of the village, Durnan felt its cold grey bleakness. The doors of the houses were closed, but here and there the fires that burned in their kitchens were reflected in the little panes of the windows.

Back in the foc's'le, Fenner sat on the form looking down at the bar. He was cleaning the finger-nails of one hand with the nails of the other. Durnan sensed that Fenner was nervous. His face looked strained.

'What's your Christian name, Fenner?'

'John. But I'm known at home as Jackie.'

'Mine is Stephen. Tell me, Jackie, what's the sudden trouble?'

'I er . . . I just feel a wee bit nervy. . . .'

'But what's made you nervy? It's just come on you like a flash. . . .'

Fenner cleared his throat. 'I heard the dockers talking among

35

themselves at the meal hour. One of them called her a tub, another said she would hardly hold together before they stowed the cargo. . . .'

'So what?' said Durnan, with a laugh. 'They talk about her just because she's black and dismal looking. Like a girl, simply because she wears a black dress doesn't mean she's not as good as one who wears a flashy dress with the rainbow colours in it. There's nothing to be jumpy about. Why, man, she's a head on her as big as ever I've seen on a deep sea boat.'

'Should I leave her, Stephen? Leave her right now?'

'If you feel you want to. But just because a few yellow-bellies of dockers condemn her . . . that's no reason for the shakes. . . .'

From the other side of the foc's'le came the snores of the two sleeping sailors.

'Listen to them lads. It isn't worrying them.' Durnan got up and ran his fingers through Fenner's soft hair. 'You'll be all right, Jackie, you'll see.'

'Should we try it?' said the mate, sitting down at the stove.

'If you like,' Durnan said.

The mate handed cigarettes round. The three of them lit up. Fenner's trembled as the mate held a match to it.

'Wouldn't you wonder Norton wouldn't stop the night here?' the mate said. Durnan grunted.

'He's an unhappy bugger, too. I don't think he gets on too well with the wife.'

'I suppose he's too fond of the bottle. Must be hard for any woman to stand that,' Durnan said.

'Yea. I don't think he's been sober one trip since I joined her, four months ago.'

'How does he keep his job?' said Fenner.

'The owners don't worry. This old thing owes them nothing. In fact it was her put them on their feet. My own father remembers her forty years ago, trading into the Bristol Channel. Believe me, Poltons wouldn't care if Davy Jones took her in his arms in the morning.' The mate stood up. 'I'll give the skipper a call,' he said, going to the bridge.

'You didn't tell him anything about Norton and me?'

Fenner shook his head. They heard the whistle go, a long blast and a short one. But it wasn't needed, for Durnan heard Norton's voice outside. He was talking to the harbourmaster and their voices were loud.

'Are you sailing tonight?' the harbourmaster asked.

'What the hell would I do in this hole of a place? I'm sailing now, in five minutes' time,' came the reply.

Norton was coming down the gangway unsteadily, now he was following the mate to the foc's'le. He was protesting about the deck cargo, but the mate kept repeating that it wasn't his fault, that he couldn't stow the cargo himself.

Durnan moved back from the glow of the stove. 'Where are you all?' shouted Norton.

Fenner stood up. The mate jerked his thumb in the direction of the sleeping sailors.

'We're leaving now,' Norton said loudly. 'There's a bit of weather outside, you'll get your arses wet; but we're calling at Cardiff to bunker. I promise you a night there, and a night in Bordeaux.' The light from the stove caught Norton's face, picking out his eyes and cheeks. Durnan could see the pain-twisted wrinkles in his forehead; they seemed to pull in his brows, his cheeks and his nose, screwing them tightly into a hollow just above his nose.

His eyes looked tired. Tired with the burning weariness that showed in them. His mouth was puckered, and his breathing was heavy, coming out from his nose almost in groans. Tearing a bit of newspaper from the table, he lit a cigarette.

'Everybody on board?' he asked.

'I think the nigger's ashore,' the mate said.

'Did you get a new hand?' Norton asked.

'Got one in Portaferry, there he is.' Durnan saw the mate pointing to him.

The news that the ship was calling at Cardiff suddenly gave him courage. Two paces from where he stood and he would be face to face with Norton. Get it over, he felt, as he moved into the light of the stove. He felt a falling sensation. It affected his eyes, but he stiffened. Now he was close to Norton, so close that he could see the hairs curling from the turf-brown wide nostrils.

'This is the new man . . .' the mate was saying.

Norton stumbled back, his hat crushing against the edge of the foc's'le door.

'Where did you come from?' he shouted. Norton's lips twisted as he bit them and his eyes widened, giving his face a stupid expression. 'You're not sailing on my ship, by the Christ's above me, you're not.'

So close to him now, Durnan towered above him, realizing what a small man he was. This gave Durnan confidence.

'Why am I not sailing?' he asked quietly.

'I'll get the police for you,' Norton said, trying to straighten his hat.

'You've no charge.'

'Get ashore, I tell you. Get ashore or I'll tear you asunder.'

Durnan remained cool. 'Look,' he said, 'I'm a bigger man than you, if the going gets rough. If I go ashore I'm taking you with me.'

The mate intervened, moving between the two of them.

'Can't this be straightened out?' he said.

Norton made to push the mate away, but the mate grabbed the lapels of his coat and held him firmly against the door. Norton tried to free himself, but the mate forced him out of the foc's'le. 'Now, look, Skipper, you're drunk, and you might as well admit it. We aren't leaving short-handed, not under any conditions. . . .'

'Who's drunk, who's drunk? . . . Take your hands off me. . . .'

'Now, Skipper, if this comes to a show down, I'll put you ashore. I'll wire the owners that you weren't in a fit condition

38

to take the ship out. I'll take her to Cardiff myself. So now, there's going to be no trouble. . . .'

The mate released his hold. There was a long pause. Norton looked as though he were crying. Then he walked unevenly down the deck.

'I'm sorry about all this,' Durnan said to the mate.

'Forget about it,' the mate said, impatiently. 'I've yet to meet the sailor who's never had a barney with his skipper.'

The pilot with the bulging eye had thrown the painter from his small boat. Fenner was making it fast as the pilot climbed on board the steamer. Joe Fish was still ashore. 'What the hell's keeping that blasted darkie?' Norton was shouting from the wheelhouse. Again the whistle went. This time, loud and impatient blasts, for Norton was still angry.

The engines were throbbing. Durnan looked to the quay. It was deserted, save for two crows that pecked at the one potato. One crow manœuvred the potato into his beak, but as he flew off it fell into the water.

The pilot was in the wheelhouse. Norton was waving his arms about and cursing. On the quay the harbourmaster waited to release the ropes. He stamped his foot and blew his hands, to chase the cold.

Joe Fish came running down the quay, carrying a small bag of rice, two loaves, a tin of condensed milk and a bottle of wine.

'Are you gonna keep us here all night, you black bastard?' Norton shouted, as the fireman struggled up the gangway. There was a chorus of shouts; let go your wire, take in the slack, haul away quickly. . . .

The bell rang, and the water roared as it churned against the quay, and in a drunken voice Norton was calling out his orders. As Durnan took in the aft ropes the water dripped from them, running in a ribbon to the port side.

She was moving from the quay with a heavy list to port. It was ebb tide and as she gathered speed she leaned deeper in the water. Fenner's face was white as he coiled the rope. Every now

39

and then he looked down the lough at the black shadows rising and falling at the rocks near Rock Angus.

Durnan pulled the cover over the capstan. It was always his habit to lean his elbows on it, and look at the port he was leaving. On every ship he did this. To him there was always the atmosphere of a farewell about it. He thought, too, if ever he was a skipper, he would toot the whistle, just to say goodbye to the port. She slowed speed to let the pilot ashore. Durnan held on to him as he climbed over the side into his punt. The pilot was in the small boat, waving his hand, heedlessly, as he swayed with the dancing movements of the punt in the swell.

The houses were gone, and where the land gathered itself into fields and knowes, it seemed to shrink and get smaller. Dimly, Durnan could see the ploughed fields, the scabby-looking furrows. He watched a cormorant hurry inland. He could hear peewits crying, but he couldn't see them, for the sky was heavy with black ropes of twisted clouds. It looked as if it were lowering itself into the sea, shutting out the land. The tattered edges of the waves threw themselves over the deck, smacking on the hatch like whipcracks.

As he came to the foc's'le, he heard Norton calling him. He stopped. A wave vomited about his feet, trickling between his toes. It sent its cold nerve up through his body, freeing his mind from the sudden alarm of Norton's voice.

Norton looked around as Durnan opened the wheelhouse door. Durnan watched his eyes closing and the twisted lips forcing their way into his mouth. An empty whisky bottle rolled with the ship's movement to Durnan's feet; picking it up he tossed it into the sea. Norton was helplessly drunk, and to keep his feet, he gripped the spokes of the wheel with all his strength. Every time the ship lurched, he fell forward. Durnan closed the door, shutting out the swish of the sea.

Norton looked at him, trying at the same time to straighten himself. 'You broke me, Durnan. Twisted this game old heart that's inside me. Judas informed on Christ. That's why I'm sailing in this bloody tub. Jazes above me, that it should come to this . . . Frank Norton, pigging in a coaster that deserted the scrap yard years ago. Many a bloody man takes a drink. Maybe he's forced to it . . .' Norton was crying, and saliva ran from his mouth to his hands.

'Jazes man, there were only the two of us saved. Couldn't you have told them it was an accident, and never mentioned the drop of whisky I had in me . . .?' Norton made an effort to swallow the saliva. Then he started rubbing his face savagely. Durnan saw this as a gesture of despair. A gesture of a man lost. Norton now dropped his head, crying like a child. Pity stirred in Durnan as he looked down where Norton's hands clutched the wheel.

'Sometimes, I forget about it. But when I saw you this evening it all came back. . . .'

Durnan came outside. Leaning on the rail he looked down at the black sea flinging itself against the ship. For the first time, he felt suddenly afraid. A great pain stabbed through his bowels, making him shiver. He was dizzy, and a ghost shouted in his mind something about the truth. He wasn't sure now that he had been right in saying at the inquiry that Norton was drunk. Black was black, and white, white, but maybe it was a good thing to mix the two of them at times . . . He felt at this moment sorry for what he'd done, whether it was right or not.

It was time for him to see to the lights. As they neared the bar, the wind got higher, carrying the water from her bow to smack it against the deck cargo.

The land was gone. The dark grey sky and the mist that the sea churned now seemed to be one. There was a silence in the sky for a moment, as if day was begetting night. Then there came a great howl from the wind, gathering darkness about the ship. Now there were only mist, sea and wind tossing the water helter-skelter. Durnan knew that scarcely a mile away there were cows grazing, horses going home, and housewives making ready warm meals for their returning husbands. But here there was just the madness of the sea and the wind, tugging, laughing wildly together in a mad melody.

Looking out he could see the long tower that marked Rock Angus, and he knew they were at the threshold of the bar. Falling on his knees, he crouched into a corner as he lit the port light. A branch of seaweed fell at his feet. He could see its bellied beads shine golden in the gleam of the port light. The wind lifted it, and tapped it fiercely against his boot. Its beads shone with the varnish of the sea, bringing to his mind the colour of his mother's coffin.

The port light recalled the tabernacle lamp. 'She's buried facing south,' the gravedigger had told him, as if the south meant something; and yet he liked it, for there was a promise in it, a promise that he found no words for.

Gripping the rail, he came towards the foc's'le.

CHAPTER SEVEN

DURNAN took his boots off.
'Did you get your feet wet?' the mate asked.

He grunted a reply, and wrung his socks over the stove. The water sizzled into white webs on the stove top.

In the yellow lamp-light Durnan saw Fenner sitting rigid on the edge of his bunk. Fenner's eyes were wide, and his mouth moved, as if he was trying to keep from vomiting.

'Why don't you roll under the blankets, and try and get some sleep?'

Fenner did not answer.

The *Glendry* was playing herself. Rising on a sea every five minutes, and flinging herself off it again with a crash.

'Will she be long clearing the bar?' Durnan asked.

The mate looked up. 'No. Norton knows all the short cuts. He's taking her through Gunn's Isle Sound. He'll avoid the tides that way. Heavy going for a while, but he knows where the shelter is. He knows this bar like the back of his hand. He was reared about it.'

'He's drunk,' Durnan said.

'He's never sober. But give the bastard his due, he's a sailor. He could smell his way into a port. . . .'

Fenner stretched himself in the bunk, but he was up again, gripping the rail.

'He's nervy,' the mate whispered.

Fenner's arms trembled and his head fell back. Durnan was sorry for him. Sorry for this boy who, frightened to death, sat clutching the framework of his bunk.

'When the ship rises, you rise with her, Jackie; when she lowers, you lower too. Don't try to stop her falling, let your body loosen, let it sway . . . motion . . . motion. . . .'

But Durnan knew that Fenner was not listening to him. He knew Fenner would sit there like a frightened dog until the weather eased, or sleep dulled his fear. He, too, had held his bunk when, on his first trip, the *West Mungo* plunged her way across the Bay of Biscay. The sailors had laughed at him. Even now, he could see Thomas, the Welsh fireman, doing a wild dance, and he knew Thomas was only dancing to quieten his fears.

'If I give you a shot of whisky, would it help you to sleep?' the mate said.

But Fenner did not answer. Durnan drew his chair close to Fenner's bunk.

'You'll have a fine time in Bordeaux, Jackie,' he said. 'Wait till you see the organs in the chapels there. . . .'

The mate left the foc's'le, saying he was going to the bridge. Durnan continued, 'Wait till you hear the priests saying the Mass in voices full of music. Not like the blokes in Ireland. . . .'

But Fenner's arms trembled and his wide eyes looked lifeless. Suddenly the foc's'le door was pushed open with great force. The mate came in. He was breathless, and his face was shiny with sea water.

43

'She's in the tides . . . She's off her course . . . Be on the alert, all of you, and stand by. . . .'

'Is it serious?' Durnan said.

'He's fallen asleep, and hasn't had a hand near the wheel at all . . .' Pointing to the bridge, the mate continued, 'I dunno what we're going to do, there's about a dozen tides meet here, and she's in the middle. They'll hold her tight, like a bloody vice.' His voice faded as he disappeared through the doorway.

The lamp-light trembled as the wind filled the foc's'le. It lifted the newspaper from the table and sent it slapping against a bunk. Tails of spray whipped in, sizzling on the stove and sending hissing clouds of smoke through the foc's'le.

Fenner jumped from his bunk, falling to the ground. He cried out in terror, 'Sacred Heart of Jesus, have mercy on me. Have pity on me a sinner . . .' The other sailors were pulling oil-skins over their naked bodies. One of them kept shouting to Durnan to take no notice of Fenner.

Tearing off his cap and coat, Durnan rushed outside. Suddenly the ship's stern rose straight up. Durnan curled his arms around the mast, burying his head in his chest.

The water poured into the foc's'le, hugging Durnan's body, lifting him off his feet. He waited, struggling to breathe, fighting the water that flooded his mouth, his ears . . . Christ, would she never settle again . . .? Was this the finish? He heard a crash, and he knew the deck cargo was toppling to the hold. The brown bags falling hammered in his brain. He heard someone cry, a loud cry; then it stuttered, and the sucking sound of the sea continued.

The ship straightened herself for a moment. For a while she danced. It seemed to Durnan as if the tides were sucking her down, like a game of seesaw. Gripping the coamings, Durnan made his way along the deck. Midway he stumbled over a bag, its rough surface rubbing his nose. He reached the companion-way ladder, and pulled himself up it, to the bridge.

Norton was bent in the corner. Durnan tried to lift him to his

44

feet, but the ship lurched, and Durnan fell on top of him. 'Listen, Sir, the cargo is spattered on the deck. She's in the tides with us. We'll have to beach her, it's our only chance. . . .'

Norton muttered under his breath, making to push Durnan away. Durnan caught his shoulders and shook him violently.

'She'll founder, Skipper, if we don't do something, and do it quick. . . .'

'I fell. I hurt myself, twisted my leg,' said Norton. 'I've hurt my head, I dunno. . . .'

'Listen, Skipper . . . She's foundering . . . Do you hear . . .? She's foundering . . . If we can run her on somewhere. You know this place . . . Tell me where the land is . . . the rocks are. . . .'

'I dunno . . .' Norton's voice died in his throat, and his head rocked, like a man weary and wanting to sleep.

Durnan knew it was useless talking to Norton. Stumbling from the wheelhouse, Durnan waited at the companionway ladder. She was deep now in the sea, the water knitting its edges in the centre of her hatch. He descended two steps, but she showed no signs of lifting herself. He plunged, feeling his body lift in the water. He reached out, clawing madly. He gripped the ear of a potato bag, and from it groped his way to the hatch coamings, pulling himself to the foc's'le.

'Were you on the bridge?' the sailor asked.

'I was. She's completely off her course. There's nothing for it but the boats.'

'Any word of the mate at all?'

'I didn't see him. Unless he's aft in the engine room.'

'It's the boats then?' The sailor's voice was nervous.

Fenner started screaming and beating the floor with his hands. Durnan saw blood trickling from his mouth.

'What about him?' he said to the sailor.

'He's been warned; it's every man jack for himself,' the sailor said, making for the door. Reaching for a heaving line, Durnan tied one end to a stanchion. If he was to save Fenner, he knew he must run a lifeline from the foc's'le to the companionway ladder. He knew Fenner would make no effort to move, he would have to be dragged. The wind eased. The ship tried to struggle free of the water that surged on her hatch. Durnan succeeded in tying the other end of the rope to the ladder. Now, he had a lifeline. The sea sucked at it, drawing him away until his feet no longer touched the ship, and in a lightning flash he hoped his knots were tied firm. He reached the foc's'le. It was empty except for Fenner, who lay crying and kissing a little crucifix, and praying loudly.

Durnan looked down at him. Blood still slid down his chin from his mouth.

'Look, Jackie, son, think of what's happening. There's still a chance if we can get to the boats. . . .'

The sea poured in, killing the last of the fire in the stove. A snort of smoke blew into Durnan's eyes making him move impatiently. Bending he knit his hand through Fenner's hair, trying to drag him to the door.

'No, no, no,' Fenner screamed. 'Dear Jesus, I believe in thee. Sweet Jesus, have mercy on me, a sinner. . . .'

'Look, Fenner, you don't want to drown?'

'I don't, I don't . . .' Fenner tried to wriggle snakelike from Durnan's grip. Curling his hands around a stanchion, he kept repeating prayers.

Lifting the shovel in front of him, Durnan slashed Fenner's hands, until they slid lifelessly from the stanchion.

'Look, Jackie, for Christ's sake listen. You'll drown me as well as yourself if you don't stop kicking.'

Durnan lifted Fenner's writhing body into his arms.

'There's a lifeline out here. Grip it and go in front of me. I'll stay behind with my arms round you. . . .'

Outside, Fenner ceased struggling. Durnan caught the lifeline and urged Fenner on until the sea filled his mouth. Then he closed his face into Fenner's back.

'Walk, man, walk. Christ, above me, you're not a paralytic.'

He could feel Fenner's body sagging in his arms. Just like a fish that had suddenly died. Lifting his knee he kicked him, urging him on. Durnan was savage with rage. He pressed Fenner's body until he felt he had cracked his ribs. Durnan felt the sea sucking his arms. Great God, would it never end? Was it miles to the ladder? Had he his hands on the rope at all? Death was winning. The sucking sea. Any minute now and they'd be away on its tongue. Christ, where was the ladder? Where was the ladder? The rope was going to break, the knots holding it would slide.

Fenner wasn't moving. Death was winning. The sea would have them. Move on, you bastard, move on. You bastard, move on. We're fighting death. Move on, move on ... Now he couldn't open his mouth. Death had won. Any minute now it would shudder down his arm snapping at his warm hands.

Was it in his body? He thought about his boot, lifting it. His shin caught something. A wild shudder went through him, causing a stap of warmth to escape through his bowels. He knew it was the ladder. The sharp edge of the step dented his shin with pain. Forcing Fenner up with his knees, he saw the port light was out. A wild urgency tingled in his head, and he realized he was on a sinking ship, and making for the lifeboats.

Down at the galley, Joe Fish, the two engineers, and the two sailors were waiting with life jackets on them.

Joe Fish was breathless, like a man who had just run a long race. His eyes oozed fear.

One of the sailors said there was no sign of the mate at all, and the chief engineer concluded that he had been washed overboard. The chief then decided who would go in the boats, and Durnan shouted, 'What about Norton?'

'He's helpless in the wheelhouse,' the chief said.

'You can't make him see what's happening,' said a sailor.

'We can't leave without him,' Durnan said, tearing up the stairway to the wheelhouse. Norton was in the corner, the sea curling around his prostrate body.

47

'Come, Skipper. We're going to make a bid for it. She's foundering.'

Norton waved his arms, trying to sing. Catching Norton under the arms, Durnan lifted him on to his shoulders. Outside the wheelhouse, Norton kicked, trying to free himself. Suddenly Durnan felt his hands clawing his throat. Norton was twisting the flesh of his neck. Durnan couldn't breathe. He tried to tear Norton's hands away. Norton was forcing his head back. Then with a terrific movement, Durnan threw him off his shoulders, and the sea flooded Durnan's body. He could see Norton nowhere.

Durnan rushed to the galley again. He had tried to save Norton, but Norton would have choked him if he had persisted, now Norton was away.

Fenner was stretched in the galley. The engineers and the two sailors were gone in the port boat. Durnan made Joe Fish lift Fenner's legs and they carried him to the starboard boat.

Now, Durnan knew, death was after them again. In the lifeboat he must grip. With one arm around Fenner. Grip, hold to anything, but grip he must. With his four fingers and his thumb, he must grip. With his mind, too. He must grip the thing he held with his eyes, with his mouth, with his bowels, with every part of him. Now Durnan was at the bow of the lifeboat. Sinking his fingers into it. He felt they might burst, but in the dark he could see his fingers fat and swollen, the blood oozing from them. The water jumped madly at him, making noises like a wild dog springing to bite. Dropping his head he called to Fenner, 'Hold you bastard, hold.'

It was dark, pitch dark, but he could see his fingers, see his body, see his mind in the shape of the red port light, and his heart pumped through his guts, shouting . . . grip . . . grip . . . grip. . . .

48

CHAPTER EIGHT

THERE was a loud surging in his head, and when this surging ceased for a moment, his ears seemed to open and close. Fish were swimming about in the dark with eyes rimmed with fire and fins and mouths coloured like violets. Then the noises came again, and jelly fish flapped around, and in their eye holes purple flames flared. Someone was laughing. A dog sat in the foc's'le with its paws curled around a stanchion. Flames came from its mouth and snorts of ashy smoke from its nostrils.

A man was yelling as bags of potatoes fell on top of him. The sea washed over the potato bags and the man was silent.

The loud noises came again, and his hand caught a cloak of seaweed. The seaweed parted from the rock and he fell among the jelly fish. Their tails tipped his chin, and he felt their slimy coldness on his lips. There was one, settling itself over his mouth to suck out his breath. . . .

Durnan heard himself cry out. It wakened him. He was aware of a man bending over him, cupping his hand on his forehead. Someone was holding his feet. Durnan's mind became quiet again, and his eyes widened. He looked up, and knew it was a ceiling he was seeing. Yet he was afraid to move lest he should fall among the jelly fish again. He could see the wallpaper in a vague way, as if he were looking at it through a pane of glass that was rain-flooded.

The man who was pressing his forehead was muttering something. The man bent, and Durnan could see his eyes. This had a strange effect, a soothing effect, hypnotic. The man was asking him how he felt. Durnan answered him, but he was only conscious of the man when his eyes met his.

Feeling around his legs, he knew he was in a bed. When he turned his head he could see bright colours. They came from a soda siphon. Again he felt he was falling, but the soda siphon held his gaze, and he pressed his heels and hips into the bed.

A woman entered the room. He tried to raise himself, but she urged him back, stroking his head, saying, 'You are still in a fever.' He felt her hands about his feet, and she left the room complaining that the water bottle was cold, and she must get it heated again.

Now he could see the room plainly. The wallpaper had flowers that recalled long ribbons of seaweed. Again the woman came into the room. This time she pushed her hand under the bed clothes until it rested above his heart. He didn't speak. He lay quiet, looking at the brass tops that bulged on the bed posts. The woman had brought a cup with her, and she was holding it to his lips. 'Take this,' she was saying, 'it's a taste of beef tea.' The liquid moistened his throat. At first he felt he wanted to vomit; the liquid tasted salty, reminding him of sea water. But as he stared at the soda siphon, the liquid became pleasant and he smacked his lips.

He looked at the picture of the Virgin that hung on the wall. The eyes and lips seemed to move, as if complaining of the heavy cloak that covered her head.

Now he was conscious of everything. But his hands felt lifeless. His elbows pointed into the sheets. His breathing was quiet, slow and steady, and his sudden awareness of it brought a feeling of contentment.

He was snug in this room. It was warm-smelling and cleanly papered. He was far away from the sea, and there was no need for him to grip any more. He could relax, move his head easily, and feel the bed beneath him. Now he was able to check the fears that lingered in his mind by reflecting on this snugness. The bed was warm, its weight of blankets and quilts weighing down on his body giving him confidence.

The woman brought him rice, codfish cooked in butter and coffee that was flavoured with brandy. Every time she was about to leave the room, she thrust her hand under his shirt until it cupped over his heart. Her hand was cool, a living thing, sensitive and alive with affection. Her long fingers curled like the petals of a flower. They moved out of a blue pullover that she wore. He thought it strange that her hands should be so beautiful and her face was plain. But then her face was strained, and in the light that caught it, it looked dark, with sunken eyes.

He was aware of her breasts as she sat on the bed feeding him. They were small, round and moved slowly with the movements of her body. She had talked very little to him, and was mainly concerned about his food, and keeping him well covered with the bed clothes. When she made the bed, he felt embarrassed as she looked at his legs, and as she tugged the wrinkled sheet from under his hips. He always wanted to turn away, to curve himself towards the wall; but she was always first with, 'Don't move. Lie still, and I'll have you covered again in no time.'

He wanted to ask her how he had got here, but it seemed an effort, for her actions showed as if she herself wanted no discussion about it. He felt now that this contentment was drugging his mind. All he wanted to do was sleep or lie still, listening to the birds' songs that came in through the open window.

He could move about now in the bed, draw his knees up, scratch one foot with the other, move his elbows, but his hands were lifeless, and he was conscious of the great heat that was in them.

Time was floating by, marked by little pleasantries; the meals during the day, her cold hand on his brow and the emotion that came with her feeling under his shirt for his heart-beats. The moon was out at night, making the Virgin in the picture nod her head. The birds were out at dawn, and somewhere at the back school children hurried through a game of football before the school opened. He got to know the doctor. This bearded man called every day, telling him that he would soon be fit again. And that he was better there than in the hospital. Then on the day the doctor told him he could get out of bed for an hour or so, he asked the doctor how he had got here.

'Your boat was picked up on Gunn's Island. The *Prince Albert*, a Portavogie fishing nabby, had pulled in there for shelter, and they found you drifting in at the dawn.'

'But where am I now, Doctor?'

'You're back in Barholm. You see, Gunn's Isle is just outside the bar. It was natural they should bring you here. I saw your case was a bad one of shock. . . .'

'But what about the others . . .?'

'Never mind, you have all the rest of your life to hear what happened to the others. Your task is to take things easy for a bit. Just to lie there and forget all about the shipwreck.'

CHAPTER NINE

DURNAN felt the cold floor. Moving to the window, he stumbled, but caught the small table to keep him from falling. The window was open, and he breathed deeply, his swelling lungs making his head dizzy.

The room door opened, and she entered with a grey dressing-gown. 'Put this about you,' she said. Then she caught his elbow and led him into the kitchen, sitting him down on a chair opposite the fire, and lifting his feet to rest on the fender.

There was a pleasant stillness about the kitchen. The red glow of the fire seemed to kindle this stillness. He was looking down at her as she sat on the low stool, with her face gazing into the fire. Her hair was uncombed and it was corded with grey, reminding him of the thread he had seen hanging from the waists of the begging women that tramped the countryside.

When she moved her head, he saw she was looking past him. Her blue eyes were wide and still, and her lips moved. They were thin lips. There was a quickness about them that was like the movements of her hands.

There were three things about her that he never tired of looking at: her hands, her eyes and her lips. Like three notes they were, and they seemed to move together when she talked.

Reaching over she curled her fingers around his foot, wanting to know if he was warm enough. He told her he was. Turning her head, she looked through the window, and the silence continued. Her sudden quietness puzzled him. Here he was, after being shipwrecked, and on his first day out of bed she sat as if they had known each other for a long time. It was her complete indifference to his sitting opposite her that made him feel that.

'Was there any others saved?' he asked quietly.

'No,' she said, facing him. 'Just you and another young lad. He's in Mathews's, further up the street. The doctor says he's coming along all right. . . .'

Turning, she looked to the window again. He could tell now that she wasn't interested, and he wondered why she should be so aloof. Now he found it hard to measure her strange behaviour with the consideration she had shown him when he was confined to bed. Yet, in the silence, he found they were getting to know each other better than if they had been talking.

Reaching for the poker, she scored the grate bars with it. 'The other lad's very young,' she said. 'Mrs. Mathews says he isn't more than twenty-one.'

'I know. Fenner's his name. Did they find the other bodies? The mate's or the skipper's?'

She drew her upper lip down, making her nose appear longer. Her eyes moved, checking something, and her cheeks flushed. After a long pause, she almost whispered, 'The skipper was buried yesterday. Two dulse cutters found his body on the rocks beyond the Gowlings. I buried him in the graveyard at Ballyphilip.' Nodding her head, she looked vaguely at the floor. 'Yes,' she went on, 'it was just a case of getting him into a coffin, and burying him in a grave that belonged to his brother.'

She smiled up at Durnan, and guessing the curiosity in his glance, she continued, 'He was my husband.' Her chin shot out, forcing her thin lips to close, making her mouth a little slit in her face. Leaning his head towards her, he spoke with quiet sincerity, 'I did my best to save your husband. You may not believe that. It's easy to make yourself a hero when the person's dead and . . .'

53

'It's all right,' she said, pressing her hand on his knee.

'I tried to carry him to the lifeboat, but he was headstrong . . . You must believe me. . . .'

'It's all right . . .' Her voice was lifeless, as if she didn't believe what he was telling her.

'I tell you, I did my very best . . .' his voice was stronger.

'Don't upset yourself. Don't work yourself into a state about it. . . .'

Now he had found the reason for her strangeness. Her husband had been drowned, and she had seen his swollen body laid in a coffin, and carried from the rocks to his grave. He wondered if she knew that he was the one responsible for her husband losing his ticket.

Yet he was aware of something about her, something about her strange face, that told him she hadn't grieved much about her husband's death. He knew she had not cried. Her face was tight and pale. It hadn't been loosened with a flow of tears. Her face seemed to him the sort that took everything in, never giving anything out. Yet it might be more painful this way. For the face that could cry plenty or laugh loud could get relief. But he could not feel that she had been sorry about her husband's death.

Looking around the kitchen, there was nothing to suggest that Norton had been her husband. There were no photographs, no pictures of ships, nothing at all to suggest the sea.

'I suppose you'll miss your husband?' he said, to break the awkward silence. She dismissed the question with a sudden jerk of her head.

'Are there any children?' She caught him staring down at her bosom. It puffed slightly as she straightened herself.

'No,' she snapped, and flattened the burning coals with the back of the hearth brush.

She lapsed into her preoccupation, looking at the window again. Perhaps she was wondering what was going to happen to her now. Rising from the stool, she felt his brow. Her hand was cold and nervous. 'You're almost back to normal,' she said. Then she laid the table for tea.

She was lively now, in the sense that she was aware of things; pressing him to more jam, telling him that it was home-made and the bread was home-baked.

She looked up quickly as the hall door was knocked. She rose and admitted a tall woman, yet she showed no eagerness of greeting for the newcomer.

'This is Mrs. Mathews,' she directed at Durnan. 'Your shipmate is in her house.' Her voice was cold, and she moved to the fire, leaving the visitor standing in the middle of the floor.

Mrs. Mathews reached out her hand to him. 'You're able to be about again,' she said. Her hand was wet, her fingers thick and clumsy.

Mrs. Mathews said, 'You had a miraculous escape,' and her eyes wandered from the table to the fire, resting on the tea pot that purred on the hob. The fact that she wasn't offered a chair disturbed Durnan.

'Young Fenner says you're great. That only for you, he wouldn't be alive the day. He says you tried hard to save Captain Norton . . .' Mrs. Mathews's eyes moved inquiringly towards her, but she coughed quickly, indicating impatience.

'The reason I'm here is that there's a man from the papers in my house, and he wants to take photos . . . So I wondered if you were well enough.' Mrs. Mathews hesitated. Durnan knew it wasn't his place to answer. He said, 'What you feel, Mrs. Norton? Do you mind if the photographer comes here?'

'If he wants to come, let him,' she said quickly.

Mrs. Mathew made her exit slowly, her head roving like a person about to buy the contents of the kitchen.

Pushing her chair back from the table, she gathered her hair into a ball. Then she cleared the table, all in silence. Sitting by the fire again, she said, 'What part are you from?'

'Portaferry. Just forty miles up the coast. I'm nearly a neighbour.'

'When you get back home, you'll drop me a line?' A smile gathered on her face.

'Yes, I will . . .' He stopped, seeing her face become still. She was looking beyond him to the door.

'The doctor said his skull was broken, like a coconut shell.' Her voice was hoarse.

'Whose skull?'

She went on as though she hadn't heard what he had said. She looked as if she were crying inside herself. 'That's what Doctor Hewitt told me. That his skull was broken, like as if someone had bashed a coconut with a hammer.'

'Whose skull?' he spoke, louder.

'Norton's,' she said quietly. 'A sad end, wasn't it?'

Burying her face in her hands she repeated, 'A sad end, a sad end.'

Durnan wanted to say again that he tried his best to save Norton, but now she was smiling, as if she had dismissed the thought completely from her mind. The front door was knocked, and she opened it. The photographer entered. He was a small man with a mop of hair and thick glasses.

'You're Mr. Durnan,' he said, reaching out his hand. 'Let me say how glad I am to see you alive. If all your young friend in the house above says of you is true you deserve a medal.'

Durnan laughed. 'And this is the woman who nursed me back to life,' he said.

'We'd better have you in the picture, too,' the man said.

Durnan watched her go to the sideboard, and tap her cheeks and nose with the puff that lay like a small pancake on one of its shelves. She pushed a red lipstick across her lips, sucking them inwards to spread the colour.

'I think you had better stand close together,' said the man, fumbling in the black box he had with him.

Durnan felt her close beside him. His hand reaching down touched hers, and when the photographer called for them to 'hold it', he caught her hand and squeezed it. The sudden flash

56

from the bulb made him press it a little tighter. Just for a moment he felt her long fingers, and she made no effort to draw her hand away.

The photographer packed his box and told them the picture would appear in tomorrow night's *Belfast Telegraph*. She asked him to have a cup of tea, but he declined. How pleasant she had been with the photographer, how standoffish with Mrs. Mathews. It occurred to Durnan to make some joke about catching her hand when she told him that the flash made her jump slightly, but she was going up the stairs quickly.

CHAPTER TEN

'YOU'LL want to go to Mathews's and see your friend,' she said. She had a bundle of clothes under her arm.

'Try these trousers, I think they'll fit you, and this is a white sweater. The moths have been at it. But the holes are in the back. If I get time, I'll draw a darning needle through them.' She left the kitchen while he put the trousers on. 'They fit grand,' he called out to the yard where she had gone.

The sweater was tight, blinding his eyes for a moment. He felt her at his back as she pulled it down. Now she was close to him, fixing it about his neck. He was looking at her fine lips. She had good teeth, flecked here and there with the red lipstick, and as she reached to his neck, her breasts gathered in her jumper, flooding up towards him. He had a sudden impulse to touch them, but she was standing away from him admiring his new clothes. She felt the clothes were too small for him, and he said that beggars couldn't be choosers. They both laughed as she rolled up the sleeves of the sweater over his hands.

'You'll need your hair straightened, unless you want to appear like a wild man,' she said. 'Sit down on the stool there and I'll run the comb through it.'

She combed his hair, catching his forelock with her fingers, sending a sweet purring feeling of pleasure through him. She was trying to curl it. 'You're not so wild looking now,' she said, pulling the loose hairs from the comb and twisting them into the fire. She opened the front door for him, and he leaned against the frame, breathing; feeling the salt air stirring in his lungs. It was low water, and there was a gentle sound from the tide, sighing as it licked the gravel. Gulls were standing at the water's edge, tickling their blue wings. Their bodies looked like young girls', their heads like hags'.

Durnan's head began to swim, as if the cold air was freezing his brain. His legs bent, and he caught the door frame, uttering a little grunt.

She led him into the bedroom, and he fell across the bed, gripping the clothes tightly. The bed started to whirl and he heard water gurgling in his ears.

It was dark when he awoke, and turning his head to the window, he saw the moon for a moment, a black knot of clouds throttling her. Slowly she freed herself, until she sprang out like a bouncing ball, flooding the room with creamy light. His throat was dry. Pushing the water bottle from his feet, he looked down at the room door, lines of light shone through at the bottom, and he knew she hadn't gone to bed yet.

What a strange being she was, her moodiness, her queer answers and her sudden questions, the cold tone of her voice, the warmth of her hands, her laugh when she had dressed him and her homeliness when she asked him to write to her. He had held her soft hand, and yet, if she knew he had sold her husband! But surely there was something amiss? Her reference to Norton's death was quiet. 'His skull was broken, like as if someone had bashed it with a hammer, just like a coconut.' Durnan felt the actual death hadn't worried her, just the awful picture of a skull broken in pieces like a coconut.

Had she not been happy with Norton? Norton, with his withered, crumpled face, glossy with tears. 'Durnan, you broke me.' Strange words for a man. Their simplicity frightened Durnan, sounding in his mind like the cry of a child suffocating.

Perhaps he had broken Norton's skull. His head, as he flung him from him, might have bashed against the deck. Perhaps he had killed Norton, in his wild effort to save him. The little scabs were still on his neck, marking where Norton had gathered his flesh into little webs. Reaching up, he touched them. They were dry and ragged, like the bodies of dead earwigs that have been dried in the sun.

A terrific heat possessed his body. His chest was wet with sweat. He heard movements in the kitchen, and the fingers of light snapped from under the door and he knew she was going to bed. He heard her slow steps up the stairs, and the paper on the ceiling puffing as she trod the floor above it. He listened, raising his head from the pillow, shutting out his heart thumps. He heard one shoe drop on the floor, then the other, and the ceiling groaned slightly, and the creaking of the bed came to him. She coughed, and then there was quiet.

He closed his eyes, and tried to sleep, but Norton's face looked down at him from behind the picture of the Virgin. He couldn't get this feeling of Norton looking at him clear in his mind. If he had a conscience, evil was pricking. Evil, it seemed, was seeking justice. Good was smug, and hadn't the same power to haunt. There was no pleasure in knowing he had told the truth at the inquiry. He had got the thanks of a dozen white-collared men, but what was the good of that? If he were before God, what attitude would God take to it? Would God say he was right in saying Norton was drunk? Or would God say that he should have acted in Norton's favour, by telling the men that everything had been all right? That might have saved Norton. The shock of the collision, and the drowning of the men, might have moved him to change his life. God had died for the evil as well as the good, and He said Himself that if He had one hundred sheep and lost one, He'd go out in search of it, never knowing what was to become of the other ninety-nine.

He threw the clothes from his sweating chest. The moon lit the room again, picking out the sad, luminous eyes of the Virgin. Somewhere a door was opened and a voice was calling out that someone was a spoiled boy. The voice was ordering in loud tones. Telling someone to gather sticks for the morning's fire. A child cried out and the door slammed loudly. The child's footsteps sounded soft in Durnan's mind, like sighs, as they trod the wet grass.

He felt himself beside the child, gathering sticks. Knowing the whins by their needles, the scabby-thorned bracken; the white dead hemlock making him shudder because of the oval-bodied slate-coloured woodlice that crawled through its satiny body. The ash tree was there with its fine leaves, making you think it was leafless.

Whin sparrows were resting in the whins. Snails lay on the bracken, slimy and cold, lazy with the fat of the dew. Soft, like the jelly fish. Grey, like the rat that has been swimming. The snails were cold, curling between your toes, making you dance with terror. . . .

The jelly fish had violet-coloured eyes, they were flapping their bodies in a dead fan dance. Norton was looking from behind the Virgin's picture, pulling her cloak from her sad face when the moon burst into the room. The ash tree was scratching its branches against the gable. The sounds were like a cross-cut saw. 'Why do you torture me? God in His Almighty mercy, look down on me. I'm no bad woman nor no whore . . . Move on you bastard, move on. Beach her, beach her . . . The water gurgled in. The water was yellow . . . It was filling the foc's'le . . . His neck was held tight. Norton was twisting it . . . Move on you bastard . . . Beach her, beach her. . . .

He heard his own voice screaming down into his stomach. The ceiling puffed and he heard her running down the stairs.

'You've fallen out of bed,' she said, kneeling beside him. He got to his feet slowly. His head was warm. He sat on the chair while she arranged the bed clothes.

'I must have had a nightmare,' he said.

Helping him into bed, she said, 'You're thinking too much about the wreck.' She curled the bed clothes about his neck.

'Maybe,' he said.

'Does the dark frighten you? If I left the lamp lit . . .?'

'No, no, it's not the dark. There's a good moon . . . I'll be all right now.'

She pulled the chair closer to the bed and sat down.

He said, 'I'm giving you a lot of trouble.'

'No trouble,' she said, pulling the dressing-gown over her bare knee. The lamp she had brought in shadowed her face, picking out her large eyes. Her hands were tinged pink at the knuckles, and her hair was gathered into a ball, marking her long neck, so smooth, not even swollen with an Adam's apple.

'Are you warm enough? There's another blanket in the drawer there.'

'I'm warm enough, thanks.' He wanted her to sit here, talking to him. He was conscious of his own lack of talk.

'You've been here over a week now, and none of your friends have come to see you.'

He said, 'I haven't any friends. I mean blood friends, like aunts, uncles or cousins.'

'You're not married, then?'

She had given him an opening. An opening for what? What did he want to talk to her about? Somewhere in his mind there were things he wanted to say. Or was it just a mood that hadn't, as yet, suggested the words? It presented itself now in a longing just to sit and look at her.

'I'm not married,' he said, looking straight at her. She dropped her head, and he felt uncomfortable with the recurring thought of having fallen out of bed. Again he was sorry for dragging her downstairs.

She said, 'I wasn't asleep, it was no trouble.'

'Do you not sleep well?'

'No.' Then after a pause, 'It's an awful thing, the want of sleep.'

'Maybe it's because you're lonely after your husband's death?'

'No. Wasn't he a sailor; never at home for months at a time?'

'But haven't you some friends? Or somebody that would come and keep you company, sleep with you?'

She did not answer the question, but looked at the window, pulling the curtain to look out at the moon.

'The moon's very clear tonight,' she said. She got up, tucked the clothes in at his feet. 'Don't bother if the lamp burns low. The flame will die itself. I trust you get some sleep, and no more nightmares.'

Reaching out, he caught her hand and kissed it. Again, he heard her mounting the stairs, this time hesitantly. Again, the ceiling puffed, one shoe fell, then the other.

Now and then he heard her coughing, and he knew she was awake. It was like a cough of pain, and he wondered if it were the pain of loneliness. The light died in the lamp, spluttering as if the wick were tired and was spitting the flame from it. The moon reached into a knowe of clouds, and its light came and went from the room as if the sky were blinking. He turned his head to the pillow, his heart beats softer and quieter. He had kissed her hand, her soft hand, and inside him he was happy.

CHAPTER ELEVEN

TWO days later, when he told her he would try again to walk to where Fenner was, she took his arm, led him through the door, and counted with her nodding head the number of houses.

'Ten doors along. You'll know the house, for the door is painted bright green, and there's a ship in a bottle in the fanlight.'

He walked slowly, and a fat old woman leaning on a half door said he had God's blessing about him, to be saved at Strangford Bar. She was ugly, with an upper lip like emery paper. She caught him looking at her lip, and she drew her hand to cover it.

Mrs. Mathews opened the door to him. Her mouth gaped wide, and she shouted, 'Come within, and be very welcome.'

Durnan made to sit on the sofa, and she said, 'Go on into the room. Your friend's dying to see you.' But she was in the room before him, telling Fenner about his coming.

Fenner was sitting up in the bed, a pillow propped at his back. Staring down at Fenner's face, Durnan thought him an overgrown schoolboy. The woman remained with them, until the smell of bread burning made her leave.

Durnan sat on the bed. Fenner was crying. 'Why are you crying, Jackie?'

Fenner tried to swallow the sigh that rose in a stutter from his chest. 'I can't help it. It's seeing you again that makes me cry. . . .'

'But I didn't do all that much on you that you should cry when you see me . . .' He ran his fingers playfully through Fenner's hair, and when Fenner drew away quickly, Durnan understood.

'Stephen, I never thought we'd live through it. My very bones shake in my body when I think about it.'

'Well, don't think about it, Jackie. A bad experience it was. I suppose you heard about the skipper?'

'Yes, Mrs. Mathews and her husband were at the funeral.'

'I'm staying with his wife. It's like something you'd read in a book. Any word of any of the others?'

'You heard about Joe Fish?'

'No.'

'They found his body about five days ago. The eyes were gone. Mathews says the crabs go for the eyes every time.'

'They buried him, here?'

'Yes, some disused graveyard, out of the town.'

Durnan realized he hadn't thought much about the others. Somehow, a shipwreck was like a passing funeral, you raised your hat and said nothing. It was the same with a shipwreck, you had been saved yourself, and that was all that seemed to matter.

'Poor Joe Fish,' Fenner was saying. 'He told me he came from a little village outside Capetown. Now he's buried in a graveyard in a tiny village in Ireland.'

'Will you go back to sea, Stephen?'

'I might, I dunno.' His eyes caught the small crucifix that almost hid itself in the hair on Fenner's chest. Reaching for it, Durnan held it between his finger and thumb.

'You believe in God now, Jackie?'

Fenner nodded, and when Durnan dropped the crucifix, he lifted it reverently to his lips . . . Mrs. Mathews came in with tea and warm treacle bread.

'Just a drink of tea, and a mouthful of bread to show welcome,' she said. As she left the room, she turned to Durnan, 'My husband's coming in for a bit of crack, you don't mind?'

When she was gone, Fenner said in a loud whisper, 'I hope he has his glass eye in. He takes it out when he's shaving, and he'd frighten you, to look at him.'

Her husband was the pilot, and he settled himself on the bottom of the bed. Durnan saw he had a habit of baring his teeth, like a playful dog.

'Wasn't it a shocking job about Captain Norton?' he said. 'To think of a man like him. That knew his way around the Cape as I know my way to bed, to be drowned at his own doorstep you might say, shocking, shocking . . .' He bared his teeth, and continued, 'But say what you like. She was a bloody death trap, that ship. Should have been in the scrap yard years ago.'

Durnan said, 'You knew Captain Norton?'

'Knew him?' he asked, with a grunt. 'I was at school with him. In the same book. We were never from each other, when we were children. As decent a man as ever breathed the fresh air of God. You seen yourself what he done for me? There was no reason for him to take a pilot, and him coming to his home port, for he knew this lough better than I did, or ever could. You seen yourself, he let me ashore, half way, just to throw the pilot fees my way. He was foolish, fond of a drink, and he lost his deep sea ticket. But wouldn't it be a funny world without its foolish folk? If there were no fools, we'd have little call for God.'

'He lost his ticket?' Durnan said, looking at Fenner.

'Aye, got a mouthful of drink and rammed another boat. There were lives lost, but it could have all hushed if it hadn't for some bloody Judas with a big mouth. Some yahoo blabbing it out at the inquiry. Some bloody religious madman . . . God, if we told the truth all the time the bloody world would cease to exist.' Mathews sucked the tails of his moustache, bared his teeth, spat into the kitchen and continued, 'God rest the poor bugger's soul; he's wherever the Almighty pleases, but he was forced into that coffin of a coaster. A man, begod, that knew more about seafaring . . .' Mathews bared his teeth with a long, 'Ach.'

Durnan looked at Fenner, but Fenner appeared not to be interested. Fenner was moving his fingers on the bed clothes, as if he were playing an instrument.

'The poor man's better off,' Mathews said.

'What makes you say that?' Durnan asked.

'A seafaring man needs a home, and Frank Norton never had one.'

'But he had a home.'

'Young man, a home of a sort. A slated roof and four walls doesn't make a home, nor does cushions on a couch, nor shiny furniture that reflects the fire. By God, it doesn't. If there's not a warm-hearted woman sitting by the fire, with life in her eyes, a smile on her face, and red blood in her heart, you may close the shanty. Begod you may pack your grip and skedaddle.'

Durnan laid his cup on the small table. Fenner turned on his side, his fingers continuing to move on the bed clothes.

'Did Norton not get on well with his wife?'

'Now who the hell could get on with thon yellow yorning?' Mathews lowered his voice, and, pushing the room door closed with his boots, he said in a loud whisper, 'I'll tell you something. Are you listening? She wouldn't let him sleep in the same bed with her. Could you beat that? What do you think of that for a

wife? Wouldn't let her man to bed with her. That's no manufactured tale, no compiled story, or hearsay. That's as true as
that cherry pipe's in my hand. I have it from Frank Norton,
himself, straight from his mouth.'

Durnan felt he must defend her and tell Mathews that Norton
was a drunkard, that he lived simply for the bottle.

'Why wouldn't she let him sleep with her?'

'Now you're talking,' Mathews said, with a grin of satisfaction.
It was obvious that he liked the trend the talk had taken.

He said, 'She's as hard as the iron that's in that bedpost. . . .'

'But . . .' interrupted Durnan.

'Let me finish,' Mathews said, stabbing the air with the foggy
mouthpiece of the pipe. As he leaned confidentially towards
Durnan his face turned to the side. Durnan was aware of the
glass eye. It was the one that bulged, and it gave his puffy face a
ferocious expression, making it like a grotesque mask. 'Let me
finish. Norton lay for three weeks in a French hospital. Now,
this is no manufactured tale, no carried story, for I have it from
his own mouth. Three weeks he lay, getting his appendix out,
and what do you think, do you know what happened when he
landed home? I'll tell you. She accused him of being with other
women and, bedamned, she still wouldn't believe him when he
hauled up his shirt and showed her the marks of the stitching in
his belly.'

Mathews shook his head impatiently, 'An evil-minded bitch,
she is. Her husband lying at death's door, and she tells him it's
because of other women. Fair play, for Frank Norton; he liked a
drink, but he'd no fancy for loose women. But no matter, God
works slow. She'll come to a bad end. She helped to ruin him.
The other bastard that deprived him of his deep sea ticket com-
pleted the ruin. Hell's fire, that he may lose the power of speech,
and may any childer that's born to him be dummies.'

Durnan knew he had no defence. Mathews believed in Norton.
Mathews, he felt, could never disbelieve in Norton. Mathews
would never admit that she was entitled to a certain belief in her

66

story. Mathews was thick, coarse and ignorant. And Durnan thought he must have lost his eye in a street brawl.

Mrs. Mathews came into the room, smiling, and pinning a brooch in her blouse. 'What's this old man been talking about? I'll swear he wasn't telling you what last Sunday's sermon was about. You didn't shut the room door for nothing, Sammy.'

'You're a nosey old woman,' Mathews said, with a disapproving look.

'What's he been talking about, Mr. Fenner?'

Fenner moved in the bed, and laughed.

Mathews said, 'I've just been telling this man, here, about Frank Norton's wife, and how she helped the poor man to his end.'

'Now, now, Sammy, don't be uncharitable. She didn't do that without help from himself.'

'She did. Sure he never hit the bottle, hard, until he married her.'

'We all know Mrs. Norton's a wee bit odd. But there's Mr. Durnan, I'm sure he finds her all right.'

Looking at her as she stood her back against the door, Durnan took a sudden dislike to her. Her eyes moved slowly, searchingly, and her lips and chin twisted coaxingly. Her voice was soft with wheedling.

'Mrs. Norton has been very good to me,' Durnan said confidently.

'Oh, aye,' Mathews grunted, 'she'll put up a good show for the stranger.'

Mrs. Mathews was making S's on her black apron with her finger.

'I suppose she's taking his death very badly?'

He knew now that she had come into the room to ask questions. The coolness with which she had been received the day the photographer arrived came back to him. Her white head was perched birdlike.

'Yes, Mrs. Norton hasn't ceased crying since she buried her husband,' he lied.

'She'll cry now. The bladder's near her eye. She didn't weep much for him when he was alive, but she'll greet her bellyful now,' Mathews said.

Durnan thought of her patting the powder on her face, and scoring her lips, and he smiled to himself. He never could imagine her being friendly with these people. She was aloof, and he felt she wanted to stay so.

Her presence in his mind was like an armour. He sensed he had got to know her intimately, yet speech between them had not been long, nor keen. But what there had been had started to sprout the buds of true friendship.

'What do you think Mrs. Norton will do about the house? Do you think she'll give it up?'

He pretended not to hear her question, and looked through the window.

She repeated it.

'I couldn't say what her plans are,' he said loudly.

'Has she any friends alive?'

'I couldn't say,' he repeated.

Mathews suddenly sprang to his feet and looked through the window. 'There's that bloody thief of a cat again,' he said, leaving the room. His wife followed him, after explaining about the small codfish that were drying in the yard.

'I saw your fingers move, Jackie, what were you doing? Thinking you were back at the organ again?'

'I was back at the organ, Stephen. Playing a "Te Deum". Every note sounded as clear in my mind as if it was a real organ.'

'What does it mean? Is it a hymn?'

' "Te Deum Laudamus",' Fenner breathed the words, as if he didn't want Durnan to hear them.

'Only for you, Stephen, I wouldn't be playing it. Isn't it strange I should be giving thanks to God, and yet it was you who saved me?' There was a pause. Fenner stared at the ceiling.

'Tell me, Stephen, did you pray to God that night? Was God in your mind?'

'No, Jackie, He wasn't.'

Fenner murmured, 'Very strange, very strange indeed.'

'What are you gonna do with yourself now? Go back to the organ?'

'Yes, I'll go back to the organ. I'll stay at home. I suppose I don't need to work, in a way . . . the folks will always see me through. But I want to earn my own living.'

'The folks?'

'My own people, my mother anyway. By the way, she was here a few times. I'd have sent her to see you, but I didn't know whether you were fit to be about.'

'You won't try the sea again?'

A little laugh stuttered in Fenner's throat, as he shook his head. 'No, I'm finished with the sea for good. But one of us will have to go to the merchant's here, and give an account of what happened. You had better go, Stephen.'

'I suppose they'll want to know what really happened. There'll be all kinds of rumours going around.'

'Yes. Mathews heard the steering went. He has questioned me often about it, but I keep telling him I want to forget all about it.'

'That's the right line, Jackie. Say nothing. But if you feel you want to, tell them the steering went, I'll talk to the merchant.'

'You won't tell them I was sprawling on the floor . . .?'

There was a childishness in Fenner's tones.

'Why should I tell them that, Jackie? I shan't say very much. As little as I can.'

'Will you tell them Norton was drunk?'

'No.'

'I'm glad, Stephen.'

'Why, Jackie?'

'*De mortuis nil nisi bonum.* I use to laugh at that tag at school. But there's times it means what it says.'

'I told them that once before, and what . . .?' Durnan got to his feet.

'Are you sorry you told them?'

'I don't know, Jackie. Times I am when people say it was the act of a Judas. But there's people would tell you that Judas is in heaven.'

'Are you going?' Fenner asked.

'Yes, but I'll look in tomorrow again. Perhaps I'll go the merchant's office tomorrow. Anyway, I'll let you know what happens.' He was moving through the kitchen when Mathews came in from the yard.

'Don't be a stranger. Drop in any time,' he said.

'Thanks, I will.'

'You heard they found the nigger's body?'

'Yes.'

'Well, when you are fit and able, just take a walk out and see where they buried the poor bugger. God help the pauper.'

'Why, what's wrong?'

'Turned the coffin on its side, because they struck a rock in trying to make a grave. Wasn't it a pity about his eyes been gone?'

'Yes, it was.' Durnan wanted away.

'Do you know what a doctor bloke was telling me? He said if I could get an eye even from some dead person, he could graft it into me. Still I would be quare looking with an nigger's eye in my head, wouldn't I?'

Closing the door behind him, Durnan paused to let the wind cool his face. Clouds were moving across the sky, their bottoms heavy with grey. The wind skimmed the water, rippling it like wild fern. The water looked green and distant. From the chimney of a house smoke flung down, spicing the air with turf and sour pine.

The fat old woman still rested her elbows on the half door. This time her hands hid her chin completely.

'Well, did you see your friend?' she asked.

'I did.'

'And is he well again?'

'He is.'

'Well, thank God for that, for he mightn't have been,' he heard her say, as he moved from her hearing.

CHAPTER TWELVE

O N the sideboard her powder puff lay slightly curled, like a biscuit softened with tea. Beside it was a small box of powder. Sniffing the powder, Durnan felt its perfume flood his nose, making him feel a strange intimacy, a closeness to her. Her comb lay on the mantelpiece, with hair circled in its teeth. Pulling a hair loose, he drew it between his finger and thumb. It was silver like a thread of frozen rain.

He sat down at the fire. Its plastered top forced the white smoke up the chimney in wrinkles. There was a strange silence in the kitchen. A dead silence. Even the light that came from the window was darkened and remote.

The door opened and she came in. 'I was at the butcher's,' she said, removing her coat. She sat down opposite him, stabbing the slack that covered the fire, until blue flames shot out and died again.

She said, 'I met the clerk from the merchant's office, and he says the merchant would like to see you.'

'Yes, Fenner was saying something about it.'

'How is your friend?'

'He's fine. Talking about going home soon.'

There was a pleasant expression on her face, a smile in her eyes. Her lips didn't share it. She continued stabbing the fire, as if begetting the blue flames was a game.

'Mr. Mathews seemed to think highly of your husband.'

'Yes, they were good friends, I suppose,' she said slowly.

'I don't think they were very good friends of yours.'

The words were out. He felt uneasy, anxious to hear what answer she would make.

'They are not, nor do I want them to be.' Then, after a pause, 'What had they to say about me?' Her eyes widened, and she was staring straight at him. Her eyes seemed to demand the answer. Her face was close to him, so close that he could see the powder beaded on her nose. All he had to do now was cup his hands

71

about her chin, and kiss her. Kiss the red lips. That was what he wanted to do. What would she do if he did?

Lowering her head quickly, she spoke quietly. 'You needn't tell me what Mathews said. He told you that Norton and I didn't sleep together. I know he did. That was Norton's topic in every pub.'

Her frankness alarmed him. Now her eyes were straight on him again, and he ground his teeth to keep his face from blushing.

'Why wouldn't you let him sleep with you?'

'That's my own business, Mr. Durnan,' she snapped as she rose and went towards the yard.

'I'm sorry, but I didn't mean to ask that,' he called after her. Her sudden snap of words had stung him. In a swift moment he realized he was only a stranger here. He was aware of an intimacy, but was she?

She came back to the fire again, leaning her elbow on the mantelpiece, quite close to him. Again, he told her he was sorry for the question.

Curving her hand on his shoulder she said, 'It's all right.'

He felt her gather the cloth slightly. Why did she grip it? Why did she stand so close to him? Why? why? And the strong urge that was in him to kiss her? He was close to a woman, a real woman, for the first time. Was he in love with her? He was. Was he?

Was there something about this love business that the sailors had talked so much about? Something so different from just going to bed with a woman? Was there something about this thing they called a home? They were a sentimental lot, were sailors, always talking about the dragging anchor, but it wasn't uppermost in their thoughts without meaning something. He had seen sailors often stopping children, asking them their ages, patting their heads. Was this their port light?

Perhaps it was. Now it was swelling through him, almost exploding. This was what he wanted. A woman, a home; this was his port light, where the anchor wouldn't drag.

She was lighting the lamp. Then she pulled the curtain.

'Will you live on here?' he asked.

'Why?'

'If I write to you, and you gone away from here . . .?'

She studied his face. 'If you feel you want to write, send your letters here. There's nowhere else I can go.'

Pointing to the lamp she told him he could burn it all night if he liked as there was plenty of oil in it. Then she climbed the stairs slowly, almost reluctantly, and he heard one shoe drop to the floor then the other.

In the bedroom he looked through the window at the heavy sky. One or two stars winked weakly, their light rust-coloured against the grey. Rain was starting to fall. He heard its heavy drop on the coltsfoot leaves. It was starting like a band. Then it beat on the upturned bucket, a slow one, two, three, of drops until it rattled the bucket. Now it was peppering down on the leaves of peppermint that grew beside the water barrel. It had started noisily, and now it was drenching the earth with a sigh that hissed. It vomited into the barrel, in a strange kind of dance.

When he turned the flame of the lamp higher the grey vanished from the room. The bed was snug. He heard movements above him. She was getting out of bed, and the slip slap of her slippers sounded on the stairs. He heard her cross the kitchen, and then a timid knock at his door. He called her in, and she entered, clutching her dressing-gown firmly at the neck.

'I want to borrow the lamp for a moment. To fix a sandbag at the back door, for the rain floods right into the kitchen if it isn't checked.'

She returned to the room with her hands shiny with rain.

'That's a dreadful night,' she said, peering through the window. 'Why don't you pull the curtains?'

She sat on the bed, turning to lower the flame of the lamp, to keep it from licking the funnel. He sensed in her slow movements that she didn't want to leave the room.

She said, 'This room is getting very shabby. I must get it done up.'

What irrelevant things she talked about. Her thoughts darting here, there and everywhere, like a wagtail. There was a sadness about her. It came from inside. The only outward sign that she cried. As she looked at the ceiling, her dressing-gown parted and he could see her soft, round breasts. He wanted to reach out, draw her to him and ask her why she was so sad, for a sudden tenderness moved in him. Touching her hand, she looked at him.

'Your hand is cold,' he said.

She nodded, appearing unaware of him holding her hand. He curled his fingers around her forearm, seeing the blood appear quickly. Her flesh was icy, and his hand warmed it.

He wanted to kiss her. Why couldn't he? His heart-beats came into his ears. He was nervous. Nervous of what? She was staring at him again, her eyes widening, making her face look as if it were coming closer to him. He sprang up, feeling his lips crushing against her teeth.

She had caught his shirt at the neck and was tugging it, half in protest but, her lips suggested, half in submission. She tore away and climbed the stairs slowly. He heard one slipper fall to the floor, then the other. He was trembling, his face burned and his hair felt as if he could tear it from his skull. He heard her coughing, coughing slowly and it reassured him. He had kissed her, and he wasn't sure if she had wanted him to. But the soft moistness of her lips were warm with fusion. His thoughts jumbled, and a coldness shivered in his back. The choking sensation came back, and he felt the room was flooding with rain. Kicking the bed clothes from him, he stumbled into the kitchen. Going to the yard, he was ankle deep in the rain that flooded the passage. The wall in front of him was damp, its skin of limewash cold, like a frosted potato. He heard her moving upstairs, and the quick decisive stab of a bar being shot into its keeper.

She must be frightened. Frightened of him. 'You needn't be afraid,' he called out. 'No need to bar your door.'

His own voice alarmed him. His head tightened. He stood

74

erect, his eyes flooded with water. Sweat was breaking through his chest, so warm that he felt he would choke. His body seemed to be rising, and he held fast to the wall. Someone was shouting and laughing wildly, like the bleating of a goat. It was a man, crouching, a brown felt hat to his chest. The man was getting smaller. His face was gathered into a grin. The man was running away from his mother. His mother was in a temper, shouting things to the man, and spits flew from her moving lips, until her words became only sounds. The man crouched into a bank and disappeared down a badger burrow . . . Durnan could not move. Life seemed to be drying up in him. His head was in a grip. Some unseen hands seemed to hold it. He had seen his father . . . a small man . . . Like a schoolmaster. . . .

Slowly the tightening in his head lessened, and he realized he was standing in water. He wanted his body cooled. He wanted air. Staggering up the passage he pulled the back door open.

The mud in the wet yard squeezed and curled between his toes, and the rain from the flooded eave dropped to his back. His knees were bending, and he clawed the wet air with his hands until he caught the slimy edge of the barrel. Steadying himself, he listened, hearing the rain from the spout tumbling into the barrel. His body was cooling, his eyes becoming clearer. He felt his feet firm on the gravel. Had he seen his father, or was it just a nightmare? Or was this father obsession starting a growth of madness in his mind?

He breathed deeply, looking for signs of his sanity in the things around him. Beyond the small garden he could see the dark hedges, shaped like the spars of dead ships. Plunging his hand into the barrel, he stirred the water, feeling its silkiness as his hand revolved. He was all right. Perhaps just a touch of another nightmare? Turning to the fields with their skeleton borders, he heard an owl hooting. Then he was conscious of the rain trickling from his hair, down his cheeks and shoulders.

Back in the room, he lay on top of the bed clothes. His feet touching the floor. His feet were warm in their covering of mud. He lay back. His body was tired and his eyes weary. He had kissed her, that was all. It had churned something within him, a promise, almost like the promise in the words of the gravedigger when he said, 'Your mother's buried facing south.' He felt these words were joyful, or in his own case, was it that he had fallen in love with a woman, a real woman?

CHAPTER THIRTEEN

THE sound of a pan, and the smell of bacon cooking, came to him when he awoke. Reaching for his shoes, he saw a dead worm on the floor, making him aware of what had happened last night.

He felt ashamed, wondering how he was going to face her, but she was calling that breakfast was ready as soon as he was ready to take it.

As he passed through the kitchen to the yard to wash, he glanced at her laying the table.

'Lovely morning,' she said, still working.

Filling the basin from the barrel, he rested it on the window sill. All around him was a great stirring of life, a freshness, a pulsing, a sweetness; yet there was no noise, no activity. It gladdened him.

'Leave the towel on the line,' she called out.

He pinned the towel, remembering how often this had happened at sea, only at sea you hung it on a greasy line in the galley, the foc's'le or the stokehole. Now he was doing it on a real clothes line, in a real house, and there was a woman calling him into breakfast.

At the table she was attentive, almost coaxingly so. There was an early morning freshness about her. Her hair was gathered into its knot, her face powdered, and when she left her bread on the plate, it was tainted with lipstick.

She ate in such a way that he knew she was enjoying the meal. There was a great calmness about her; it soothed him, but when he thought of how she had behaved about her husband's death, it left him wondering.

There was not a visible tear. Just an acceptance that he was dead and there was nothing more. She could feel like that about last night. Bolt her bedroom door and shut the incident completely from her mind.

He told her he would like to see the merchant this morning.

'Do you think you're able to make it?' she asked.

He said, 'I think so.'

Gathering the tablecloth, she took it to the yard to shake it.

'Had you another nightmare last night?' Her voice came along the passage.

'I er . . . I think I must have had. . . .'

'I was down early this morning. I looked in, and you were lying on top of the bed clothes. I tucked you back in bed.'

'But my feet,' he heard himself almost shout.

'Yes, they were muddy, I sponged them, but you slept on, never as much as moved an eyelid.'

'Good God!'

'What is it?'

'My muddy feet. . . .'

'You were worse the day they brought you from the wreck. Forget about it.'

She tidied the grate, sweeping the cinders into a little bank.

'I heard you up,' she said. 'I was up myself, fixing the skylight. It rattles if there's any wind. I thought I heard you shout something. . . .'

'No, I . . . must have been sleep walking . . . I dunno,' he was confused with sudden relief. The handle of the skylight could sound like a bar being pushed home.

'I'm sorry . . .' he heard himself mutter.

'If you're ready, I'll direct you as best I can to the merchant's,' she said.

77

She pointed to a building that rose high above the small houses. It had tarred shutters and whitewashed walls.

The fat old woman was leaning her elbows on the half door, her hand fondling her chin.

'You'll soon be fit and well again,' she said.

'Yes,' he murmured, walking on.

'Well, thank God for that,' she called after him.

The morning was fresh with silent urgency. How grand it was to be able to walk again, to hear your feet on the road. Not to be frightened to breathe, and to feel the sea was out there but you were far away from it.

He called at Mathews's house. Mrs. Mathews bade him enter. Fenner was fully dressed, in a new suit, new shoes and new shirt.

'What do you think of this gentleman?' Mrs. Mathews pointed to Fenner. 'Up this morning and away to Mass.'

Durnan saw Fenner motion him into the bedroom.

'I'm going home in an hour or so's time, Stephen, and it occurred to me that you might like to come. We could drop you at your place. Mother was here and made the arrangements. Anyway, she's crazy to meet you. I've tried to keep the meeting as far away as possible, but she's a fuss pot.'

Coming as it did, Durnan was slightly shocked. Now he must go home. He seemed to realize it for the first time. He had no right to think otherwise. Fenner repeated the offer.

'Very good, Jackie,' he said. 'But first I must see what the merchant wants. That's where I'm going now. Would you care to come?'

'Thanks, Stephen, but if you can manage on your own, I'd be very pleased.'

'Well, all right. I'll look in on my way back, and let you know. Thanks, too, for the lift in the car.'

'We'll wait for you,' Fenner said.

Outside the house he met Mathews. 'I'll walk up the street with you a bit,' Mathews said. Before Durnan could say anything, Mathews was beside him.

'I suppose you're right glad your shipmate's well again?'

'Yes.'

'You'll get a medal for saving him. But save as you did he'll die young.'

'What makes you say that?'

'Did you ever look at his finger-nails? Pink as a buckie rose they are. That's a bad sign.'

'Why is it a bad sign?'

'I'm telling you it's a bad sign, and I know.'

As they walked, Durnan saw it was his small eye that was now visible. A fisherman sitting on an upturned tub drew Mathews's attention to the nets he was sewing.

Durnan walked on, glad to be rid of Mathews. On reaching the merchant's office he was asked to wait by an oily clerk. Durnan sat down in the small office. On its walls were pictures of ships, and shiny advertisements for farm implements, and a golden eagle with the word INSURANCE printed across its breast, and underneath it a text saying *The Lord is my Shepherd.*

The oily clerk reached Durnan a tract, saying, 'You might be interested in that, sir, but if you aren't there's no harm done.'

Durnan looked at the pink paper. It preached the follies of strong drink. Durnan crumpled it, and threw it into the fire opposite.

'No offence meant,' he said to the clerk.

'None whatever,' the oily clerk smiled.

The merchant entered the office with his hand outstretched. 'You poor, poor soul. Glad I am to shake your hand, and you alive.' The merchant had huge eyebrows. Durnan found it uncomfortable to look at his face because of this. But he had a habit of talking into your face, Durnan discovered, and his oniony breath was revolting. Thus Durnan dropped his head as the merchant continued. 'And poor Captain Norton! Such a man, such a man. Well, well, well. But I'll not detain you. Sit down, my son, sit down.' Durnan was glad of this to escape the breath, but the merchant had drawn his own chair up, as if he intended to whisper to Durnan.

'You must be weak after all you've been through. Now, it's about the question of an inquiry. If there is one, as no doubt there will, you'll be called. What are you going to say? In your opinion what caused it? The bad weather no doubt. The treacherous storm, like a thief in the night it crept up. The east wind. The ship couldn't weather it, she couldn't fight it. Did the steering go? I heard so. Did I hear correct?'

Durnan decided to remain quiet. His tag would be that the steering went; it would save so much useless talk. The merchant was going on. 'She was good leaving port; as settled in the water as a hen on a nest of eggs. Ran into dirty weather and couldn't fight it.'

'The steering went,' Durnan said.

'That's your story, my friend. Keep it like that. Simple and straight, no frills, no frills.' He felt the merchant's hand on his shoulder. He could see the ship, too, with her heavy list to port, and the deck cargo. But what did it matter?

'The steering went,' he repeated.

'You've a clear mind, my good friend, a clear mind. And a simple story to tell. Neat as a matchbox she was leaving port. Sitting in the water like a sleeping swan. But the steering went, and the steering to a ship is what sanity is to a man . . . but I'll not detain you further. It's a thing you'll want to forget. I was once in a motor accident, and if ever I think about it my head spins again, just like a top . . . but come to the inner office for a moment.'

The merchant selected a key from the bunch that hung from his pocket, opened a safe and took out some money.

Counting the money he said, 'A little gift of ten pounds; buy yourself and your friend some clothes. No doubt his story will be the same as yours. The great thing is, that both of you are alive and well . . .' The merchant held out his hand. 'If you are here much longer, don't be a stranger. Why not come to church on Sunday. There'll be a seat and a hearty welcome for you. We have a special preacher. A man from the wilds of Nigeria, telling us about the Lord's work in that pathetic land. . . .'

Durnan stopped dead in the middle of the street, crumpling the notes against the lining of his pocket. Why couldn't he accept the merchant's money without further thought about it? A motor horn sounded and he ran to the footpath.

In Mathews's, on the way back, he told Fenner what had happened, and taking the notes he counted five, offering them to Fenner.

'I don't want them, Stephen. I should be giving *you* money. But you won't find my people ungrateful, you won't. . . .'

He said, 'You must take them, Jackie.'

'I don't want them. I have friends, a home, parents, and you have nobody.'

Fenner was right. He had nobody.

Fenner said, 'If you've made up your mind to come with us, the car will be here in about an hour. If there's anything you'd like to see to . . .'

'I'll come, Jackie.'

'Well, I'll send the car along for you.'

'Jackie, do you think I should offer some of this money to Mrs. Norton?'

'I dunno. Maybe you should. I suppose it depends on what sort of a woman she is. I mean, does she act as though you ought to pay her?'

'I'll offer her some, anyway.'

He did not quite know himself what kind of woman she was. But now he was going to shake her hand in farewell. He was filled with expectancy. Expectancy of what? What would or what could he say to her? He would shake her hand, offer her some money. And what then? In his mind he could hear the car purring. He was pressing her hand. Would she tell him to hurry on, not keep the car waiting? Would he kiss her, and say he was in love with her? Or was it too soon after her husband's death? Anyway that's what he'd do.

CHAPTER FOURTEEN

SHE was not in the kitchen when he entered. There was a thick lifeless quietness, broken now and then by a spewing and cracking noise from the fire. The walls seemed to be dead. The table was bare, save for a small vase of wallflowers in the centre. The hearth was swept clean, and there were wet patches on the kitchen floor where she had circled the floorcloth. In the room the oilcloth was shiny and smelt of soap, and outside the window a fungus-coloured wallflower was forced against the window by the wind. The clothes were off the bed, and the tick curled end to end. Points of yellow feathers jutted through it. The bed gave the impression that it had not been slept in for a long time.

He had wondered often at the thick silences that came on the house. He felt, now, he had found out the reason. There was an absence of homely intimacy. She seemed to wrap the intimacy up every time she cleared the table, or fixed the bed, or cleaned the hearth. All this brought about the feeling of strangeness that was part of the silence. He liked her tidiness. It was remarkable to notice it in the walls, on the pictures and in the furniture. All these articles were spotless, as if some unseen person had taken them away at night and cleaned them. For never did he see her do it. He was beginning to know now what Susan King meant when she said, you couldn't make a house out of a barn, but you could make a home.

He heard movements upstairs. He listened, and the footsteps ceased. They sounded as if coming from next door. Then he heard them again, slowly coming down the stairs. Lifeless and heavy they came; the lock clicked, and she entered the kitchen.

Moving to the fire, she sat down, prodding it unconcernedly. 'Did you see the merchant?' she asked.

'I did.' Her question recalled the money. Already he felt nervous.

He said quietly, 'I'll soon be leaving.'

'Where are you going?' She did not lift her head, but kept watching the scraps of coal she was gathering into the fire with the poker.

'Fenner's mother is taking him home in a car, so it'll be a good chance for me too. . . .'

'You're going home?' she asked with sudden attentiveness.

'Yes, home. Or what's called home . . .' His throat was dry.

'But do you feel you're strong enough? If you are bird alone, and going back to a damp and empty house . . .'

He moistened his throat with effort, and told her about Robert and Susan King.

She nodded her head, her eyes turning her face to the fire again. He kept staring at her, trying to discover why she had been so quiet upstairs. Perhaps she was praying.

'When are you leaving?'

'The car should be here soon.'

'You'll take the clothes I have for you. There's a bag belonging to Norton you can pack them in. Keep the bag too.'

She hurried up the stairs. The moment was yet to come, the shaking of her hand and the offering of money. She returned with the clothes and the bag, and when he packed them he toyed with the cord that hung from the choked neck of the bag.

'Well, better sit down until the car comes,' she said.

He sat facing her again, suddenly conscious of his clouded mind. Now there were no words, nothing he could say, and so much he wanted to say. His brain throbbed, as if his heart had reached up into it. Any time now the car would be here.

He said feebly, 'I'm like a beggar, going when I'm served.' The echo stabbed into his stomach, making him gasp for breath when he thought of what he had said.

What were the things he wanted to say? Christ, they were within him. Did he want to say that he loved her? Did he want to kiss her? To embrace her? Did he want to ask her to marry him?

She was trying to smile, and her eyes seemed to say that she

83

understood what was in his mind. Her silence was preparing the way for him. His face flushed, and to avoid her gaze, he said, 'I owe you a lot for the way you attended to me.'

'Do you?' she asked quietly.

'I'd like to give you some money . . .' he stammered.

'I don't want any money. You'll need it yourself. Keep it. Get yourself some new clothes,' she said.

'I'd rather you'd take it. . . .'

'But I don't want it, Stephen.'

She had said his name for the first time. The sound of her saying it gave him confidence.

'What is your name?'

'Winnie.'

'Winnie, I'd rather you . . .' But she was laughing, her thin red lips parted. Reaching down he caught her hand, and kissed it. She made no move to withdraw it. This recalled the incident of last night.

He said, 'I'm sorry for last night.'

'Sorry for kissing me?' she asked with a smile.

'No, not for that . . .' but he was lost for words in the great thaw that had so quickly set in.

'It was my fault as much as yours,' she said. 'I told you a lie about the skylight. It was the door you heard me bolting.' She saw her words had stung him, and added quickly, 'But it's all over now and there's nothing to be alarmed about.' Her smile reassured him.

The door was knocked, and a car horn sounded quickly. Gripping her shoulders, he kissed her. 'Would you marry me, Winnie?'

'Yes.'

'Sometime. But I'll write to you . . .' The knocking and the car horn became louder. As he made to open the door she stopped him. 'Better rub the lipstick away,' she said, crumpling her handkerchief to clean his lips. But he bent and kissed her again, and she shook her head with mock impatience.

84

'Seriously, you must clean your lips; what'll your friend think?' She moved away and opened the door. Fenner entered. 'You ready, Stephen?' Durnan introduced him, and they shook hands.

Fenner said, 'We have the car and I felt we might look at the grave of Joe Fish. Mathews says it's just a mile or so out of the town.' Fenner carried the bag to the car. Durnan shook her hand. 'I'll write,' he whispered. 'I'll write tomorrow. Yes, I will, tomorrow. . . .'

As he was getting into the car Fenner warned him to look out for the flowers in the seat.

'Mother brought them for the Mathews,' he said. 'I thought it would be nice if we could put them on old Joe's grave.'

Mathews, in front, directed the driver. They stopped at an old graveyard, and inside the gate they turned abruptly to look at where Joe Fish was buried.

It looked as if they had laid his coffin on the flat earth and covered it with soil. Mathews explained about the rock, telling them they couldn't go deeper and that it was a crying-out sin to leave the grave as it was.

Fenner laid the flowers in the centre of the grave and quoted: 'Home is the sailor, home from the sea.' Then, falling on his knees he crossed himself and prayed for the soul of Joe Fish.

At the foot of the grave Durnan saw a rat-hole. He pointed it out to Mathews. Mathews crossed to the hedge, and stripping a long branch came back and pushed it up the rat hole. It thudded lightly on the coffin, like a timid knocking on a door.

'God help the pauper,' he said.

Fenner was full of writing to the Sailors' Society about it, but Durnan answered him in nods and grunts, for his mind was back with Winnie.

As they moved out of the graveyard Mathews pointed to a vault. 'Do you see that vault? The people in it are over one hundred and fifty years old. I know, for one day there was a wheen of us curious about it, and I lifted the top off it. That's a

85

remarkable thing to do, for there must be five hundredweight in it, it's solid granite. I lifted it myself, so I did. I'm the strongest man in these parts, and do you know why? This is a remarkable thing I'm now going to tell you, my mother kept me on the breast until I was four years old. She was the strongest woman that ever mothered a child. . . .' But Durnan wasn't interested, nor was Fenner, for they were both silent as the car drove back to the village.

CHAPTER FIFTEEN

MRS. MATHEWS came to the door and invited Durnan in for a cup of tea. He refused, but Fenner said, 'Come on in, Stephen. I want you to meet mother.'

Fenner introduced him to a little woman in a fur coat and a hat made from the same kind of fur.

'No, no, I'll not shake your hand, but throw my arms round you, and hug and kiss you,' she said. After pecking kisses all over his face, she cried, 'God and His Mother bless you.'

Fenner said, 'Come, Mother, don't make a scene.'

'He saved your life, and do you want me to greet him as if I were sorry about it?' Her small black eyes looked lifeless as the tears dimmed them.

'Jackie, did you thank Mrs. Mathews for her great kindness?' Fenner slunk into the room, pretending to look for things.

Mrs. Fenner took her purse from her handbag and handed Mrs. Mathews two twenty pound notes.

'What's this for? God bless me, forty pounds, a small fortune.'

'Take it and say nothing. If I had to bury the brat, it would cost me three times that. Come now, put the notes away, and not stand there like somebody waiting on the hangman. Don't look as if you'd stolen them. . . .'

Mrs. Mathews beamed down at the notes before she pushed them into a delf ornament on the mantelpiece.

Fenner came from the room. 'I think we're ready now, Mother,' he said. Durnan caught his eye winking him out to the car.

'Stephen, that wee woman thinks I am still a child. Talk as little as possible about the ship going down, or she'll fuss and cry, and feel us all over to make sure we're really alive. You know what mothers are.'

Mrs. Reilly's words flashed in his mind, ' Pulse of my heart. . . .'

'What's keeping you, Flo?' Fenner was calling out from the back of the car.

Durnan laughed loudly.

'What are you laughing at?'

'I'm laughing at you calling your mother Flo.'

'That,' said Fenner, smilingly. 'I call her that when I'm in a good mood. She's the best soul in the world, but too fussy, and she can never say goodbye without taking an hour over it.'

Fenner's words nearly brought tears to Durnan's eyes.

She was getting into the car. Into the back seat beside her son, urging him to tie a scarf about his neck, to pull the rug well over his knees. 'Are you comfortable in front, Stephen? There's room here at the back for another, but it's best to travel with plenty of room.'

Durnan assured her he was all right.

'Flo, darling, will you quit fussing? Anyone would think I was an invalid or a bit of rare china. I'm all right.'

'You're not all right, Jackie Fenner . . .' She broke off, to wave goodbye to the Mathews family, crowded round the door.

She said, 'Stephen, when you've seen your own people you must come and spend a holiday with us.'

'Yes, Stephen, you must. It never occurred to me to ask you,' Fenner added.

Searching in her handbag she took out a card and handed it

over to him. He read the words: Glasslough Arms Hotel, Glasslough. Proprietors J. & J. Fenner.

'A postcard any time to that address. Can you come in a week's time?'

'Yes, I'll come. I'll . . . ' he was recalling the kiss.

'Let us have your address in case you need coaxing to come.'

The driver eased the speed of the car while Durnan wrote his name and home town on a slip of paper. During the lull the driver lit a cigarette, and the smoke wafted to the back. Fenner started coughing, slowly at first, then his head bent, and his forehead was red, and his eyes seemed to bulge. A shower of phlegm came from his mouth as his head rocked to and fro.

'Johnny, put your cigarette out, it's too much for him,' she said. Her face twitched to stem the tears that peeped from the corners of her eyes. She started wiping her son's mouth with a handkerchief.

'I wish to God you wouldn't fuss so much. I'm all right. . . .'

'You're a stubborn son, Jackie Fenner. You've got that chest back again.'

Fenner closed his eyes, resting his head back against the cushion. There was silence now. The little woman bit her handkerchief and rubbed her eyes.

The car raced on, slowing where a cow fed on the roadside, halting to let a dozen ducks walk unconcernedly to the other side, skimming the hedges where a stubborn farm cart refused the allotted space. The kiss seemed far away. Durnan couldn't remember it, and yet it wasn't half an hour ago since he put his hands on her shoulders. Rubbing his lips, he found traces of the lipstick on his handkerchief, and he hurriedly stuffed it in his pocket. The car curved round a sharp bend, tilting him against the door. He knew the bend well. Now it was only a matter of minutes and he would be home.

'I live beyond the village,' he told the driver.

'Well, let me know where to turn and when. . . .'

They were in the village now, crossing the market square.

A few cows stood tail-swishing near the grey barn that was known as the Market House. Now they were going down Ferry Street, down the steep hill that led to the shore road. His heart sank. It was always the same, every time he came down this street after being away. He was filled with a sudden sickness, trying to vomit and knowing there was nothing to come up. He felt it was a sickness of the mind that flooded down into his stomach, causing a vomit of despair.

And voices came into his mind, shouting. Where did he get such a fancy name, Stephen Durnan?

'Round this corner, right or left?' The driver asked.

'To the left, and straight ahead. A mile beyond the last house.'

Fenner and his mother would be away in a little while. Stephen Durnan. Sure he doesn't know where the hell he came from, and that's the truth. He knew they said that in the small houses they were now passing. But in Norton's he had seen his father. He knew that image would come again, the man with the felt hat rushing away. He knew it would fly into his mind, as the perfume of a flower flew into the nose in a field, yet when you searched for the flower you never could find it.

'Far along?'

'Yes, just around the red banks,' he said, groping on the floor for his bag. 'Better not attempt the loanen in case of a puncture. It's thorny and rough.'

The car stopped and its two doors opened. He pointed up the loanen to the cottage.

'That's where I live, when I'm at home.'

'For God and His Holy Mother's sake, don't go sailing again,' Mrs. Fenner implored.

'Now, now, Flo, be sensible. What would happen if no one went sailing?' Fenner said.

'Father of wit, you're there,' she laughed. She made Durnan promise that he would come to them in the course of a week or two, and as he closed the car door after her, she bade him promise again. Even as the car moved away, she called out, 'Don't forget . . .' She waved her hand, trying to get her tear-sodden hand-kerchief to flap. He watched the car snort dust from its wheels until it rounded the bend. He let his bag lie against the grass bank that fringed the bottom of the hedge on the road. The heavy clink of a hammer reached his ears, and looking to the beach he saw the bent figure of Robert King on the deck of the *Summer Breeze*. Near the vessel pitch was melting in a bucket that rested its wrinkled body on a ring of stones. When Durnan sniffed the air, it was tainted faintly with the odour of melting pitch.

He was half way up the loanen when he saw the white smoke feather from the cottage chimney, and he knew Susan was there.

She was bent over the fire, stirring a pot, when he entered.

'Did you get back?' she asked, not turning to look.

'I did, Susan.'

'Ach, Stephen, it's yourself. Didn't I think it was Robert when I heard the latch click.' She pulled a chair to the fire and pointed to it.

'I'm making a taste of stew. Robert found a brace of whaups; he said they fell at his feet after he heard the shots. So I'm afeared the shooters may search with sorrow for them. For in that pot they are, and in that pot they'll remain. I'll put in another couple of spuds, and you can have a bite with us.'

He knew she hadn't heard about the wreck, or she would have talked about it. There was contentment in her face as she peeled the potatoes.

'Keep your eye to the pot, and move the lid when it boils over. I must run down to the beach to Robert. You know, he's not able for the caulking himself. He's killing himself trying to get her decks tight afore the winter comes with the rains.' Tying a grey shawl about her head, and with another warning about the pot boiling over she left the kitchen.

Durnan removed his coat and stretched himself on the sofa. He was at home again. What was going to happen? What was he going to do? Go back to sea? No, not for a while. There was no great hurry in his mind. Not the sense of urgency he had always felt when his mother was alive. There were twenty pounds in the post-office. He had lost his book, but he knew that Miss Gelston, the postmistress, would be able to fix things for him. He had the ten pounds the merchant gave him . . . thirty pounds in all . . . enough to keep him for a long time.

He could live comfortably on the thirty pounds. The rent of the cottage was two shillings per week. He could manage well on one pound a week. He could get a stone of flour and a pound of currants and Susan would bake bread for him. He could borrow Robert's punt and fish as many codling and lythe as would do for him. He could go to the fields at the back of the cottage and snare a rabbit, and there was shell fish galore beyond the Point.

He wanted a rest, after tramping the seas since he was thirteen. It was warm and he opened his shirt, recalling to his mind the cold of her hand as she rested it above his heart. She was a woman. A woman that was inside him. Even now she was close to him, almost breathing on his cheek. She was lonely. Did she let him kiss her because she was lonely? Mathews's story might have been wrong, just an act of bluff on Norton's part. She was right in refusing to sleep with him if she thought he had been in the hospital for something other than his appendix. Women knew more than men in this sort of thing, a wink was as good as a plain-spoken statement to them.

He urged his head further into the back of the sofa. He was thinking of a woman for the first time in his life, thinking seriously. No other woman had ever troubled him. He had gone ashore, often, with the other sailors, but on these visits he had never showed any eagerness for women; if he got one, well it just happened, if he didn't . . . well, it was just the same . . . never any regrets, nor longings.

It was never the foremost thing in his mind. He hated brothels. Even in France, where it seemed as natural to visit them as it did a pub in England or Ireland. No . . . women were there . . . if it happened . . . that was that . . . he didn't go chasing them.

He would write to her, telling her how lovely it was when he kissed her. Was there another woman he liked better? No, there wasn't. No one else in his mind, never was. No, Winnie was within him, part of him. Everything about her, her eyes, her lips, her hands ... He would write to her. He would marry her. Take her home here ... The pot boiling over forced him to his feet, and his head was slightly dizzy as he walked to the fire.

CHAPTER SIXTEEN

'STEPHEN, son, the postman was just telling me about it, this very minute. Indeed if this wasn't Friday, and pension day, I wouldn't have heard it at all,' Robert King said, stretching out his gnarled hand that was freckled with pitch beads.

'There was just you and another lad saved. Sad, sad. . . .' He shook his old head.

'Poor Stephen, and me thinking you had got a run home for the week-end,' Susan said, as she ladled the stew into plates. She complained that the whaups were young and that their flesh was boiling through the pot like feathers tumbling in a breeze.

Robert poked through his plate until he forked out a piece of dark flesh. Nibbling it from the fork, he smacked his lips, and addressed Susan.

'Susie, me old hen, but that stew's very tasty. Isn't it, Stephen?'
Durnan turned a mouthful of the hot food and nodded.

'Their flesh would remind you of a hare, although it isn't as dark in colour,' Robert said.

'They're grand for making a pot of broth, but just what you'd know on the strong side. It would take you standing by to skim the grease,' Susan said.

'That stew is fit for a king. That we may never have worse,' Robert said.

All through the meal Robert talked, telling how tricky the bar at Barholm was and of how the *Moss Rose*, a ketch of seventy tons, was lost. He demonstrated, with his fork in the stew, how she fought the wind, until Susan impatiently got up saying, 'Would you just listen to that old blow? You'd think he was aboard the *Moss Rose*, and him only quoting hearsay.'

'Susie, my old cigar, you're always trying to take this good husband of yours down a peg or two.' He winked at Durnan.

'Get this cup of tea into you, and away to the finishing of your caulking,' she answered.

There was something very kindly in this winking habit of Robert's. It made Durnan like the little man more. His tiny slits of eyes hid themselves every time he laughed. Susan's bluff manner acted like a magnet on Robert. She would call him an old fool, a silly old whigmaloorey, an old blackguard and a rapscallion, but in turn she enjoyed the long litany of names he had for her. They were devoted to each other. They lived within each other, no two were ever closer.

It was Robert who had shown him his first compass, taught him how to read it, and told him the port light was red and the starboard was green, taught him to make his body strong by turning the winch in the *Summer Breeze* and climbing the rope ladder that reached to her mast.

Now, he remembered, it was Robert had brought about his hankering for the sea. He knew, too, that Robert would never admit that a steamship berth made a sailor. Robert belonged in the sailing ship. Looking at him now, Durnan felt that his eighty years of life had been grudgeless.

He was a happy old man. Happy in every sense. Loved the life he led in his own *Summer Breeze*, with Susan always in the cabin, his counsel, his guide, the only other person in his world. The little eyes spoke of the lively life that was still within him. They seemed to capture his nature, stealing the smile from his lips, to keep it shining always. His face looked twisted, as if his eyes, tired of the smile, had gathered his mouth and cheeks into a pucker of flesh. His flesh was brown, like brown paper that was meat-stained with flecks of blood.

'Come, husband, the rain will be down on us, and you blathering there, like a travelling tinker. Take yourself off and finish your caulking.' Susan was pinning a grey shawl about her head.

'Stephen, son, I never get a minute's peace with this nagging woman. It was the unfortunate day for me when the devil forced me to ask her to marry me.'

'It was out of sympathy and pity that I gave you myself. I brought my pigs to a purty market.' She had Robert's coat from the door, forcing his arms into it, pulling it down about his hips.

'Put a scarf on you, or you'll get the cold,' she said.

'Afraid of losing me? Take good care of me, good men are scarce.'

'If you get the cold you'll keep me awake all night with the coughing.'

Robert was moving through the door, laughing and clapping his hands.

Susan looked after him as he moved down the loanen. 'He's getting no younger,' she said. 'You know, Stephen, if anyone heard us going on like we do, they'd think we weren't happy together. But you know I talk like that to him for his own good. He likes me to boss him. Makes him feel he's a young fellow. If I told him he wasn't able for the caulking, he'd take to the bed. You know his eyes aren't good. He's using a mallet, and he'll smash his thumb as sure as God. . . .'

She cleared the table. Then she took the bed clothes from the room.

'You'll need these aired,' she said, arranging the chairs round the fire and covering them with blankets.

'Have you any notepaper, Susan?'

'Deed and I haven't. I used the last sheet All Souls' Night. I sent in the list of our dead for prayers. Are you needing it in a hurry?'

'No, Susan. Maybe I'll go into the village now, and get some.'

'Well, if you're going to the town I'll be as far as the loanen foot with you,' she said.

He caught her arm as they walked. She was looking towards the *Summer Breeze*. Robert was on his knees, puffing the fire under the bucket.

'If the rain comes we'll be flooded out. He has her deck as naked as a winter ash,' she said.

Durnan said, 'Well, Susan, you needn't worry. My cottage is there and you're welcome as long as you like to stay.'

She thanked him, and hobbled down the beach, and quickening his step he hurried towards the village.

He decided to go to the post-office. He could talk to Miss Gelston about his lost book. It was Friday, and the office was crowded with old age pensioners. Some were folding the ten shilling notes carefully, others were wrapping their books up in brown paper that looked soft and silken from usage.

One old woman was holding a pound note to her weak eyes, and exclaiming, 'It's little enough for two to live on, but sure half a loaf's better than no bread. God love "Lord" George. Protestant and all as he is, it's many a Hail Mary I've whispered for his Welsh soul. Only for him we'd all be in the workhouse.'

'Now, now, Mary, you're served. There's others to come, so move off and keep the counter clear,' the postmistress was saying.

Durnan stood waiting, watching the two women behind the counter beetle the books with their heavy stamps.

One old man took a long time to make a straggling X on his form. All this fascinated Durnan. His life at sea had no variety, no great closeness to living things.

A child kept tapping the counter, crying out, 'I want my granny's pension. Cafolla's here and she'll give me a penny for ice cream.'

Miss Gelston shook Durnan's hand and said she was glad to see him safe and well. She was a tall woman, with inquisitive eyes, and her hair was built on her head like a coiled rope. When he told her about losing his book, she motioned him into the kitchen saying she had something to tell him.

'That won't be hard to fix,' she said, when she heard the full story. 'But there's something else. Now don't look so alarmed. You've done no harm or anything like that. This little matter I want to talk to you about is to your advantage.'

Durnan wondered what on earth it could be. Why she should bring him into the kitchen to talk about it.

'It's a matter of one hundred pounds, that your late mother has deposited here. I think I'm right in feeling that she intended you to get it.'

His head swam at the sudden news. He said, 'She never mentioned anything to me about having saved that money.'

'Of course, her end was sudden. . . .'

He nodded, looking straight at the postmistress.

'She got little time to settle her affairs. When the heart snaps everything is over. But there's no one else for the money. Do you know if there is?'

Was there? He couldn't answer that. He knew of no one. Perhaps his father . . . the man with the grey felt hat . . . The postmistress continued, 'Your are her only flesh and blood. Your father might turn up, but it was your money that built the little nest egg.'

Strange that this woman should mention his father. Did she know anything? He knew his mother had worked as a cleaner in the post-office when he was at school. Perhaps his mother had talked to her about it.

'Still, I don't think there's any danger of that,' she said, with an air of finality.

'Any danger of what?'

'Any danger of your father turning up.' She slurred the words, sounding as if she were sorry for mentioning his father. She changed her tone, 'However, I think we can take it that you are her only kith and kin, or whatever you choose to call it. So I see no reason why you shouldn't get the hundred pounds, plus whatever interest has accrued.'

'Did my mother ever talk to you about who my father was?'

'Never.'

The door was knocked and the postmistress got to her feet.

'Leave the matter entirely in my hands and I'll see that everything is all right. Meantime, don't be a stranger when you're passing the office, look in now and then, and we'll let you know how things are progressing.' She reached out her hand. 'Don't look so troubled. You're a hundred pounds richer since you came in,' she said.

Outside, he breathed deeply when he thought about the money. A hundred pounds. Then there was his own money, and the ten pounds he had in his pocket. He was rich.

He met the harbourmaster and asked him into Jane Whorry's for a drink.

When Jane saw him she sang again, this time with greater gusto:

> Ramble away, ramble away,
> Are you the young man
> They call Ramble Away?

'Your rambling days were nearly over, Stephen,' she said.

'It's hard to drown a sea dog,' the harbourmaster said.

After the third round of drinks the harbourmaster said, 'Any washing you want done don't hesitate to send it along to my brother Andy's. He has five of the finest daughters that ever breathed the fresh air of God.'

'You may soon take a wife yourself, Stephen,' Jane said.

Durnan felt gay. The drink was fogging his mind, and he wanted to laugh. Yet he knew he must watch himself lest he burst into hysterical laughter, and tell Jane that he was thinking of taking a wife. He checked himself, suddenly, for the words seemed on the tip of his tongue. They were there, ready to be spoken, 'Yes, Jane, I'm getting married. To a widow woman.'

He thought he heard Jane answer, 'A widow, Stephen? She'll have all the more sense.'

A tramp who had been standing at the top of the counter came down to him, asking if there was a doss house in the village.

'Now, now, Barney, you know well enough where the lodging house is. Don't come any soft Arthur stuff here,' said Jane. Durnan gave the tramp half a crown. The tramp spat lightly on it and left the bar. The harbourmaster ordered another drink. Durnan realized he was getting drunk. He rested his elbows on the counter. His chin shot out, and his eyes were warm.

'I'm getting drunk,' he said.

'Nonsense,' said the harbourmaster. 'All you need is cup of black coffee and the full of your lungs of fresh air. Come along to my brother Andy's with me.'

Durnan steadied himself. He was near the door when he thought of Robert and Susan. He must bring them a drink. Poor old Robert, trying to stuff the rotten sides of the *Summer Breeze* with pitch and oakum. He called for a bottle of whisky, telling the harbourmaster who it was for.

'A decenter man couldn't drink your health,' the harbourmaster said. He felt the little man grip his elbow.

'Come on to Andy's and you'll leave it as sober as an archbishop.' Durnan wanted to go home, but the harbourmaster wouldn't hear tell of it.

'Are you there, Sina?' the little man called out, as they entered. A fat woman appeared, with a duster in her hand.

'I fetched Stephen Durnan along for a cup of black coffee. You know Andy's wife? Sina Maxwell to her own name.'

Durnan sat on the sofa, feeling he was going to be sick.

'Make yourself at home,' the little man was telling him, 'and the house of parliament is at the head of the garden, if you're so inclined.'

Sina was hurriedly removing the women's underclothing from the line that stretched across the fireplace.

'A modest woman. A modest woman. Lead us not into temptation . . . Do you see anything, Stephen? She's frightened of the harmless clothes putting bad notions on us.' Sina shook her hand at the harbourmaster, telling him that he had an eye for evil.

'She has five of the finest daughters that ever trod shoe leather, Stephen. If you're looking for a wife, you might go further and fare worse.'

'If Stephen Durnan wants a wife he'll pick one for himself, won't you, Stephen?' He laughed at her question.

'Your Harriet would suit him down to the ground,' the harbourmaster said.

'Listen to that old matchmaker. He never sought a wife for himself,' Sina said, preparing the coffee.

'I had no call to seek a wife, when I had such a good sister-in-law as you.'

Durnan gulped the coffee. It cleared his mind, sobering him. He got to his feet.

'You're not going, so soon?' Sina said.

'Yes, I must. Thank you for the coffee.'

'Nonsense, it was nothing,' the harbourmaster said.

'Now that you've been in once, come again. If it's lonely for you at home come in here. There's always fun with five girls that's fond of singing and a game of cards and crack that's lively with laughing. Nobody wears a long face here. So if your heart needs lifting drop in any night,' Sina said.

'She's right,' the harbourmaster agreed. 'I use to sail in a French barque, and I had shipmate that always maintained that a meal without wine was like a day without sun. So I say, a house without song is a house without joy. So heed Sina. The welcome's not from the teeth but from the heart.'

Sina inquired if he would be able to walk home himself, and the harbourmaster offered to assist him, but he was through the door calling out goodbye and that he would call again.

Nearing the slip, he watched children playing. They threw a stone to each other, singing loudly:

> Mrs. M'Lean, had a wee wean,
> She didn't know how to nurse it,
> She give it to me, and she give it to you,
> Till its poor wee belly burstit. . . .

Thrusting his hand into his pocket, he took out what money he had, and, moving into the ring of children, scattered it in the air.

CHAPTER SEVENTEEN

'HOW long ago is it since you were drunk, Robert?' Pushing his cap back on his head, and wrinkling his brow, Robert said, 'You're asking me something now, Stephen.' Staring into the fire, Robert repeated the question, 'How long is it since I was drunk?' Then as if the fire had given him the answer he looked up quickly. 'It's easily ten years ago, since I was happy in the way that whisky makes you.'

'Would you like to get drunk tonight, Robert?'

'Say drunk easy,' Robert answered, his eyes laughing, shaking his head, making his ear-rings dance.

'I'm getting married, Robert.'

The words were out. All evening they had rested on his tongue, and now he had spoken them. The image of her lips came to him, and she was crying out that she was lonely. Taking the whisky from his pocket he ripped the covering from the cork.

'What else would you do but get married, now that your mother's in the clay?' Robert said.

He pointed to a cup, motioning Robert to fetch it. He filled it with whisky. Then he remembered about Susan, and he called into the room where she was making the bed.

'Come out, Susan. Come out and get a sup of whisky.'

'Stephen's getting married, and he wants us to drink his

health. Come out, old girl, and wish him well,' Robert almost shouted.

Susan eyed the whisky and a smile came on her old face.

'There, there, there,' she said, with a wave of her hand, as Durnan poured out the whisky. 'Bless my soul, you'd have me singing if I took all that whisky.'

'Why wouldn't you sing? It's good if it makes you sing,' Robert said.

Durnan said, 'Put it into you, Susan. It isn't every day you get your heart lifted with whisky.'

She nodded, curling her bony fingers around the handleless cup. Her face suddenly changed as her lips moved rapidly, and she coughed loudly, her head shaking quickly. Robert looked up at her, hiding his eyes in laughter. She caught the edge of the mantelpiece. Her eyes were fixed, suddenly drawn to the lamp-light. Leaning back, her face assumed an expression of stupidity.

'Many happenings,' she said. 'First you bury your mother, you nearly bury yourself, and now you're getting married. I hope it isn't a slut from these parts?'

'It isn't, Susan.'

'I'm glad you went further afield.' She staggered from the mantelpiece, falling forward. Durnan caught her arm and seated her in a chair opposite Robert.

'My head's light, son. I'm not used to whisky. It takes the feet from under me. No, son, I'm not used to whisky.'

'Listen to her, Stephen, and her could drink me under the table,' Robert said.

'God forgive you, Robert King, you've a lying mouth.'

Her head fell helplessly against the back of the chair.

Robert continued to blind himself with laughter. With an effort he pointed his finger at her.

'You're drunk, Susie. You're drunk, you strumpet.'

'Mebbe I am and mebbe I'm not,' she muttered, almost to herself.

'You're drunk, Susie, and there's no sense in denying it, and your husband isn't far behind you. Yes, Susie, you're as full as a tick.'

Susan kept moving her head, and her lips muttered as if she were talking to someone in the ceiling.

Robert stood up. He began speaking in a strange accent. A mixture of English and American. 'Did ever I tell you, Stephen, about the one regret of my life? It happened in Hong Kong, to a friend of mine. Jack Postlewhaite was his name. It was the custom in those days if you wanted to join the navy you hung your shirt on the yard-arm. Well, poor Jack, when climbing up, didn't he fall to deck? He was dead when they picked him up. That night, Stephen, he appeared to me. As plain as you are now. One regret. One great regret. He was gone before I could ask him what the next world was like. . . .'

'Another drink, Robert?'

'Well, just a thimbleful.' Durnan had heard Robert tell that story often. Now Robert was staggering about the kitchen.

'I'll get a sailor's funeral, Stephen. I'll die when the tide's full. Yes, Stephen, I'm one of the few of the old brigade. Get aloft there, gale or no gale, brace that, brace that . . . Stephen, old son, I'm gonna sing. The Spanish chieftain on the banks of his own Guadalquivar.'

'Robert King, it was never in you to sing a song well. But scrake, oh aye, you can scrake like a corncrake in harvest time,' Susan said.

Durnan looked at Robert, squeezing the laughter from his eyes with his fingers. Susan's head was bent over the arm of the chair. Her nostrils were wide and brown reminding him of the colour of his mother's shroud. Even in the darkness, for the lamp shone from the mantelpiece to light only a small part of the kitchen, he could see the live things that recalled her immediate presence. They all seemed to be charged with life, and were only waiting until she would come again for them. They were not the big things in the kitchen, the chairs or the table or the dresser, but the little things: the bunch of black thread that hung from the mouth of the calendar, the hat pin that was stuck in the wall, and the band of cloth that hung near the mantelpiece that she used to tie around her head when her headaches came.

He would burn them, and there would be nothing left, nothing that was living. He lifted the thread, but it was caught inside the paper belly of the calendar; then unhooking the calendar, he saw a spider dart up the wall. He burned the calendar. He pulled at the hatpin but it was tight, and he eased it like a loose tooth, before its beady top came away from the stem.

Robert was singing in a shaky voice, 'Lay the Spanish Chieftain dying'. Susan was moving her head forcing the words of 'Two Little Girls in Blue' up her throat. 'One was your mother, I married the other . . .' Her throat dried, and as she moistened it the strings of flesh in her bent neck looked as if they were going to break.

She stopped singing and staggered towards the room.

'Are you off to bed?' Robert said. But he didn't wait for Susan to answer. He went on singing, pointing dramatically to the floor, as though the 'Spanish Chieftain' lay there.

There came a loud noise from the room. 'Something has happened in the room, Robert. Mebbe Susan has fell.' Durnan had to shake the old man's shoulder to get him to listen.

He heard Robert's voice in the room. 'Susan, old girl, what's happened to you? Come, old pet, try and get to your feet. Come, try and get your arm around my shoulder, lift now . . . Stephen, would you come here a minute? Susie has fell.'

She was lying on the floor, her face hidden among her hair, her clothes above her yellow shiny knees.

'Could you lift the creature into bed?' Robert was saying. 'I don't seem to have the strength, Stephen.'

Durnan lifted the withered body to the bed. Robert kept repeating that it was the wee taste of whisky that took her feet away, and that she was the best creature that ever God put breath in. Durnan pointed to her shoes, and Robert started removing them. Her legs were bare and crooked, like barkless bortree branches.

'You didn't hurt yourself, old pet?' Robert was asking, as he bent to sweep the hair away from her face.

Susan's hand fell flat across the pillow and she murmured in her throat, 'No flustering, Robert. I'm all right. I cowped at the end of the bed, reached out too short, but I'll be all right. Go outside with Stephen and sing your bellyful.'

Robert forced her head higher on the pillow. Her mouth opened, showing her two front teeth that were rough and coloured like the outside of a limpet shell.

'Let me take off the rest of your clothes,' Robert said, tugging at her skirt. But she lay with her mouth open like someone paralysed. Robert was unable to pull the skirt over her hips and he kept repeating, 'Susie, old hen, ease your body up until I get your skirt off.' Sweat glistened on Robert's brow. 'Stephen, mebbe you could take her things off. I'm not able.' The old man sat on the bed, struggling for breath, and wiping his forehead with the end of the quilt. Durnan peeled off her skirt, her red petticoat and the knitted skirt that was next her legs. Then her blouse and the shortened pullovers and shirts from the upper part of her body, until he came to where the brown paper was soft and sodden on her chest.

'Let the paper be, Stephen. She's troubled with her chest, and she swears there's a cure in brown paper.' But Durnan had moved the paper, looking for a moment at her withered breasts, reminding him of bladders that were windless and wrinkled with the heat of the sun.

'She'll get a good night's rest, and the wee jorum will make her sleep. But I hope she hasn't hurt herself bad.'

'Wait till the morning, Robert, and if there's a pain you could fetch the doctor.'

'I could, Stephen; that would be the right thing to do.'

'How do you feel, Susan?' Durnan bent over the bed.

There was no answer. She lay with her mouth open with sleep snoring in her throat.

The old man nodded, and knelt down by the bed in a dazed

104

manner. Crossing himself, he chanted loudly: 'Our Father Who art in heaven, hallowed be Thy name, Thy kingdom come . . .' He bent his head, burying his face in the bed clothes.

'Good night, Robert. Good night, Susan,' he said quietly. But the old woman lay with her mouth twisted, and Robert kept his head bent. Little movements showed in the back of his neck. Durnan didn't know whether he was praying or crying.

Durnan felt tired. The fire was grey and sleepy. Feeling inside his pocket he took out the notepaper. In a vague way he counted the sheets and the envelopes. He couldn't write to her tonight. His mind was asleep, and there was a sense of far awayness about everything. He knew if he were in bed he could sleep. He undressed, and pulled the bed closer to the window, so that he could see the stars. They were burnished, like polished bronze. Would she ever be in this bed with him? Why not? He lay back, writing on the space that seemed so little between him and the stars. His soul wanted to soar. He was lonely. She was lonely. Lonely as the heron on the beach, that was coughing on the beach. Now it was coughing its way to the bog, its wingflaps sighing in the night air.

CHAPTER EIGHTEEN

WHEN he awoke Robert's hand was on his shoulder.
'Come, Stephen, I've brought you a cup of tea, and a fried mackerel. I met Mahood, the hawker, and he had a box full, so I bought three. Come, eat it before it cools. It's as crisp and fresh as dried dulse.' Durnan sat up in bed, looking at Robert arranging the breakfast on the bamboo table.

'You'll soon have a woman of your own doing this for you,' the old man said.

'What's that you say, Robert?'

'It took the mouthful of whisky last night to loosen your

tongue. I wished you well last night when I was beside myself with whisky. I'm cold sober now, and I wish you well again.' Robert moved to the door. 'Susan's as stiff as a poker this morning. She hurt her side, and it's as black as your boot. She won't hear tell of fetching the doctor. Well, if you want any more tea, Stephen, give a hello into the kitchen.'

Durnan ate the meal, dressed and started to write the letter. But words wouldn't come. He chewed the end of the pen. All he wanted was to ask her to marry him . . . he had asked her that . . . but they must fix a time, and it must be soon. He could send her a telegram. Why not? But Miss Gelston would read the telegram. He didn't want that. He wanted things kept quiet. Again she might not be keen on an early wedding on account of her husband's death. He got up from the chair, looking through the window. On the telegraph wires on the road two crows were moving nervously. Quickly they flung themselves from the wires. It suddenly struck him, that he could telephone her. He could go over the fields to the coastguard station, put through a call to the merchant's office and wait.

He put on his coat. Robert asked him if he was going to the village and would he bring out a bottle of Sloan's liniment. He told the old man he was going to make a telephone call at the coastguard station.

Robert said, 'They're a good set of men over there. Ask for Bickerstaff, he's the chief boatman. He's a Yarmouth man, and one of the best. Say I sent you, and you needn't be alarmed. . . .'

Durnan crossed the field at the back of the cottage, and took the path that led to the knowe. Climbing a gate and two roughly built stiles, he came in view of the whitewashed building that was the station.

A coastguard was digging in a garden when he approached the building. Durnan stopped, and the guard waved his hand in salute. They always did this, greeted every passer-by.

'Could I see Chief Bickerstaff?'

The man threw the spade from him, and came down the garden.

'I'm Bickerstaff,' he said, buttoning his shirt to shut out the mass of red hair that curled on his chest.

'I'm Durnan, from the cottage across the fields. Robert King told me if I spoke to you you might let me use your telephone.'

'Certainly, of course, why not?' The coastguard bent to clean the soil from his boots. 'The women folk don't like the place messed up on them,' he said, smiling. 'Just follow me.'

Bickerstaff showed him into a small office. Durnan found the merchant's number, and dialled it. He was nervous. He was always the same when using the telephone. A voice said, 'This is Maxwell's, produce merchants. . . .'

'This is Durnan. Is that Mr. Maxwell speaking?'

'Yes, yes, yes, Mr. Durnan, of course. . . .'

'Would it be possible for me to speak to Mrs. Norton? I mean could you get her to phone me here at this number?'

'What is your number, Mr. Durnan? I'll send someone for her.'

Durnan gave the number.

'Good, good, if you hang on there, you'll get a tinkle from me, either to say Mrs. Norton is coming, or she's not. So just hang on there . . . Oh yes, one thing, in case I forget. There'll be an inquiry into the sinking of the *Glendry* on Thursday next. You haven't received any notification of it?'

'I haven't.'

'You will in due course. But your story is a sound one. The inquiry is being held in Belfast. Just a preliminary one. But your story is simple and straight. Sitting in the water like a sleeping swan, isn't that it?'

'Yes.'

'Well now, if you just ring off I'll call you back and let you know whether Mrs. Norton is available. . . .'

Durnan replaced the receiver and came outside. The coastguard was sharpening a sickle. 'Did you get through all right?'

Durnan told him he was waiting on a call back.

'You must be Durnan from the *Glendry*?'

Durnan nodded, and Bickerstaff went on to talk about the ship, inquiring if it were true that the steering went. Durnan told him it was. (Would she be at home? She would have his message by this, if Maxwell delivered it by car or bicycle.)

'We thought Norton might have beached her. He knew that bar better than anybody,' the coastguard was saying.

'The steering went and she was at the mercy of the tides.'

'Yes, and they are tides there. It's a proper graveyard for ships, that place.'

The telephone rang. 'That's likely your call now. But let me answer first, just in case it's officialdom,' Bickerstaff said with a wink.

'Yes, it's for you,' he said, holding out the receiver. Durnan heard the door close. He was alone. She repeated herself three times before he knew her voice. He inquired how she was and if she was still lonely.

'What do you think?' she said.

'Do you know why I phoned you?'

'No, I do not.'

'Is there anyone there? I mean, anyone to hear what you're saying?'

'No, there isn't.'

'You said you would marry me. . . .'

'Yes, I did.'

'When, Winnie?'

'When you want me to.'

'Could it happen soon?'

'Any time you say.'

'I was frightened, seeing Captain Norton is just a little while dead. . . .'

'I said I'd marry you when you wanted. . . .'

'Could I have a talk with you?'

'Yes, whenever you say it.'

'Could you come to Belfast on Thursday next? The merchant

108

says there's to be an inquiry. So if you ask him, he'll let you know where it's to be, and I could meet you there. . . .'

'Yes, I'll do that. Mr. Maxwell has just come into the office. Is there anything you want to say to him . . .?'

'No, there isn't. You'll marry me, Winnie?'

'Yes, yes, yes.'

'And I'll see you on Thursday in Belfast . . .?'

'Yes, yes . . .' Her voice faded and a purring noise stung into the receiver. She was gone. He had heard her speak, and now she was far away, as the day he had kissed her.

'I owe you some money for that,' he said to Bickerstaff.

The coastguard pointed to a tin lifeboat. 'Drop what you like into that,' he said. When Durnan put his hand in his pocket and found it empty, he remembered throwing what loose money he had among the children last night.

The coastguard had moved out of seeing distance, but when Durnan approached him, he said, 'We collect what little money we can for the Institution. It's most worthy of it.'

Durnan felt slightly ashamed, and taking a note from his pocket he handed it to Bickerstaff, saying he couldn't get it through the olit in the boat.

The coastguard thanked him, after inquiring if he could afford what he gave.

Durnan turned down the gravel path that led to the road. This meant he had a two miles' walk to the cottage. But he wanted to walk, to get rid of the sudden excitement. Stripping a hawthorn rod from the hedge, he flogged the tall grass on the roadside as he walked. He slashed out at the dandelions, and sliced the heads of the red-seeded dockens.

There was a mad delight within him. He wanted to jump in the air and cry out that he was happy. He would meet her on Thursday, and they'd make plans for their wedding. Soon he would have her eyes, her lips, her body, every part of her, a real woman, his wife. . . .

He found himself uttering strange sounds, and laughing like

a horse neighing. He sat down on a grass bank, feeling the cold swell through his trousers. This steadied him, forcing him to sort out the mad medley of thoughts in his mind.

He was calmer as he walked up the loanen to the cottage. At the door a dead heron lay on the step, its neck curled like a hook. Robert was stirring porridge when he entered.

'Did you get using the telephone?'

'I did, Robert.'

'Well, even if you are in the village don't bother about the Sloan's liniment. I walked down there to the *Summer Breeze* and I found a dead heron on the beach. I'll pluck him and squeeze the fat from his joints. There's nothing's as good for pains and stiffness as the fat of a heron.' After licking the porridge spoon, the old man went on, 'A strange thing, Stephen, a dead heron. You'd only see it once in a lifetime, and maybe not then at all, if you were not lucky, just like a dead donkey.'

Durnan knew Robert was in a wandering mood. That he would go on talking about the birds he had seen when trading to South America, and the strange fish that looked like human beings.

'Is Susan any better?' Durnan asked.

'The stiffness is there. It's hard to kill. I'm making her this taste of porridge. She's dying to have a crack with you, Stephen, about the wedding. Old as she is, she's young of heart, with an ear for hearing about love and fal de dals,' Robert whispered with a wink.

'I'll go in and see her,' he said.

CHAPTER NINETEEN

'IS that yourself, Stephen?' Susan made to rise, but Durnan pushed her forehead back gently.

'Take it easy, old girl,' he said.

'I'm old, Stephen. Eighty-one years of age come the next

dulse cutting. No shame for my joints to be stiff. God, son, fitted me out well when He was at it, and sure He knows I'm grateful.' Her face was covered with her grey hair·and she tried to puff it from her lips.

'Robert tied my hair up for me this morning, but sure he's buttery fingers. Unless it's a sailor's knot of some kind, he's as useless as the unborn babe.' Durnan gathered her thin locks, twisted them through his fingers until they stood on her pink head like tufts of wool.

'You're kind, Stephen, just like your mother before you. Has the girl you're going to marry long hair?'

He had to think, seeing for a moment her shapely neck.

'Yes, Susan, I think her hair is long; I'm not sure. . . .'

'Far better to have long hair. Not like the scaldy women you see in these parts. You'll be bringing her home soon after the wedding?'

'Yes, Susan, I hope in a fortnight's time.'

'What else would you do? Maybe tomorrow the stiffness in my side will be easier and I'll be able to walk down to the *Summer Breeze*. Robert tells me he's come great further with the caulking. You'll need the place to yourself, son. You'll want to clean it up for your bride coming home.'

Durnan now knew that Susan had been thinking about things. He said, 'Don't worry, Susan; there's no need for you to hurry away from the cottage. You can stay here until you're fit and well again.'

'I'll be suppler sooner than I say, for Robert's going to rub my hinch with heron's fat. Think of him, Stephen, finding a dead heron. I don't like it son. It's before something. A lock of nights before your mother died ·there was one perched on the bowsprit of the *Summer Breeze*, and he cried out loud. . . .'

'Surely, Susan, there was nothing remarkable about that?'

'Wasn't there? Mark you, he cried, and him standing stiff on his stilts of legs. Other times they cry when they start to fly, but never when they're stock still. . . .'

He knew not how to answer Susan. She believed in these things. A crying heron, or a picture falling, or a robin hopping into the house, would send her praying to God, asking His forgiveness for her sins.

'Robert heard it, too, and we knew it was before something. But your mother's happy. She got the priest and the holy oils on her head and feet.'

Susan paused, moving her head. She was breathing noisily. The room was quiet, a kind of secret quiet, a quiet that seemed to be loud. Durnan felt that Susan would die soon, not because of the dead heron, but there appeared in her eyes a conflict. It seemed as if her eyes imprisoned her soul, keeping it from leaping from her body. The quiet was coaxing, charged almost with an intimacy. He felt he could ask Susan any question at all.

Robert's voice came from the kitchen, singing 'The Spanish Chieftain'.

'Would you just listen him. He imagines he can sing, too, that's the fun of it. If he knew a song it would be the less matter. But he's humming that dirge since the day and hour I married him. And if it was to save his soul, he couldn't tell you the words of it.'

The singing ceased and the kitchen door opened and closed, Robert had gone outside. Durnan drew his chair closer to the bed. The silence was in the room again.

'Susan,' he said, softly.

'Yes, Stephen, son, what is it?'

'Did you know my mother very well?'

'I did son, I did. For twelve years, ever since we beached the *Summer Breeze*.'

'I suppose you know she wasn't married?'

'I did son. But I never made it my business to talk or even hint about that.'

'I suppose, she never told you ... I mean, she never talked about me?'

'No, Stephen. Only times I would be asking her about you,

and how you were going on. But further nor that, your name was rarely mentioned.'

'She never dropped a word as to who my father was?'

'Never, son. Never once in my presence. Besides, son, I never made it my business to inquire. God never blessed Robert nor me with any children, and I never like to mention other people's to their faces, lest they thought there was spite in my talk.'

'She never told me, Susan, and God knows I asked her about it often enough.'

'I hope it didn't make you nurse a grudge against her? She was your mother, Stephen, and I'm sure she was shamed many times carrying you.'

'It was never rumoured, Susan, who he was?'

'I heard your mother was housekeeper to a schoolmaster, and it seems his own wife was sick in the hospital, so they were together . . . But that's only hearsay from a travelling woman that wandered the countryside selling thread, and needles and *Old Moore's Almanacs*.'

'And did she tell you that?'

'She did. But I think there wasn't a tooth of truth in it, for that's how she got her bread and butter, finding out things about the folks here, so that she could pour it into ears that welcomed scandal. She tried it on me, telling me what I've told you, before I had time to order her from the *Summer Breeze*.' She ceased talking, as Robert came into the room with an egg cup filled with the dead bird's grey fat.

'Three rubs of this Susan and you'll be able to jump a five-barred gate,' he said, laughing.

Durnan came into the kitchen, sat down at the table and, smoothing the notepaper, he started to write.

'Dear Winnie.' He repeated the name over and over again. He couldn't say 'My Love' or 'Darling Winnie', like in the letters he had read in the Sunday papers. Even writing to his mother, he never could finish it as he had been taught at school, 'Your loving son,' for he never felt like that.

His letter would be practical. No love or kisses. Just a straight-forward note to say how glad he was that she was going to marry him. Bending again to the notepaper he wrote:

Dear Winnie,

I don't know just what to say now, but I am very glad that I phoned you, and that things have turned out as they have. I am writing this in my own kitchen, and it is quiet, just like your own. Now, I think it would be best if you made all the plans, as to when and where we can be married. Anything you suggest, no matter what it is, will suit me. You can come and live here in my place if you want, or I can sell what furniture's here and go and live in your place. So whatever you say will suit me. We could get married as soon as you like, as I have been left a few pounds by my mother, not much, but enough, I think, to get married on. I am looking forward to seeing you on Thursday. Maybe by then you'll be able to let me know how you want things.

What should he write now? *Yours Faithfully* or just *Yours, Stephen Durnan*? Hurriedly he scribbled *Yours, Stephen*, and slid it into the envelope. If he hurried down, to the road, he could catch the postman returning from his rounds.

Ten minutes he sat waiting, and then the postman appeared round the bend. The postman stopped.

'I want you to post this for me.'

'Sure thing. I'll stamp it for you. Never mind about the money. It's as little as I can do for you, after you giving me the goat. She's doing well. A grand milker and the nipper's punch proud of her.'

Durnan said, 'I'm glad she's milking well,' and saluted as the postman rode off.

She would have the letter tomorrow. She might answer it immediately. Perhaps at this moment she had her plans made. He knew women could do this sort of thing much better and quicker than men.

Robert was approaching, bending now and then in the loanen to pull a dead twig or to free his trousers from the clinging bracken.

'I think the weather's going to be fine for a time,' Robert said. 'I might get her deck finished. I have just a square around the cabin to do.'

He told Robert he would light the fire under the pitch bucket for him.

Robert unwrapped the brown paper parcel he had with him. A rag smelling of paraffin oil and the feathers and bones of the dead heron fell to the ground.

'I'm for burning them,' he said, pointing to the feathers. 'It's best, for the smell would fetch the rats if I buried them.'

Durnan went on his knees and lit the fire. Flies were buzzing around the bones and a yellow cleg circled on to Robert's boot. Then it darted off, flying straight at the corny beak of the bird. The long legs reminded Durnan of stems of honeysuckle. They hadn't lost their cherry redness. Its feet looked frosted although the nails were silvered. 'Bird alone.' She had used that expression. Surely, if any bird had earned that name, it was the heron. Surely if any human beings had earned it, Winnie and he had. Her life was silent among the human clegs like Mathews and his wife, and the neighbours that never spoke, nor came to see her when Norton was drowned.

Now, that loneliness was dying. Flying into nothingness, like the smoke that poured from under the bucket. A great joy came within him, as he heard the bones spit and crack in the fire.

'The pitch will soon be melted,' he called to Robert.

Robert was on his knees, raking the timber joints with a blunt wood chisel. Durnan found a screw-driver and knelt beside the old man. Woodlice tried to curve themselves to freedom, but as they peeped from the newly opened seams, Durnan flattened them into shapelessness.

Robert beat the deck in a dreamy fashion, almost as a sleepy child would beat the chair it sat in.

'You're day dreaming, Robert. What do you see? A full-rigged ship, bound for Australia, ready for the tussle round the Horn?'

The old man nodded. Pulling the neck of the jersey further up his neck, he said, quietly, 'It's Susie, I'm thinking about, Stephen. She's done. . . .'

'Nonsense, Robert. She'll be out of bed in a day or two, and as hale and hearty as ever. . . .'

'She won't, Stephen. Here we are caulking these old decks. And how many more winters . . . ?' Robert rubbed his eyes. 'Yes, Stephen, she's done. That knock she gave herself the other night twisted something. It has affected the heart. I know. I know too well. My hearing isn't so good, but I laid my ear to her chest last night, and heard the slow beat of her heart, like as if it was labouring, the slow unwilling beats, Stephen; her heart wants to rest. It wants to stop, it's tired . . . She bid me get the priest for her. That's a bad sign.'

The old man started crying. His face gathered and the amber-coloured tears spread themselves down his broad cheeks. Looking at his face now, Durnan couldn't believe he was crying. He was like an old clown, making faces. Gathering the ragged cuff of his jersey, Robert wiped his eyes, blinking quickly to banish the tears.

'You'll carry her down for me, Stephen? Frail as she is, son, I haven't the strength for it.'

'Carry her down where, Robert?'

'Down here, aboard the *Summer Breeze*. Maybe tomorrow. She's talked to me about your wife coming. She knows a thing or two, Stephen. Knows a wink's as good as a whole rigmarole.'

'You know, Robert, she can stay up there as long as she likes.'

'But you don't know Susie. She has a proud spirit, and hates troubling folks. She said to me, it wasn't the right thing for her to be lying there and you wanting to limewash the house and freshen it up for your wife coming.'

'But, Robert . . .'

'I know what's best for her, Stephen. I know she'd rather be aboard the *Summer Breeze*, so, son, to please us both, you'll carry her down.'

Robert bent to his work again, and Durnan took this sudden movement as meaning that the old man didn't want any more talk about Susan.

They worked on in silence. Now and then the old man brought his hand to his eyes. Then, shaking his head, he continued to rake the seams, letting the woodlice escape over the broad deck of the vessel.

CHAPTER TWENTY

ROBERT got to his feet at the sound of an approaching farm cart. Going to the bow, he called out to the driver. 'Are you passing through the village, Andy?'

'I am. I'm for Stranovalley, taking this sow to the boar.'

'Would you hop off the cart when you get to the curate's door, and ask the curate to come to the *Summer Breeze*?'

'To be sure, I will. Who's ailing?'

'It's Susan. She give her side a bit of a knock, and she'd like to see the priest.'

'I'll do it, Robert. Have him out right away,' the driver said, urging his horse forward. When he was gone Robert said, 'A good soul, is Andy. He's servant man up in M'Giffert's.'

Robert went below, calling up to Durnan to catch the articles he was going to hand up. A folded tablecloth, the crucifix and a brass candlestick.

'These things are for the priest, Stephen. You'll stand by, son, when he comes out, to help him. You know, I'm sure, what's to be done. I'm going to tell you the strangest thing, Stephen. You didn't know, I warrant you, that I was born and reared a Protestant?'

Durnan shook his head, but suddenly he remembered seeing the old man on his knees; how he crossed himself, saying the 'Our Father'.

'But I saw you praying on your knees. . . .'

'Susan taught me to do that. Made me cross myself, every time we left on a voyage. "Bless yourself, in God's name," she would say, "Catholic and Protestant alike must ask His blessing." ' Robert frosted the candlestick with his breath and polished it against the sleeve of his jersey.

'Sure I wouldn't need to be in the room with him, Stephen?'

'No, Robert. He'll hear her confession and anoint her.'

'Anoint her?' the old man asked, wide eyed. 'Susan called it something else, a queer name that I never heard before.'

'Extreme Unction?'

'Aye, that's it.' There was a touch of wonder in his voice, as if the name fascinated him, making him curious.

'That's a queer strange name, is it not, Stephen?'

'I suppose it is. It is a sacrament.'

'What does it mean, Stephen?'

The answer to that question was fresh in Durnan's mind, for it was the question the priest had asked him when he was being examined for Confirmation.

'It's the sacrament of the dead, Robert. The priest gives her communion. Viaticum, it is called, which means food for the journey.'

In his mind, Durnan could see the priest handing him his red card, which meant he had passed, and would be confirmed, making him a strong and perfect Christian. Twenty or more years ago it was.

'Why do they call it food for a journey, Stephen?'

'I don't know. They say it makes the soul ready, strengthens it for the long journey from the grave.'

The old man's face went white and his mouth gaped open.

'She's going to die, Stephen. When she asks for that she must feel she's going to die.'

'Have a titter of wit, Robert. She's not going to die. If a man makes his will on a Monday, it doesn't mean that he's going to die on Tuesday.'

'But this is different, Stephen. Susan wouldn't ask for this thing, unless she felt she wanted it badly, needed it badly.'

'Maybe, she wants to confess her sins. There might be something troubling her. Something on her mind that she'd like to talk over with the priest.'

'There could be nothing on her mind, Stephen. Isn't her and I as close as two clam shells? Couldn't she tell her bit of trouble to me . . .?'

'You must understand, Robert, that Susan's a Catholic, and she has a certain feeling about things.'

'What things, Stephen?'

'Lots of things . . .' Durnan was unable to answer the old man.

'But, Stephen, to confess her sins. What sins would Susan have to confess?'

'I don't know, Robert,' and to stop him asking further questions Durnan laughed, and added, 'Theology isn't in my line, Robert. You'll find Susan will be all right.'

But he could see that Robert's mind was disturbed.

'But, Stephen . . .'

'Look, Robert, are we going to finish this patch of deck? If the rain comes the cabin will be flooded. . . .'

'Let it be,' the old man answered. 'I want to take these things up to Susan.'

Durnan watched the old man cross the beach and climb the loanen. Then, falling to his knees he started to stuff the timber seams that were naked around the cabin. When he finished it, he went downstairs into the cabin to hide the tools. Robert had converted the bunk, so that there was room for both of them. Durnan felt the bed. It was hard, the mattress stuffed with straw. There was a strong smell that recalled the sea. It was mixed with tar and the air was damp and heavy. Durnan looked at the steep stairway, and saw he would have to be careful how he carried her down. There was no reason why she should leave the cottage, but perhaps, as Robert said, she was independent, and had spirit.

On deck again, he looked towards the lough. Mackerel were playing and the water shivered near the shore as the herring fry swerved to avoid landing on the beach. If he launched Robert's punt he could go fishing and get a mackerel or a codling for tea. Behind him he heard footsteps on the gravel, and turning he saw it was the curate.

'I'm looking for Mrs. Robert King. I'm told she lives in this boat. This is the *Summer Breeze*?'

'I'll bring you to her,' Durnan said, coming down the ladder to the beach.

As they walked up the loanen Durnan told the curate what had happened. But the curate appeared not to be interested, for he kept picking his way lest he should dirty his black shiny shoes.

As they reached the house, they met Robert coming out with a dish of water.

'She bid me wash her hands and feet for your coming, Father,' Robert said, as he scattered the water among the hawthorns. The curate passed quietly into the room. Durnan motioned Robert to the chair opposite his own.

'I think I have everything on the table. I set them at Susie's bidding, so everything should be all right,' the old man whispered.

The low drone of the Latin words came from the room as the priest administered the sacrament of the dead.

Robert remained silent, his mouth open, his hand covering his brow. Durnan thought of his approaching marriage. He would need a new suit, new shoes and new shirts and underclothing.

'Isn't it a strange job, that of a clergyman,' Robert was saying, 'to be working with people when they are just born, and working with them when they're getting married, and standing by them when death's near hand?'

Robert's words made Durnan think of his own baptism. Where was he baptized? Could he get a certificate? He wasn't sure whether he needed this certificate.

He could ask the curate when he came from the room.

Robert bent over and whispered, 'Tell me, Stephen, do you have to pay anything?'

'No, Robert, not a thing.'

The Latin drone ceased, and they could hear the priest telling Susan not to worry, that God was giving her sufficient time to make peace with Him.

'Could I go in now, Stephen?'

Durnan nodded and the old man left the kitchen.

'I'd like a word with you, Father,' Durnan said to the priest as he came from the room.

'Yes, what is it?'

'I'll walk as far as the loanen foot with you, and tell you what it is.'

He saw the curate had a habit of twisting his mouth, and shooting his eyebrows up in a superior fashion.

'I'm getting married, Father. . . .'

'Yes?'

'I don't know whether I have any baptismal lines, at least I don't know of any. . . .'

'What age are you?'

'I'm thirty-three, Father.'

'You're thirty-three, and you know nothing of your baptism?'

'I know nothing about my certificate. . . .'

'But surely you were baptized?'

He hadn't expected answers like these. He expected help, and it seemed he wasn't going to get it. The curate never slackened his pace. He kept walking, taking long strides to avoid the soft mud. Durnan saw he was a dandy of a fellow, for near his ears flecks of powder showed where he had dusted his face after shaving. His woolly black coat was theatrical, and he kept twisting his mouth.

'You haven't answered my question. Don't you know whether you were baptized or not?'

The tone of condescension in his voice spurted a flame of anger in Durnan.

He said loudly, 'Look, Father, it's nothing to me whether I have a certificate or not. I want to get married. I'm a bastard, a by-blow, a love-child, or whatever the hell you like to call me . . . I need lines saying I was baptized . . . a docket like one you'd sign for receiving a ton of potatoes, and I must have it. . . .'

The curate stopped, 'My dear fellow,' he began, but Durnan had already left him, saying he would see the old Canon about it, that the old Canon would understand.

Returning to the cottage, Durnan hesitated at the door. Five minutes would take him over the fields to the Canon's house. This was something that must be seen to at once, so why not do it right away? He was at the back of the house on his way over, when he heard Robert call his name.

'Susie wants to be shifted tonight,' the old man said. 'I've tried to put her off, by telling her the bunk is damp, but she won't hear me at all, Stephen. There hasn't been a fire in the cabin this long time, I've told her, and she bids me go at once and kindle one. So I must let her have her way, Stephen. She's old, and God knows mightn't ask me to do much more for her.'

In the kitchen, Robert shovelled live coals from the fire into a bucket and rushed down to the *Summer Breeze* with them.

Durnan sat on the sofa, feeling that he had perhaps better wait until hearing from Winnie before he went to see the Canon. He knew that custom had it that a marriage took place in the bride's parish, but he was not sure in her case. She might want the wedding in Belfast. She might be afraid of what the neighbours would say about her getting married again, and her husband only fresh in the clay.

He would like Fenner for his best man. She could have her own bridesmaid. They might even go to Fenner's hotel for the honeymoon. He felt that if Mrs. Fenner knew about his wedding she might insist on this. Thursday coming he would see Fenner and mention it to him.

Susan was calling him, and when he entered the room she pointed to the chair by the bed.

'I want to give you a wedding present, Stephen. Some sheets and two red silk shawls. I bought the shawls in Troon, in Scotland, more years ago than I like to recall. We traded to Troon for many's a year, and there's a great kindness with the Scotch.'

He thanked her, and asked her if she wouldn't be better staying on in the cottage.

'No, son. A body's better in their own corner. I'll make Robert get the presents for you, when we go on board.'

Robert returned with a pair of socks. Turning back the bed clothes he put them on Susan's feet. Then he rolled her body in a blanket and quilt.

'Come, Stephen, we're ready.'

Durnan lifted her body, and her hair hung down.

'Better put my cap on you, Susan, it'll keep the cold from your head, and hold your hair up,' Robert said.

As they neared the door, she told Robert to look out and see there was nobody about.

'Not a sinner,' Robert assured her. 'Only two corbies on the beach filling their mouths with gravel for ballast on their flight across the lough.'

Outside, she kept her eyes closed, complaining that the light was too strong for them. Robert led the way, about five yards in front, looking back every minute and repeating, 'Keep to the edge of the bank, Stephen, and there's no fear of you losing your feet or slipping.'

When they reached the vessel and were on the deck, she lowered her head saying, 'You've made a brave job of the caulking, old one.'

Robert laughed, 'Not so much of the "old one". Your *Summer Breeze* is now as tight as a fiddle.'

At the cabin entrance, Durnan had to curve her body to get it through the narrow opening. She gave a little groan and muttered, 'Mother of God, this pain . . .' Durnan saw beads of sweat on her yellow brow.

He laid her on the bed. She sighed loudly, and said, 'God bless you, Stephen. You'll prosper. You were kindness itself. If kindness has a mark, son, it's in your face, so it is.'

'You're home again, now. Are you content?' Robert asked.

'A body's bones rest better in their own place, don't they, Stephen?'

'I suppose they do.'

There was silence, only the sounds of Susan moving in the bed. Then raising herself slowly, she said, 'Robert, wind the alarum-clock, and not stand there with your two hands the one length.'

CHAPTER TWENTY-ONE

THE housekeeper told him he would have to wait until the Canon had finished Mass. She showed him into a room that was bare, except for a crucifix and a picture of the Archangel Michael driving Lucifer into the bottom pit of Hell. The floor was stained black, and a goatskin stretched its silky hair underneath the chair at the head of the table. The table was long, with a red sash in its centre. It reminded Durnan of the red shawls Susan had promised him as a wedding present, and which he hadn't got as yet. Perhaps the old girl's mind was wandering. Well, if he never received them, it was nice to think of her intention.

This room smelt of turpentine and bees-wax, and there was a great stillness in it. It seemed to Durnan a room apart from the rest of the house, almost a large confession box. Even the chair Durnan was sitting in was so arranged that it faced the one at the head of the table; and the table itself showed where the Canon's elbows rested as he listened. There was a deadness about the walls, a shut-in-ness, that frightened him a little. In this room, Durnan knew, the Canon met sin, face to face. Here there were no dark corners as in the Church confessionals, where you could whisper your sins unseen. This was where the Canon brazened things out with you. Where seducer met seduced, and raper met the raped. And the shut-in feeling made it worse. Even the windows with their frosted panes reflected only the dark shadows of the ivy leaves, making them look like skeletons.

Supposing the Canon was like the curate and kicked up a fuss about his baptism? Good God, it wasn't his fault that this should be so. But he remembered the Canon as a soft-spoken man whose favourite words were those urging his people to pray hard, 'And lay up treasures of grace in the kingdom of heaven, for themselves.' Yet old age could sour people and make them cranky. . . .

A dog was barking playfully some distance away. As the barking came nearer, Durnan heard a voice saying to the dog, 'Now, now, Barney, take it easy, take it easy. This is the only soutane I have, and the tails of it doesn't take kindly to your teeth.' The door opened and the Canon came in the room.

'I don't know you, and I suppose I should.' The old priest smiled as he sat down, sweeping his hand over his bald pink head.

'My name is Durnan. You knew me as a boy, but I've been at sea this long while. . . .'

'Yes, yes, it's young Durnan. You served my Mass, didn't you? You're a man now, and didn't I read something in the papers about you?'

'You did, Canon.'

'Well now, what is it you came to see me about?'

'I'm getting married, Canon.'

'Well, don't look so frightened about it. Dammit, I thought you had come to tell me you were after committing a murder. You're getting married? Well, continue from there. . . .'

When the Canon heard his story, he said humorously, 'I don't think your case calls for excommunication, and there's no cause for worry. But tell me one thing, and this is very serious. The right answer to this question will make matters easy, the wrong answer will complicate things dreadfully. . . .'

Durnan waited, wondering what the question could be. The Canon lowered his head, and stared straight at him.

'Tell me,' he said, 'you haven't a wife tucked quietly away in some port? Say a barmaid in Cardiff, or a fish-gutter in Aberdeen, or maybe a waitress in Liverpool?'

'No, Canon, I haven't.'

'Well, now, sure that's the right answer to that all important question.'

'I haven't, Canon.'

'Man alive, don't look so serious. I think the Irish are losing their sense of humour. Too many Hollywood pictures, I think that's the cause of it. If you'd said you had a wife tucked away, we'd a' had a bit of fun. I remember . . .'

The Canon told a long story about an Irish sailor that came to him in Paris. Then he shook his head, as if mention of Paris had revived fond memories.

'Have you ever been in Paris?'

'No, Canon. Any time I've been in France it was in a coaster, and that means you never get a night or a day to go sight-seeing.'

'But next time you go, take a week off and visit Paris. The Continental Church . . . But where were we? Yes . . . about your wedding . . .?'

'Yes, Canon.'

'Find out where your wife wants the marriage to take place. Does she belong to this parish? I should have asked you that before.'

'No, Canon. She belongs to Barholm.'

'Well, if she wants the marriage in Barholm, just let me know, and I'll fix things for you. Again, if she wants it, say, in Belfast, I'm known there too . . . Anyway let me know where she wants it. Let me know a day or so before the event. So now, wipe the misery from your face, and smile for a change. If you died with a face like that, I wouldn't read your burial service. And now I think it's time an old man like me had his breakfast, don't you?'

The Canon held out his thin soft hand. 'I trust you'll be happy. Come and see me as I told you.'

The outside gate groaned as Durnan shut it. The sound of children singing reached his ears, and he walked up the road to the school. The children were rushing from the school to the field opposite, tossing a ball in the air. On the ridge of the school roof crows were perched nervously, with their heads cocked in a listening manner. Durnan knew they were waiting for the scraps of bread dropped by the pupils. These same crows were doing this when he was at school. They were the same crows. They seemed to have been there since the school was built. With warty beaks and feathers missing from their wings. They made him feel there was a great sameness about life, that somehow the real things never changed, that everybody did the same things, just like the crows. He had alarmed and worried himself over his baptism; now it didn't seem to matter; at least, not as seriously as he thought it would, for the Canon had eased his mind about it. He felt sure now that the Canon knew all about him. That his mother had whispered her sin many times into his old ear. 'Canon, I had a child, and I'm not married. I was unfortunate. The father was . . .' And the Canon he felt had told her to pray to God and ask His forgiveness and to say her beads as often as she could, and that he knew she was sorry for her sin. . . .'

The Canon, he supposed, knew there were thousands of cases like his mother's all over the world. He knew he must deal with sin, and perhaps that was why the people liked him, and said about him, 'Oh, the Canon? If you told him you murdered somebody, he would say, "You didn't mean to do it, I'm sure. . . ." '

Two boys were approaching him, swinging a pail. He knew they were going to the well in the field for drinking water. They would bring the full pail back to the school and the pupils would dip the rusted tin into the pail and drink. He had always curled his lip over the tin, for some of the boys had sore mouths. One boy had called him 'Horsey' for doing this, because he sucked the water through his teeth. One of the boys shouted at him, 'I know you. You're Stephen Durnan and I've got your goat. You gave it to my daddy. She's grazing beyond the bank in Tully-board if you want to see her.'

The other boy asked him for a butt of a cigarette. Durnan watched him suck the cigarette through a nervous finger and thumb.

'You must be the postman's boy.'

'Yes, I am. I was glad to get your goat. The doctor said its milk would be good for me. I've to get eggs too. I'm sick and sometimes I can't breathe.'

'He's lucky,' the other boy said. 'There's times he doesn't have to go to school and he doesn't get slapped for it either.'

Durnan looked after the boys as they went towards the well. The shoulders of the postman's son gathered and crouched.

Durnan felt he was lucky, for he was sound of wind and limb, had never had a day's sickness in his life. He had many things to be thankful for, and good health was one.

On his way home he stopped at the clay banks. If he brought some clay back with him, he could mix it with lime and cream-colour the outside and inside of the cottage. Nearby, a worn grain sack was hanging over a line of barbed wire. Lifting it he spread it out, and with a flat stone he dug into the clay, plastering it in a hump in the middle of the sack. There was lime in the out-house. He could put it into the water barrel, let it melt, then thin it down with sea water. Sea water was best, for the salt in it kept the lime from rubbing off. He would boil the clay in a bucket, and as it bubbled pour it into the lime. He could buy cement and fill the holes at the base of the walls. He could tar the bottom of the walls about a foot up, and wash the floors with paraffin oil, to make sure they were clean and fresh-smelling.

Winnie would curtain the windows. Change them completely from the dull grey coverings his mother had on them. So dull they were, they looked like long torn spiders' webs. She would plant flowers in front of the cottage, wallflowers to bloom against the walls, puddles of pansies and spreads of primroses.

Hardy flowers that would thrive and stand against the wind that blew from the sea. He knew she would fit in to the cottage, that she would always be there, smiling, walking, poking the fire, sweeping the floor, making the dry tea hiss as she poured the boiling water on it, unhooking the kettle as it spewed into the fire, her powder puff lying on the dresser like a tea-softened biscuit, the perfume of her powder and the scarlet red of her lipstick. She would be with him at night, her one shoe dropping to the floor, then the other, and the creaking of the bed as she got in beside him. They could talk about everything, lie in each other's arms . . . Maybe there would be a child—who knows?— maybe twins. They would have a father and he'd be proud of them. . . .

As he walked the bag knocked against his knee. He could see the clay was melting. It was shaking in the bag like a huge jelly fish, and it sweated through the sack in beads that were lacey like lemonade froth. As he hurried homewards the cottage came in sight. It looked grey as mountain sheep and just as lifeless. In his mind he could see its walls cream-coloured like a biscuit, its window sashes painted bright green, its spouting red and its window sills painted mast colour.

As he came down the field, he could see someone staring through the window at the back of the cottage. It was Robert. Suddenly he left the window and started pushing the back door.

Durnan called out, 'What is it Robert?' The old man didn't appear to hear him, for he kept rushing from the window to the back door, in a bewildered state.

Again he called out, as he neared the cottage. This time Robert saw him, and shaking his hand he answered, 'Come quick, Stephen, son, come quick.'

CHAPTER TWENTY-TWO

'WHAT'S wrong, Robert?'
'It's Susie,' the old man gasped. 'There's a young doctor come aboard the *Summer Breeze* and he says Susie must go to the hospital. Stephen, will you come down?'

As they walked to the vessel, Robert told him that earlier in the morning Susan took so bad that he was frightened, and walked to the town for the doctor.

'I went up for you, Stephen, but you weren't there.'

The young doctor was on the deck when they arrived. He was trying to remove a fragment of tar from his grey flannel trousers. Robert descended the stairs to the cabin. The doctor looked at Durnan.

'Are you any relation of the patient down there?' he asked.

'No, my name's Durnan. I'm from the cottage above. I'm neighbourly with these people. . . .'

'Have you any influence with the old woman?'

'I might have, I dunno. What is it you want me to do?'

'Talk to her about lying in that rat-hole of a cabin. I'll get her into Newtownards hospital, for she can't remain down there. Have you seen where she is?'

'Yes I have, but er . . .'

'There's no air in the place and there's a smell of pitch or tar that would kill anything. She's almost choking. She'll cough up what's left of her lungs if she isn't shifted soon.' The doctor bent to scrape his trousers again; under his breath he cursed, for the tar was now on his fingers. Robert was climbing the stairs. There were tears shining on his cheeks.

'Susie won't go, Stephen. She says it's the poorhouse he's sending her to . . .' The doctor looked up quickly. 'It isn't the poorhouse but a first-class hospital, where she'll get first-class treatment. Good God, man, you can't leave her down there. Why there's neither sanitary arrangements nor anything else. It's my duty to have her removed to hospital, otherwise I won't attend her. In view of that I'll lodge a complaint with the Local Authorities.' Robert returned to the cabin. The doctor closed the penknife he was using on the tar, now he was running his fingers through his oily hair.

'What is her trouble, Doctor?' Durnan asked.

'Her heart's affected, and the incessant coughing is making things worse. That's why she must be shifted at once. Go down there and get a whiff of the tar and it'll nearly choke you. She'll definitely have to go to hospital, for I won't attend her down there. . . .'

'I understand, Doctor. But you must know how it is with old people like these. . . . They have their own funny ideas about hospitals. . . .'

'Ignorant prejudices are things I won't tolerate. Either she gets out of there, or I'm forced to get her out. . . .'

'If I brought her to my cottage, Doctor? She was there before for a while . . . If I brought her there would it suit you?'

'Bring her anywhere there's fresh air, anywhere at all, as long as it's far away from that rat-hole. . . .'

'Very good, Doctor, I'll talk to her and see if she'll come back to my place.'

'If you remove her, tell her husband to let me know.' As the doctor descended the broad ladder that reached to the beach, he muttered, 'Good God, tar everywhere.'

Durnan watched him pick his steps on the wet sleechy beach, his brown shoes sinking in the soft dead sand.

Finally, he started to run and slammed the door of his car in temper.

Robert was seated on the bunk. His feet rested on the floor, and nearby was a small bath of water. Susan lay on the bed, her face looking at the small port-hole that stained the grey light it borrowed, making it tawny. There was a strong smell of tar.

'Where did the tar come from, Robert? It wasn't smelling as strong as this last night.'

The old man had difficulty in speaking, for the tar caught his breath, forcing the words down his throat again.

'I tarred around the floor last night after you left, Stephen. Susie said there was bugs, but I don't believe it.'

'Aye, there was one as big as a spider,' said Susan, turning in the bed. 'It went over my face, and I bid him disinfect the floor with tar.' She breathed noisily, causing a whistling in her nose.

'It was a spider, Stephen,' Robert protested.

'It was no such thing, Robert King. I say it was bug, and I'm saying what's true.'

'Well, if you say it, it's right, for it was your face it trod on,' Robert said. Then he lifted the bath and went up the stairs.

'He's washing one or two things for me, Stephen. A nightdress and two shirts. It annoys me to see him do it. But he's a good creature, Stephen. There's times I wonder why God sent me so good a husband . . .' Suddenly her head fell back on the pillow and she started to cry.

'I'm going to no hospital. I'll be carried out in the four boards first, before I let them take me there. It's the poorhouse, that's what it is, in spite of all his flowery talk. What right has he to order me from the *Summer Breeze*? He's a foreigner, come here with a fancy tongue in his head. But he'll shift me to no poorhouse. He won't, he won't. . . .'

'Look, Susan, it's not the poorhouse. It's what's called the County Hospital.' As he spoke, he reached over and lifted the hair away from the sweaty brow.

'It's the poorhouse, the poorhouse. I'll not go. I want to end my days here. If death's to come to me soon, it can find me in the *Summer Breeze* easier than in a hospital.' She wriggled her head, coaxing a fresh breath into her mouth.

'But, Susan, you can't stay here with the tar catching your breath. Why you can't get air, even now, and it's smarting the eyes out of you. Now, listen to me; if I carry you back to the cottage, will you let me?'

'Stephen, son, I can't go living and sponging on you. . . .'

'You're not sponging. I'm only asking you to let me bring you back to the cottage.'

'You're kind, Stephen, like your mother before you.' She closed her eyes, forcing the lids together.

'Come, Susan, are you agreeable to come to the cottage? The doctor will attend you there, and there'll be no more talk about the hospital.'

She bit her lip, and the crying shivered in her throat.

'I'll go and tell Robert I'm taking you back to the cottage.'

She rubbed her nose, and crushed her head closer to the pillow. Durnan looked down at her as he moved to the cabin stairs, but she made no answer.

Robert was washing, pulling, tugging and squeezing the shift, holding it before his eyes and ducking it again like a cormorant in the suddy water.

'She's agreeable to come back to the cottage, Robert.'

'It's dacent of you to take all this trouble, Stephen.'

'Nonsense, Robert. Let you go up to the cottage and make the bed ready for her. The clothes and things are just as you left them.'

Durnan wrapped her in the blanket, and when he got to the deck she said, 'Stephen, son, would you rest me here for a little? I just want to take a look at the *Summer Breeze*.'

He laid her on the deck, covering her naked feet, and stuffing his folded coat under her head. She pointed to the hatch. 'There it is,' she said. 'It held stones, and coal, and flour and bricks. And there was one time it carried salt. It was queer, Stephen, to look at the salt; it was just like a floor of snow, only it shone with more colours. And there was one time we loaded pit props in Killyleagh for Maryport . . . Did you ever load pit props?'

'No, Susan.'

'A strange cargo. We had to build them on top, right into the bow. They were tree arms, about your height. And I remember one that had the remains of a chaffinch's nest on it. It was sad, Stephen, to think of it going under the ground, for ever, like as if it was human and was being buried. And there was another one with a hole in it, and there came a great screeching from the hole, and the docker that handled it was frightened of the screeching. And when I looked into the hole, I could see the mousey head of a blind bat. Just a blind bat, Stephen, no bigger than a field mouse, and as harmless, but the screeching that came from it scared the docker and, afore I could stop him, he had hurled the branch over the side into the sea, and then the screeching stopped, for the poor black thing was drowned. Wasn't it queer, Stephen, for a man as big as you are to be frightened of the bat?

'It was, Susan.'

Again the tears were flooding her eyes. She shook her head.

'Come, Susan, you'll be catching cold if you lie there much longer. Besides the deck is too hard for you. . . .' Through her crying, she murmured, 'The *Summer Breeze*, the *Summer Breeze*.'

He bent to lift her, but she caught his arm. 'Look,' she said, 'there's Larry,' pointing to a gull that had settled on the deck. It had one leg and a stump, and it cocked its head and moved forward at the sound of her voice.

'Stephen, will you see that it gets a morsel of food night and morning, or maybe some fish-guts? . . .'

As Durnan carried her to the cottage, she told him about the gull, how she had fed him every morning and evening for the past nine years, and that she had named him Larry. She said that the bird knew every word she uttered, and that he was timorous and unsure of himself, and he was frightened of crows.

When she was in bed, she asked Robert to heat the brick and put it at her feet. Then Robert took a letter from his pocket. He handed it to Durnan saying, 'I was nearly forgetting, Stephen, but the postman gave me this for you this morning.'

Durnan opened the letter. It was from the shipping agents, asking him to attend the inquiry on Thursday morning. As he noted the address, Durnan was happy, for soon he would see Winnie again.

CHAPTER TWENTY-THREE

THE following morning Durnan melted the clay, and Robert went to the beach for salt water for the lime. Then the old man cut the whiskers of grass that grew at the bottom of the wall. Now and then he would go to the kitchen door, and call in, 'Are you all right, Susie my pet?'

Tomorrow was Thursday, and the thought filled Durnan with ecstasy, making him playful and merry, as he splashed the cream-coloured lime into the holes. Towards midday, he asked Robert about food, and when they found they had nothing but bread, Robert said he would go to the Point and get some limpets and fry them in oatmeal.

The old man was only gone about half an hour, when he returned with a half bucketful of shell fish. Durnan worked hard. Already the lime wash was drying on the walls, transforming them, and just as he finished the gable, Robert called out that the meal was ready.

Robert asked him when he was going to paint the windows, suggesting that he might paint the doors, for his sight wasn't good enough for him to assist with the windows.

Durnan told him he was going into the village to buy some clothes, and that he would get the paint when he was there.

Durnan called at the post-office, and the post mistress advanced him twenty pounds. In Lawson's the drapers he bought a suit, a blue suit, with a fine white stripe running down every inch of it. He bought a white shirt with two collars, and a tie with red bars that recalled the funnel of a steamer. The attendant showed him socks and asked him about a pair of pyjamas. Durnan had never had pyjamas. Always at sea he had the dirty habit of turning in wearing his inside clothing. The men he sailed with regarded pyjamas as an effeminate garb.

'Yes, I'd like a pair of pyjamas,' he heard himself say.

'What size?' Durnan knew the attendant had him. But the

sailor in him came out. 'The biggest size you have, they always wash up. . . .'

'Not these,' the shopman insisted. 'But I think size nine would do you.' He was glad to get away from the shop, stopping at Jane Whorry's to buy a bottle of whisky.

Tomorrow he would be with her again, and they could talk about their wedding, and if they got a chance of being alone together, he would kiss her and press her close to him, for now a warm desire was within him.

He hurried homewards, looking out at the calm face of the lough, and he thought about the long nights in winter, when the wind howled, shaking the windows of the cottage. She would be with him, beside him, with his arms around her. There would be snugness, peace in his mind, a new rhythm in his life. Already he felt a great rebirth in himself. The old shadows were gone, his bastardy, the death of his mother and his yearning for his father, the shipwreck too . . . these things meant nothing now. Tomorrow at the inquiry he would tell them that the bloody ship sunk, saving herself from the scrap yard, and there was no use weeping over spilt milk.

In the loanen he met the doctor, and inquired about Susan. Again the doctor started cursing the *Summer Breeze*, calling it the black hole of Calcutta.

Robert was finishing the job of cleaning the lime warts from the windows. He rubbed his hands with butter, saying he couldn't stand the dryness of them after the lime. Durnan filled him half a cup of whisky. 'Would Susan like a nip, Robert?'

'Would it be right to let her have it, Stephen, after seeing the priest and getting the holy oils on her?'

'A thimbleful wouldn't do her any harm.'

'Whatever you say, Stephen. If she takes it herself, I have no objections.'

'A hair of the dog that knocked you down, Susan,' Durnan said as he entered the room. Robert had started to sing 'The Spanish Chieftain'.

136

Durnan lifted her head, pushing a pillow at her back. She tried to smile as he held the whisky to her lips.

'Listen to him,' she said, 'at that old dirge again. You would think God hadn't put another song on this green earth.' Then she coughed as the whisky trickled down her throat.

Durnan unwrapped his parcel, and, calling Robert, he spread the new suit on the bed.

'What do you think of it?'

Robert felt the trousers with his finger and thumb, and said the stuff felt strong and that he hoped he would live long after being married in such a splendid suit.

Susan had to have the coat held up in front of her, and she said that navy blue was always decent and respectable looking, and the white stripe in it gave it a bit of colour. She went on to talk of her own wedding, of how she knitted Robert's jersey.

'Full of dropped stitches it was, Stephen,' Robert said, closing his eyes with a smile.

'You were a dandy that morning. Weren't you, Whistling Rufus? Stephen, you'd have taken your dead end at him, varnishing the peak of his sailor's cap with vaseline.'

'All to be nifty for you, and where did it land me? Bound hand and foot to the hardest woman in Christendom.'

Durnan stood up. 'Will you be awake early in the morning, Robert?'

'Name the time and I'll be up, Stephen, if you want me to rouse you.'

'Would you give me a call about six or thereabouts?'

'Certainly,' Robert said.

'Good night, Susan.'

'Good night, Stephen.'

'Good night, Robert.'

He took the trousers and shook them several times in an effort to take the lines out of the legs. He put on the coat and swung his arms quickly to take the stiffness out of it, he rolled up the vest, for he disliked wearing a new suit for the first time.

In bed he held the whisky bottle to his lips and drank slowly. He breathed quietly, feeling sleep caressing the back of his head. He stretched his legs, feeling the cold of the sheets. Then his cheeks burned, and he slept.

Robert wakened him, telling him that the morning was grey with dark shadows in the sky. He had made oatmeal porridge for the breakfast, and what was left of the limpets, with three razor fish he had boiled.

When they finished breakfast Robert said to Durnan, 'I'll walk as far as the loanen foot with you. Susan wants me to feed Larry. It'll be a change for him to get fried limpets.' The gull was waiting on the bowsprit, poking his beak into his blue breast. 'He's waiting for you,' Durnan said.

'Susan has him spoiled,' the old man replied.

CHAPTER TWENTY-FOUR

A CLERK showed him into a large room, with a table in the middle of it. He was the first to arrive. Mrs. Fenner came next. She told him that Jackie was down with a bad cold, and that she had come merely to apologize. They talked a long time, and as the men seated themselves at the table, she moved away after whispering that he might come and have lunch with her.

He said, 'But I'm expecting a friend, Mrs. Fenner.'

'Well, you can bring your friend along,' she answered.

Now the dozen men were seated around the table. Clearing their throats, fidgeting with their pencils and trying to look important. What a disappointment they were going to get, Durnan thought, if they felt they were going to drag up in all its detail the sinking of the *Glendry*. They called on a tall man at the head of the table to speak first. Then a small man, with gathered shoulders and eyebrows like a hedgehog, started to question Durnan. This man had a habit of knocking his teeth together, and he seemed to distrust Durnan's answers. The merchant sat in the far corner of the room blinking his eyes and licking his lips.

'The cargo was properly stowed, Mr. Durnan?' the merchant asked.

'It was,' Durnan replied.

'You're positive?' the small man inquired.

'Yes.'

'What makes you positive?'

'Because I was present when they loaded her. I was checking the cargo.'

'Are you an expert on how to stow a ship's cargo?' Durnan took a dislike to this small monkey of a man. Banging his fist on the table he said, 'Look, gentlemen, the bloody ship's steering went, she was at the mercy of the sea, and she wasn't able to fight it.' A murmur filled the room, and Durnan saw Mrs. Fenner nod approvingly at him.

The small man got to his feet again, running his finger and thumb up and down his silver pencil. Durnan knew that this hunched-back fool would twaddle all day, pestering him with stupid and silly questions. Clearing his throat loudly, Durnan spoke directly to him. 'Gentlemen, it's just a waste of time for us here. I've told you the plain truth. The ship left port, got into trouble and foundered.'

'Yes, yes, yes, that seems to be exactly what happened,' said a soft-voiced man who kept pouting his lips. The men started talking to each other in low tones. Then one of them asked Mrs. Fenner when her son would be fit to appear. She told him in about a week's time. They whispered again to each other. Then the soft-voiced man shook Durnan's hand, and said they'd call him again when Mr. Fenner was able to appear.

Durnan followed Mrs. Fenner from the room. A porter was approaching. 'Are you by any chance Mr. Durnan?'

'That's me?'

'There's a lady to see you. She's in the waiting-room.'

139

She was reading a paper when the porter opened the door. She looked up, and Durnan reached for her hand.

'It is nice to see you again,' she said.

He introduced her to Mrs. Fenner, who insisted that they must come to her hotel for lunch. Durnan looked at her clothes. She was wearing a broad-brimmed hat that had a red band. It did not suit her, for it made her face small and yellow; it hid her eyes and her brow. Once, when they crossed a busy road, he caught her arm, squeezing it gently, but she walked quickly, almost heedlessly.

All through the lunch she kept her head down. She seemed shy and in one of those moods that made him think of her being far away. But perhaps she was like himself, she wasn't used to hotels, and the waiters and the diners fussing and rushing here and there made her uncomfortable.

After coffee, Mrs. Fenner wiped her lips with a small handkerchief and said, 'Well, Mr. Durnan, when are you coming to see us? I needn't go back and face my son lacking a definite answer. So make up your mind and let me know when I come back.' She excused herself and went to the door with 'Ladies' painted on it.

He said, 'Should we tell Mrs. Fenner about our wedding? We could go there together and spend a few days when we are married.'

'No,' she said, keeping her head bent. Then she fingered her gloves, and added, 'He's your friend. You can go and spend a few days with him.'

'But why won't you come, Winnie?'

'I just don't want to come. That's all.'

He thought she wasn't thinking of the approaching marriage at all. Perhaps there was something worrying her? After all, her husband was only dead a short time, and the thought of marrying again might have upset her mind a little. Had it been two or three years since his death she would have acted differently. Her mind was not as clear as it should be, and there was all this noise about, knives and plates, and a child crying, and an organ playing outside with its shadow reflected on the window that faced them. He knew that, like himself, she was a stranger here, huddled at the table like a frightened cat in a corner. She would be all right if they could find some quiet place to talk.

Mrs. Fenner returned to the table. After a pause the little woman said, 'Any of you people want to spend a penny? The Ladies is over there, and the Gents is downstairs to the right.' Winnie got up, fingering her hat, and left the table.

'Don't be shy about it. If you want to go, go.' He smiled as he stood up.

Mrs. Fenner continued, 'I haven't run an hotel all these years, without knowing what to say and when to say it.'

A woman standing outside the Gents with a child asked him if he would take her little boy in. He took the child's hand, and as he bent over the little boy to loose his pants, he sniffed the perfume from the child's hair. Then a shivering came into his stomach, stabbing a pain into his bowels. It seemed to lift and hurl him dizzily through space, and he felt the wet tattered edges of a petticoat flapping against his legs. He saw his legs red and bulgy, and he gathered the wet tails of the petticoat over his knees and knelt on the cold floor. A voice was shouting, 'Stop your creeping, boy. Get on to your legs and walk.' It was his mother's voice. Her dark figure leaning over him with a cane barking in the air before it stung his legs.

Durnan released the child, and let the hot water in the hand-basin run over his wrists. He thought his mind had freed itself of these childhood shackles, but touching the child just now had brought back a moment, an awful moment, of his own childhood. Why was it so near? That he could feel the wet petticoat that rubbed his legs, and hear the bark of the cane as it cut down on them. Christ, what a miserable childhood he had.

The little boy was tugging at his coat, crying out that he had finished. Mrs. Fenner and Winnie were shaking hands when he got to the table.

'Now, Mr. Durnan, I want your answer. Once and for all, when are you coming to see us? This is Thursday. Why not come down on Saturday? You can stay the week-end for a beginning.'

He promised the little woman he would come on Saturday.

'Come first to Belfast, and make sure you arrive in time to catch the bus at half eleven.' And shaking his hand, 'We'll be watching out for you. And the lunch is paid for.'

Winnie and he were alone, but the noise continued, and a wireless had been turned on, filling the room with the full blare of a brass band.

He said, 'Should we find some quiet place where we could talk?'

'All right,' she nodded, and rose from the table.

Where they were to search for quietness in this busy city, Durnan didn't know. But he felt if he took a tramcar to its terminus, they must come to the city boundary, and beyond that there must be the country.

On a near-by pole, a sign said: ALL CARS FOR FALLS PARK STOP HERE BY REQUEST.

A tramcar approached and they boarded it. Her broad hat seemed to make her self-conscious, for she kept fingering it, and now a little dent was beginning to show in its brim. When they reached the park it was quiet, with a wide field that stretched far away to the mountains. Inside there was a wall with seats of plank fashion jutting out. Women with prams were sitting on the seats nearest the gate, but further up the path there was a vacant seat.

When they sat down, Durnan looked towards the next seat at an old man paring his corns with a razor blade. Winnie was heedless of the old fellow. Suddenly he shook his fist at Durnan and shouted, 'You won't flee from the wrath to come. There'll be no dancing in hell nor no pictures, and when the rich man calls for a drink, God won't heed him, for he didn't heed God when on earth.' The old man then pulled on his boots and went off, crying, 'Give an account of your stewardship'. Winnie remained heedless of him. Durnan heard her mutter something, and again her fingers went to her hat.

'What was it you were saying, Winnie?'

There was a long pause before she turned her head and said, 'Nothing.'

'Funny old man that. He must be a bible-thumper. Belfast's full of them,' Durnan said. It wouldn't have surprised him, if she hadn't heard a word the old fellow said. He felt he had to say something to take her out of her reverie. He had brought her here in order that they might plan for their wedding.

'Were you lonely when I left, Winnie?'

'I was. Just a little.'

'I suppose you wondered, the day you got the telephone message?'

'Yes, I did.'

'Were you surprised when I asked you to marry me? I mean so soon after your husband's death?'

'I didn't expect it so soon. But it's all one in the end. Marry me tomorrow or two years hence.' She smiled, but it disappeared as quickly as it had formed.

'I was with my own parish priest, Winnie, and he says it is the custom to get married in the bride's parish.'

'And what happens if the bride doesn't want the wedding in her parish?'

'You don't want to get married in your own, Winnie?' She shook her head.

She said, 'I was thinking, maybe, we could get married here in Belfast. You being a sailor would make it easier.'

'Yes, I'd be agreeable to that, Winnie.' After a pause, Durnan continued, 'Yes, Winnie, we could do that; in fact the Canon at home would fix it for us. What about a groomsman and a bridesmaid?'

'We don't want any fuss, do we?' she asked.

'I was thinking of asking Fenner.'

'I'd like it as quiet as possible. If we get married in a Belfast church there are always people there to act as witnesses. As I say, we don't want any display. Does it matter who is bridesmaid or groomsman?'

She was right. After all, they were the two that really mattered. After the wedding the witnesses were usually forgotten about.

'Would your priest fix it for us in a Belfast church?'

'He would, Winnie. I'll see him about it, first thing when I get back home.'

'Very good. Now where are we going to live?'

'That's a matter for you, Winnie. Though I'd like it to be my place.'

'Let it be your place then. When I return, I'll see the auctioneer and sell my own stuff. Isn't your place furnished?'

'Yes, Winnie, I think we'd have everything we need. If we haven't it would be fun buying new things as we went along, it would give us a feeling of building our own home.'

She looked away quickly, as if something on the mountain suddenly caught her attention.

'Winnie, are you sorry you said you'd marry me?'

She looked straight at him. 'No. Did I say I was sorry?' After a pause she said, 'Aren't we making arrangements for it?'

'Yes, Winnie, we are. When can it happen?'

'As soon as you can arrange it with your priest. Tomorrow, if it can be done so soon.'

Her eyes were shadowed with blue, a deep blue that spread over her cheek bones. Her face was pale and her head shook a little.

She said, 'I feel awfully cold. Let us walk back to the bus station, and I can get an early bus. I'll call and see the auctioneer about selling out. The sooner it's all over the better.'

She pulled her gloves further up her wrists, arranged the scarf tighter round her neck, and just as she turned to lift her handbag, he gripped her shoulders and pulled her towards him.

144

She dropped her head quickly, and the wide brim of the hat scraped his nose and chin.

'What are you doing, in broad daylight?'

'But Winnie, only to kiss you. We're alone here.'

'We're not. Look at the women further down.'

She was walking away before he could answer. Outside the park gates she said, 'Should we take a bus or tram to the city centre, or would you rather walk?'

There was a kindlier tone in her voice.

'I think we'll walk,' he said, glancing back to look at the women with the prams.

He felt she was right about the broad daylight, for had he kissed her these women might have thought she was just a tart he had picked up. He was glad now that she had refused his kiss.

He said, 'I'm sorry, Winnie, for what happened just now . . . It was unthinking of me. . . .'

'Don't let it trouble you,' she answered.

She ceased walking fast, taking an interest in the shops they were passing. Then she stopped, looking through a window at a pair of gloves.

'Would you like those gloves, Winnie?'

She nodded and they went into the shop, but the gloves were not her size, and she refused the assistant when he suggested another pair. Durnan eyed a powder box under the glass of the counter and he bought it. She slipped in into her handbag and thanked him.

He discovered, as they walked, that her step was proud and firm. Her flat-heeled shoes clinked on the flagstones with determination. That was what her clink–clink suggested to him: a woman, firm, determined, unshaken, a fighter.

'As soon as I get home, Winnie, I'll see the Canon and ask him to fix a church in Belfast for us as soon as he can.'

'Yes.'

'And you'll go straight home now and see about selling your things, and the day we're married you'll come to my place?'

'Yes, but you must let me know a day or two before the wedding.'

'Yes, Winnie, I'll write to you, and let you know everything.'

He shook her hand as she got into the bus. Then he made his way out of the station. He did not look round. He didn't think it right that he should. They were just a pair of showless lovers. They had long passed the stage of courtship. They had clear minds, wanted to get married, without show, without fuss.

CHAPTER TWENTY-FIVE

ROBERT was cooking herring, and as they sat at the table, the old man talked about the herring coming into the lough. But Durnan was heedless of his talk, for he was hurrying through the meal so that he could cross the fields to see the Canon.

'What great hurry is on you?' Robert asked.

'I'm going over to see the Canon.'

'A fine old man, the Canon. Do you know what he told me, Stephen, one time he come to see Susan? That I'd have to be a Catholic before I could be buried in the same grave with her. That's queer, isn't it?'

He pretended not to hear the old man, rushing to the room to inquire of Susan how she felt. Then he hurried from the kitchen and over the fields.

The Canon shook his hand and said, 'Well, now, what's your trouble this time?'

'Well, Canon, we have decided to get married in Belfast, and we want you to fix the church for us.'

'So you want a city wedding. We aren't stylish enough for you.' He could see the Canon's smile, and he knew the old man was joking. He pointed a seat to Durnan.

'Of course, before we do all this, we must know a little something of the bride-to-be.'

'She's a Barholm woman, Canon, and I'm sure her parish priest would tell you anything you want to know about her.'

'I have an inquiring old mind, and just to set it at rest, I think we'll give the parish priest at Barholm a little tinkle and lend an ear to what he has to say. Would you agree to that?' Again the Canon was smiling.

Moving to the door he called to the housekeeper to get Father Breen on the phone. The old man sat at the table again, and offered Durnan a cigarette.

'You're doing the wise thing, Stephen Durnan, getting married, now that your mother's gone. A man like you needs a wife and home. I daresay no man needs a home more than a sailor, despite the fact that he's seldom in it.'

'Will you be able to fix a church for us, Canon?'

'That isn't the hardest thing in the world. I think we'll be able to manage it. Mind your cigarette ash, for this old woman I have as housekeeper is a total terror. She would pass by a spider's web should it be as big as a sheepskin, and mourn all night over the tiniest flick of ash.

The housekeeper knocked on the door, saying the call was through.

'What is your girl's name?'

'Winnie Norton.'

'And does she live in the village itself?'

'She does, Canon.'

The priest closed the door, and Durnan wondered what questions and answers would now pass between the two clergymen. He supposed they made all this ado about things, in case of bigamy. He settled himself back in the chair, and from somewhere came the loud laughing voice of the Canon. Perhaps they were laughing about Winnie, her being a widow for such a short time. He was right, for when the Canon returned, he said, 'Well, Father Breen tells me she's a widow, and that she isn't very long a widow.' The laugh was still on his face.

'She is, Canon.'

147

'She'll have all the more sense. Still, I've been a long while marrying people, and it's one of the quickest in my experience. But I don't blame you. It's a bad thing, a very bad thing, to toy long with the idea of marriage, propose to the woman and get it over as quick as you can. Well, you are all right, the bride's all right . . . get a church and the wedding's all right . . . isn't that it?'

'Yes, Canon.'

The Canon opened a drawer, took out a sheet of notepaper, and started writing.

'When would you like the wedding, what day?'

This was Thursday, and he remembered she had asked him for a day or two's notice. Next Friday would do.

'Friday next, Canon.'

'Very good, Friday it'll be. I'll get in touch with the right people. Any particular church?'

'No, Canon, we just want it quiet.'

'Well, take this letter to the Church of the Holy Innocents, in Belfast. I'd suggest a good time would be about ten-thirty in the morning. The P.P., there, is a good friend of mine; in fact, he's my nephew.'

'Thank you, Canon. You are very kind. . . .'

'Nonsense, man. That's my duty. That's what we're all here for, to help each other. If people would only realize that, what a happier place the world would be.'

'That's true, Canon.'

'Well now, I don't want to lecture you. You're a man, and I'm sure you've knocked about the world a good bit, but perhaps a word or two mightn't be out of place at this moment. You are about to be married. Marriage is a great sacrament, so, son, approach it with a clean heart and a clean mind. Ask God to bless your union with children. Be honest with her, and faithful to her. Share with her all you've got, whether it be much or little.' Suddenly, the old priest took a torch from his pocket, and shone it on the window.

'Do you see that, in the window?'

'Do you mean the bird sitting on the nest?'

'That's the Pelican in her piety. She would feed her young with her own blood. Remember that symbol, if God blesses you with children.'

The old priest's hand reached out. 'Good night, now. And God bless you.'

As he ran over the fields he felt in his pocket for the letter, just to make sure it was there. The word piety seemed to whisper through the breeze that came from the sea. It was a lovely word, and when he sounded it aloud he felt it was a real word, a word that God himself had made specially. It was a word you wanted to whisper. Robert had the lamp lighted and was sweeping the hearth when he arrived.

'I think Susie would like a word in your ear, Stephen.'

The room was dark, and Robert followed after him with the lamp. Its yellow light picked out Susan's withered face, showing her lips black. The bed creaked as she tried to lift herself.

'It's a parcel I have for you, Stephen. There it is at the end of the bed. Undo it. It's the wedding present, the sheets and the shawls. I love to call them silken shawls. . . .'

'Reminding you of the Spanish Chieftain,' Robert laughed.

Durnan unwrapped the sheets and spread the shawls on the bed.

'They're lovely, Susan,' he said.

'Red shawls are not the fashion now, Stephen. More's the pity. But they'll do to spread over the cot when your weans come. I think it's lovely to see a wean happed in red silk.' She started crying loudly, 'I'm done, I'm done . . .' Her head fell back on the pillow.

Robert bent over her. 'Susie, old pet, we're old, and if God didn't bless us with weans he gave us kind neighbours. If we never had weans to bring us joy, we never had them to bring us sorrow. . . .'

Durnan tiptoed from the room, leaving the old woman crying and the old man trying not to.

149

Susan must have bought the shawls years ago, for as he held one of them to the light of the fire, he saw it peppered with moth holes. But he put them away in the room, so that Robert wouldn't see them.

'I have something for you too, Stephen,' he heard Robert say. Robert was holding a hand-knitted jersey in front of him.

'Susie knitted this for me, close on ten years ago, and I want you to have it.' The old man measured the jersey against Durnan's body and said, 'It'll fit you well, Stephen, for ten years ago I was as full in the chest as you are.'

'Thank you, Robert; it is very kind of you.'

'Mind, Stephen, in all fairness to you, it wasn't always in my mind to give it to you. But sure, Sunday and Saturday is all one on the *Summer Breeze*, now that she's beached. Isn't it sad, Stephen, when people cease to be fond of clothes? It's a sign they are near death.'

'Not at all, Robert.'

'Ah! but yes at all. But don't think it unmannerly of me offering you the jersey, because I'm past caring for wearing it myself.'

'Why should I? It's a splendid jersey, and would cost a lot of money if I went to buy it in a shop.'

'But, Stephen, I never was a liar, and the truth about that jersey was that I was keeping it to dress me when I was dead. Is that queer now, me offering it to you, with thoughts like that connected with it?'

'No, Robert.'

'Susan tells me that Catholics must wear shrouds. She told me that, when I questioned her about the brown rig that draped your mother. It's sad to me sometimes, Stephen, to think I won't be buried in my fisherman's cap and jersey. The apostle Peter was a fisherman, and I think it's a kindly nod he might have for the likes of me . . . but there . . . Susie tells me I must become a Catholic, if I'm to be laid in the same grave with her. Is that right?'

But Durnan was thinking of the jersey Robert kept for his death bed, and had now made him a wedding present of it. He burst out laughing.

'What are you laughing at, Stephen? It's no laughing matter, I can tell you. Sure, it wouldn't be any harm putting me in the same grave as Susan?'

He could see the old man was serious. There was an earnestness in his voice.

'Will it be hard for me to become a Catholic, Stephen? I can bless myself, and say the Our Father and the Hail Mary, and the Creed, for Susie learnt me all them prayers.'

'Does Susan want you to become a Catholic?'

'Susie never mentioned religion to me since the day and hour we were married. She taught me prayers, the only ones she knew. You know, Stephen, at sea people don't feel the same about religion as they do on the land. On the land they never seem to find God, so they must fight about Him all the time. But at sea you can see Him everywhere, in the water, in the moon, in the stars, and you can hear Him in the wind . . . He's always there, like a strong but silent friend.'

'You're right, Robert.'

'Stephen, what will they do to me, to make me a Catholic? I've often wanted to broach it to Susan, but I was always afraid to mention burial to her, seeing she's a few years older than myself.'

'Likely they'll baptize you, Robert.'

'Pour water over my head, like they do with a new-born child?' Robert removed his cap, and feeling the bald centre of his head that was coloured like a pancake, he said, 'Pour water over here, Stephen?'

'Yes, I think that's what they'll do.'

The old man was puzzled about the whole thing. Durnan, to change the subject, said, 'Where did you get the herring we had tonight?'

'Before noon, I seen the herring come into the lough, so I

151

launched the punt and jigged about a dozen of them. Half of them I gave to the roadman for helping me with the beaching of the punt. Stephen, son, if only we had a net we could slip up the lough the night and get ourselves a cran or two. Do you hear me?'

He hadn't and he said, 'What was it, Robert?'

'If we had a net or two, we could get a few cran tonight.'

'But we've no boat, Robert.'

'Isn't my punt there?'

'She's too small, Robert.'

'Small, if you're looking for big fishing and big money, but there's room enough in her for two nets and twenty or thirty pounds' worth of herring; and that's as much as any Christian would want.'

'Have you ever fished herring in her?'

'Susie could tell you something about that that would open your ears. Four years ago, in two nights we got forty-five pounds' worth of fish in her.'

Durnan became suddenly interested in what the old man was saying, and he questioned him as to where the herring went to when they came to the lough.

'Beyond the Jackdaw Island you can fish them. Fine plump herring, as full as a pigeon's breast. Susie had a great smell in her nose for fishing. She could nearly hear them swimming. I'm gameball, yet, Stephen, for a season's fishing in the lough.'

'We have no nets, Robert.'

'Nets aren't the hardest things to get. You can buy them in plenty from Portavogie.'

'Are you going to blather there all night?' Susan called from the room.

'She wants me to rub her side, Stephen; it pains her when it comes this time of night. But think about the herring. You could stay at home a long while and fish.'

Stretching himself on the sofa, Durnan thought about what Robert had said. Surely, if Susan and he could fish in their small boat . . . and there was always the chance of buying a bigger boat. A good season's fishing would mean a lot. It would keep him at home, now that Winnie was coming. Bringing the lamp to the table, he wrote to Winnie, telling her what the Canon had said, and asking her to let him know when she could arrive in Belfast.

In the room he held the lamp high to pick out the cobwebs in the corners and the dark patches on the walls. Tomorrow he would colour the room, wash the furniture, and take the new blankets from the drawers and hang them outside to air.

In bed, his mind was active. Robert's talk of fishing made him eager. He could see himself pulling the nets with the silver-bellied fish shining in the dark. He could hear the cough of the seals and the heavy splash of dog fish. He could feel his legs wet and his hands tingling with heat, and the damp fleshy touch of the rope as they lifted the anchor, his feet warm with excitement as they headed her for the long sail down the lough from the fishing ground. He was urging the little boat ahead, giving her full sail, hearing her tear the water, watching a herring doing its last dance in the net. On and on, down the lough, hearing the distant sigh of the tides circling the islands. He was swinging the boat, taking her straight across the lough, nosing her for the beach below the cottage. He saw himself, cold and wet, flecked with herring scales, walking up the loanen, standing at the door of the cottage, smelling the warmth of the kitchen.

Winnie would be there, asking him if the catch was a good one. Urging him to a good meal, leaving him to clear the table, then getting into bed beside her, lying with his arm round her, hearing the licking of the water on the gravel, and the cry of the curlews as they hurried inland from the sea.

CHAPTER TWENTY-SIX

IN the morning the rain wakened him. After breakfast he took the bed apart, removed the pictures from the walls and cream-coloured the room.

Robert suggested a skirting of tar on the bottom of the walls, and covering himself with a bag, he went down to the *Summer Breeze* to fetch some. When Robert left the house, Susan called Durnan into the room.

'Stephen, it's something very special I want to talk to you about.'

'What is it, Susan?'

'It's about Robert. Did you ever know that Robert was a Protestant?'

'Yes, he happened to mention it one day last week, when we were working on the *Summer Breeze*.'

'What was he saying, Stephen?'

'Nothing very much. He just happened to mention it.'

'It worries me, Stephen, for I'd like him to be buried with me, when his time comes. Would you mind having a talk with him about it? I don't like bringing clergymen about the house, they have a funny way of talking about these things.'

'All right, Susan, I'll have a word with him. Supposing I sent him in to you, couldn't the pair of you thresh it out between yourselves?'

'I suppose we could. But somehow it'll seem strange for me to talk about this with him. You see, Stephen, it'll all seem so strange to us. Like two strangers we'll be.'

'It won't be that hard, Susan.'

'Ach, it's queer that folk can't be left themselves to decide things. I'm not a learned woman, son. I can scarcely write my own name, but I don't feel God would say against Robert being laid in the same grave as me. . . .'

'Let me talk to Robert, Susan, and you'll find everything will be all right.'

When the old man returned with the tar, Durnan called him into his bedroom and said, 'Robert, Susan was talking about you, just now. Would you go in and have a crack with her? Come to some decision as to what's going to happen.'

'I'll do that, Stephen. But look, one thing, Larry is standing on the deck of the *Summer Breeze*, cold and hungry looking; I must fetch him down some crumbs.'

'I'll bring the crumbs to Larry, if you'll go in and talk to Susan.'

Durnan was glad of any excuse to get away from the conference which was to decide Robert's religious beliefs.

Picking up the bag that had fallen from the old man's shoulders he pinned it across his own, got some bread and came outside.

The rain stung down into the lough, making a soft sighing sound as its million needles stabbed into the water, causing a grey mist. The one-legged gull was perched on the deck, his white feathers crumpled and his leg shiny.

Durnan threw the crumbs to it, but it didn't move. Only the small stump shook. A few crows hovered round the boat. Then the gull was suddenly active, falling on the deck as the movements of his beak at the bread threw him off his balance.

Looking at the vessel Durnan realized she was doomed. What would Robert do with her? Sell her for firewood? Susan, he felt sure, would never rise again from the bed in the cottage. If she did, she could never live in the *Summer Breeze* again, for she could never climb the way to and from the cabin. Everything about the vessel spoke of death. The patched decks, the withered bowsprit, the bits and pieces of her deck furniture broken up for firewood. Even the one-legged gull spoke in terms of decay, of usefulness long past, of helplessness. But Robert and Susan could stay with him until their days were finished.

When he returned to the cottage, Susan had everything arranged. Robert was to be baptized. But the old man looked worried, and Susan kept waving her hand in the air.

'Ye would think he was going to get a tooth out or face a firing squad, to see him,' she said.

'Will he just pour water over my head, Stephen?'

'That's all, Robert.'

'He's uneasy, Stephen. He thinks the priest is some kind of a witch doctor, going to torture him, or make him walk on fire. Isn't the Canon just an ordinary man like himself, Stephen?'

'More or less.'

'It isn't as though he was a stranger,' she went on. 'Sure you know all the prayers. Didn't I teach you them all?'

'You did.'

'Well, sure there's nothing more to worry about.'

But Robert looked more bewildered, and Durnan tried to change the talk, but Susan was full of it.

'He'll need a sponsor, won't he, Stephen?'

'A what?' Robert asked.

'A sponsor, or a witness. Maybe you would act for him, Stephen?'

'Yes, I will. Any time he cares to fix it, I'll act as witness.'

Robert followed him into the kitchen, and sat opposite the fire.

'I suppose, Stephen, I'd need to be dressed when I'm being baptized?'

'Well, you could hardly go with the clothes you're wearing. Not that there'd be any objections, but since I remembered you, Robert, you were always pretty nifty.'

'Would I have to take me ear-rings out, Stephen?'

'What for?'

'I heard a preacher man in Cardiff saying that ear-rings were pagan things. Because they wouldn't come out, Stephen, unless they'd lance them out.'

'No, Robert, you won't have to take them out.'

'There's one other thing, Stephen.'

'What is it?'

'If I am to be baptized, and if I must go in my finery, would you lend me the jersey I gave you as a wedding gift?'

'Certainly, Robert.'

'I hate asking you for it, Stephen, after me giving it to you with a keepsake air about it. But it's the only decent stitch I have.'

'I'll leave it out for you, Robert.' The thought of Robert's jersey brought to his mind his visit to Fenner's. Tomorrow was Saturday and he must be on his way to Fenner's.

'Yes, Robert, I'll leave out the jersey for you, and when I come back next week we can talk more about your baptism.'

'Are you going away?'

'Only for a day or two, Robert. I'm going to stay with the young fellow I saved in the *Glendry*.'

He packed the small case, folding the pyjamas neatly in the corner. This was the first time he'd ever worn them. He was going to an hotel, a real hotel, where everything was clean and fresh. It was going to be a new experience, an experience poles apart from any he had ever had before.

This was going to be his first real holiday. What a difference it was going to make. What a change from the lousy ninepenny-a-night dumps he had stayed in while leaving a ship or waiting to join one.

Everything about him must be clean. He felt he must wash himself from the head down, every part of his body.

He filled the big tin bath, stripped off his clothes and stood in the middle of it. He lathered his body with soap until he was able to draw his finger through it, leaving marks like tram lines. He washed his hair until the rinsing water changed from grey to clear, assuring him that it was dirt free. Then he sat by the fire and cut his toe nails. He knew he must be particular about his feet, for he had a habit of kicking the clothes off himself at night. Usually in the morning the bed clothes were on the floor, and he felt that Mrs. Fenner might look into the room while he slept, just to see if he was comfortable, for she struck him as being that kind of woman.

Now everything about him was spotless, and a great heat filled his body. Outside the rain was falling, and when he opened the door the breeze blew some on his chest.

He moved out until the rain peppered his body, keeping his hand on the latch, lest Robert should come out, and on finding him standing naked in the rain, might think he had taken leave of his senses.

A thrush was singing somewhere near and a robin flitted on to a hawthorn just opposite where he stood. The song of the robin was sad, almost a lament for the quietness of the evening. The song of the thrush was irregular. The rain seemed to upset him and he flew past the cottage, his wings making a curious trembling sound.

Durnan moved his arms, and a longing to run down to the lough and swim seized him, but as he stood the wind became stronger, and the robin ceased his singing, and flew off in search of shelter. Darkness was in the sky, a heavy rain-sodden darkness. In the kitchen he dried his body. The heat returned when he got into bed. He lay back, smelling the fresh smell of the coloured lime that was drying on the walls, and he forgot he hadn't used the tar to make a false skirting at the bottom.

CHAPTER TWENTY-SEVEN

DURNAN heard the bus conductor shout, 'Fenner's Hotel.' Mrs. Fenner had said she would meet him but there was no one about, except a tramp who, with his hand to his ear, was singing a ballad about a Boston burglar.

She appeared at the door, and came rushing over, 'Stephen, Stephen, you're here, and not a soul standing by to greet you. You must forgive me, but we're filled out and . . . I trust you weren't waiting long.'

Taking his arm, she led him into a small room, and calling to a waiter she said, 'Walter, get Mr. Durnan something to eat. There's some fried chicken put aside for him. Polly has it. But bring him soup first, and a bottle of stout. Or would you like whisky, Stephen?'

'Stout, if you please.'

She pointed to a table. 'When you've had something to eat, you can go upstairs and see Jackie. He's getting up tomorrow.' She was fanning her face with her hand. The waiter returned to the table with soup.

'Walter, bring some cigarettes — or make it cigars,' she said.

Durnan tried to protest, but she waved her hand, saying, 'Nonsense, man, you're here as my guest, and only the best is good enough.' Durnan's mind was confused. The soup was in front of him, and spoons and knives and forks surrounded his plate.

'Come now, take your soup before it's cold,' and taking a spoon she cleaned it with a white cloth she carried and put it into the soup, 'Go ahead and don't talk.'

Never before had he had a meal like this. The chicken was piled on his plate, and underneath it were thick slices of red soft ham. The potatoes were chipped, and looked the colour of gold.

The sweet seemed to contain every fruit under the sun, and then the waiter brought cracker biscuits and large squares of cheese.

When the meal was finished she brought him upstairs. Pointing to a door with the word 'Gents' painted on the glass, she said with a smile, 'I don't have to tell you what that's for.' Then she took him along a corridor, and showed him his bedroom.

'Now if you want a wash up I'll call for you in five minutes or so and take you up to Jackie.'

Durnan looked round the room. It was papered with a clean cream paper. A border of blue ran along the picture rail, and continued down the corners of the room. The ceiling was cream, and the carpet was blue. The bed seemed to bulge. Yet, when he felt it, his hand weighed it down like a mass of dough. Its pillows were spotless, so were the sheets. How glad he was he had cleaned himself so well. Even now, he wasn't sure whether he was clean enough. In the corner near the window there was a wash-hand basin, with towels folded over its bottom bars. He washed his hands, and was drying them when she entered the room.

'I hope this room is to your taste,' she said. 'The last person to sleep in that bed was a Bishop, so it should be sanctified.'

She took him up more stairs, then pausing at a door she brought her fingers to her lips, and, with a wink, she knocked the door. 'Guess who's here, Jackie,' she said.

Fenner said, 'You're very welcome to my home, Stephen.'

'I'll leave the pair of you now. I'll send you up another drink, Stephen.'

'But, Mrs. Fenner . . .'

She was hurrying out of the room saying, 'You protest too much. Don't annoy me.'

'Well, Jackie, how do you feel now?'

'I have nightmares. Sometimes, I believe, I scream. I feel I do. But the others say they never hear me. I'm getting up tomorrow.'

'It's just the aftermath. I've had one or two myself.'

'Tell me, Stephen. I never got it quite clear about Norton. What really happened to him?'

'I was trying to get him from the bridge. He wouldn't move, so I lifted him on to my shoulders. It was my intention to carry him to one of the boats, but outside the wheelhouse he started twisting my neck with his hands. I couldn't stand the pain, so I hurled him from me.'

'You hurled him from you?'

'Yes, I couldn't stand by, and him trying to choke me, could I?'

'No, you couldn't. You tried to save him, anyway.'

'I did.'

'How many have you saved in your time?'

'I dunno.'

'Come, Stephen, I'm curious. I really want to know.'

'I saved a man in Truro, dived in after him. I saved Norton . . . and that's all,' he said hesitantly.

'And you saved me,' Fenner said.

'Did I?'

'Of course you did. Do you realize I was paralysed with fear? It was awful, when you started to drag me away from the stanchion. That's three lives you've saved.'

'I suppose it is, only the last time I tried to save Norton, well I've told you what happened.'

Mrs. Fenner returned with a bottle of stout. 'I suppose you've seen your photograph,' she said.

She switched on the light, and held the newspaper in front of him.

'You're not such a bad-looking fellow, and the woman is the skipper's wife.'

'Yes, that's right.' He felt he would have to tell them about the wedding. He just couldn't keep it from them, they were so kind and decent about things. After all, a wedding was nothing to be ashamed of. Everyone had a right to know about it.

'Yes, that's the skipper's wife,' he said, trying to take the whole thing casually. 'She nursed me back to life, and I'm marrying her next Friday, if all goes well.'

'Next Friday!' Mrs. Fenner exclaimed. 'Let me offer you my best wishes, and may you never do worse than we wish you. Now, Stephen, tell me, what can I get you for a wedding present?'

'Nothing, Mrs. Fenner, I don't . . .'

'We'll talk about that later. Could you not get this fool of mine a wife?' But Fenner was laughing at her, 'Poor Flo, mad for grandchildren,' he said.

A waitress appeared and told her she was wanted. She left the room saying, 'My goodness, no rest for a wicked old woman.'

Fenner's father and his two sisters came into the room. 'We have a lot to thank you for,' he said.

'Mother tells us you're being married next week,' one of the girls said.

The talk dragged on. Every now and then Fenner's father pressed a button and the waiter came with two stouts. One of the girls played the piano which stood in the far corner of the room, and Mrs. Fenner came in to say that tea was ready.

How funny, Durnan thought, to sit down and eat a whole lobster. At home he had seen them often and often, but he had never tasted their flesh, and he supposed the men that fished them were the same. That seemed the odd thing about fishermen, the poor ones. They always lamented their poor food, yet it never struck them that occasionally they should eat one of their own lobsters or salmon, or a few of their clams and oysters.

After tea there was more stout, and more playing on the piano, and two other men came in and they played solo until it was nearly midnight.

As he lay in bed, Durnan felt this was the beginning of his new life. This really was life. Not an abundance of it, but enough of it to show him that he lived almost like a human animal. People like his mother had never found out much about life. They had never troubled to find out about it. Things came to them, and they never questioned from where or why. That was the curse of the poor, this stupid fatalism. They took no action or say in the making of their own lives. Everything was directed by God. God's will was strong and there was no moving against it. If God willed they lived in poverty, they did so. If God willed they should be dirty, they made no effort to clean themselves.

Durnan knew that this short holiday would do him more good than all the sermons ever preached by men with rows of letters after their names. It warmed his soul, just to live for a brief while in an atmosphere of enough. In an atmosphere of clean beds, of knives and forks, white tablecloths and flushing lavatories. He would enjoy this holiday with something of a spiritual feeling; he knew he'd have a bath in the morning, with big rough towels to dry himself, a decent breakfast, a good lunch, contented people, manners, kindness, comfort.

His mother could have had many of these things, if she hadn't been such a slitherer. But then there were hundreds, thousands of people like his mother. It was this stupid fatalism, that God had nothing to do with. They were to blame themselves.

In the morning a waitress brought him his breakfast to bed. She told him that Mrs. Fenner said he could come to Mass at eleven o'clock with them.

The waitress opened the door that faced the bed, but she turned after she looked into the room. Durnan followed her with his eyes. He thought this door was locked, or that it was another wardrobe, but now he could see it opened to a bathroom. The waitress said, 'Yes, the towels are there, if you feel like a bath.' Then she lifted his shoes and left the room.

When he finished his breakfast he smoked a cigarette, then he stripped off his pyjamas, and filled the pink bath with water, letting the two taps run, until the water felt so that he could lie in it. There was a long brush, and he rubbed soap on it and scrubbed his legs. The sensation made him laugh, made him laugh out loud. God above, what a life! Old Robert could talk about his baptism, his Christian baptism, but Durnan felt this to be a social baptism. This would make a man ambitious. Fill him with a longing to strive and work for things. Never would he have this feeling in his own dull cottage. It wasn't a case of putting a beggar on horseback and he'd ride to the devil; it was just that he was getting a little of the other side of life. He was beginning to understand what people meant when they spoke of their more fortunate brethren as losing their heads, when, after saving a few pounds, they built themselves big houses, with bathrooms and things.

He dried himself, and plucked the stopper from the hole to let the water run away. Now that the bath was empty, he saw a mark around it where the water had reached to, the mark was definite, just like the Plimsoll line on a ship. It was dirt, and he felt ashamed, wondering what the waitress would think when she came to wash the bath. He took the long brush, soaped it, and turning on the water washed the greasy line away, leaving the bath as clean as when he first got into it.

He dressed, and as he fixed his tie the girl returned with his shoes. They were well polished. He was combing his hair when Fenner entered.

'Did you sleep well, Stephen?'

'Like a log. Your mother's going to kill me with kindness.'

'Don't be silly. Come on, you'll have to put up a bit of a show. We're taking you to Mass. Mother thinks, well, I mean, she doesn't know sailors are . . .'

'Is the chapel far away?'

'No, just down the street. I'll take you to the organ loft. I'm playing . . .'

'Bit of a change from the concertina in the *Glendry*.'

Fenner laughed. 'What's your favourite music Stephen?'

'Why?'

'Provided it isn't jazz, I'll try it as a voluntary.'

'You mean you'll play my favourite song?'

'Yes, if it isn't jazz. I must draw the line, you know.'

'Do you remember playing on the concertina "My Singing Bird"?'

'I do.'

'Would you play that?'

'I'll play it, Stephen. In fact it's a favourite with myself.'

Mrs. Fenner joined them downstairs, and as they walked to the church men coming from the early Mass lifted their hats and caps to the little woman.

All through the Mass Fenner played, his jaws moving and his eyes looking as if they were seeing into some strange dreamy land. The music was sad, like the music he had played that day on the ship when the sailor told him to stop it. The choir sang softly. The words slowly came back to Durnan, recalling the days when, as a boy, he had served Mass.

'Et Exspecto Resurrectionem Mortuorum . . .' sang the choir. Durnan knew it was the Credo they were singing. Then the Mass was over and Fenner played 'My Singing Bird'. As he played a mood of freedom swelled through Durnan. He was conscious again of his rebirth, starting with this great whiteness of things, and the thought of Winnie. This tune was a symbol, a symbol of freedom.

'If I could catch my Singing Bird' — he felt he had caught his; his struggle, his reaching out was ended. Now his soul would have pattern. The music ceased and he felt a little dizzy, but his mind cleared, and he knew the pattern was fixed.

On Tuesday he told Mrs. Fenner he must go home. He knew there would be a letter waiting for him from Winnie. The little woman said, 'When he had done so well, why not finish the week?' but he told her he must go as he had things to see to.

'Well, if you must go, you must. But mind, Stephen, nobody is chasing you away,' she had said.

He was having tea for the last time; grilled salmon with fried potatoes. Mrs. Fenner urged him to eat more, and beside his leg she left a little case.

'What's this?' he asked.

'Open it when you get home, and you'll see what's in it,' she said.

At the bus, too, when her husband and she and Jackie were seeing him off, she pushed a carton of cigarettes into his hand, and told him to be sure and bring his wife with him next time he was coming. And when he shook her hand she was crying, and he wanted to call her Flo.

'God and His mother, bless you,' she said.

'God bless you too, Flo.' He had said it, and now the bus was moving off, with the three of them waving him goodbye, and Mrs. Fenner wiping her eyes with the napkin she had in her hand.

On the road back a gleam of dying sunlight warmed his face, making him drowsy. Would his own home ever be like the one he had just left? He would try hard, do his damnedest to make it just a little like Fenner's. Try to bring into it the ring of laughter, the freshness and the clean smell of comfort that seemed to be everywhere in Fenner's, even in the stables outside the house.

At Belfast he found he had an hour's wait before his bus left for home, and he inquired the way to the Church of the Holy Innocents. He saw the parish priest, who told him the Canon had been in touch with him, and it was arranged that his wedding should take place on Friday morning.

CHAPTER TWENTY-EIGHT

DURNAN had scarcely entered the cottage when Robert shook his hand and said, 'Stephen, we're like millionaires here, now.'

'Why, Robert. Have you found a fortune?'

'It's yourself, man. Go into your bedroom and have a look at what come for you in a motor van.'

'What on earth are you talking about, Robert?'

'I'm just saying, go into your bedroom, take the lamp with you and see for yourself.'

Robert followed him into the room, and pointing to a new bedroom suite said, 'Well, Stephen, old son, what do you think of them?'

'Where did they come from, Robert?'

'That I couldn't tell you. There come a motor van here, and the driver of it asked me if Stephen Durnan lived here. I said he did, so he planks the furniture in the room, after making me sign a paper to the effect that they were received in good condition. It reminded me, Stephen, of signing for a cargo.'

Durnan thought, Winnie might have sent them on, but after opening this drawer and that one he came to the wardrobe; inside the door a little card hung from the handle, and on the card it said, 'From Fenners wishing you and yours long life and happiness.'

'They are well-mannered folk, with kindness of heart, and no stinting of their money roughness that sent you them things,' Robert said.

'They are everything you say, Robert.' Durnan examined the furniture, nervous with sudden delight.

'Robert, if we just had a carpet on the floor?' he said.

'Fly high, boy, there's nothing like it, and you making a start in married life.'

The shiny furniture reflected their shadows in the lamp-light. Robert pointed to the corner and said, 'See, Stephen, I flattened an Oxo tin and nailed it over that mouse-hole; they won't chew their way through that. And I washed the floor all over with paraffin oil, just to make it fresh. And there was a hole near the fireplace, the size of a hazel nut, and I poured tar down it, just in case there might be woodlice or cockroaches in it.'

They left the room, and Durnan remembered about the small case. When he opened it he found a bottle of whisky, a roast chicken and a bottle of port.

Robert eyed the contents and shook his head.

'This is another present from the same people,' Durnan said.

'It's kings or the descendants of kings you've been with this short while,' Robert said.

'Get out three clean plates and make some tea, and we'll have our supper in the room, Robert. Could Susan manage a bit of chicken, Robert?'

'A bit of the breast, Stephen. It wouldn't be too hard on her old molars. I think she only has the two left.'

'Very good, Robert, a leg each for us, and the breast for Susan, with a nip of whisky in the tea to flavour it.'

Durnan propped the old woman up in the bed, and putting a little stool over her knees, laid before her a plateful of white chicken.

As she ate it her lips moved like a rabbit's.

'That's nourishing,' she said. Robert said, 'Fingers were made before knives and forks,' and he curled the leg around his mouth with his hand. Durnan asked Susan if she'd like some whisky in her tea, and she said, 'Sure I might as well. One is good without the other, but both are better when they're together.' Then she pestered Durnan with questions about the furniture, where it came from? And who gave him the whisky? Was it his wife's people? Had they money? — until Robert started the 'Spanish Chieftain', and she fell back in the bed with laughing.

'Look at him, and the grease shining from his lips.' But the old man waved his arms and shook his head, and his smiling eyes were lost in his face as he sang.

Durnan sang too, crying as his voice swelled out the words of 'My Singing Bird'.

'I never knew you had such a grand voice, Stephen,' Susan was saying, and for her benefit he sang the song right through to the end.

During the short time that remained before the wedding, Robert went about still humming the 'Spanish Chieftain'. Now and then he would say, 'Stephen, the herring are in the lough, man, if only we had a net or two. . . .'

Durnan laughed at him, but Robert made signs with his hands. 'Man Stephen, I'm keen to be lowering the nets. . . .'

Durnan worked hard, with Robert lending what little help he could. They cut the hedges, cleared the front path and filled the holes in the loanen with gravel. Durnan brought the gravel from the beach in buckets, and Robert, with a fire shovel in his hand, spread it with the eagerness and delight of a schoolboy.

Then a letter came from Winnie. She had received his, and was pleased to know that he had arranged everything. She had fixed with the auctioneer to dispose of her things, and she was only keeping the bed clothes and one or two little personal things that she would send on. She felt that her things wouldn't sell well, as the neighbours about the place were funny about buying from certain people. She signed her name 'Winnie Norton' and, in a postscript, added she would arrive in Belfast at ten o'clock on Friday morning, and that she would wait for him at the bus station.

He re-read the letter, trying to deduct what she meant about her neighbours being funny about buying things from certain people. People like the Mathews might boycott the auction, for no other reason than that they didn't like her. Irish people could be like that. Carry their dislikes to stupid extremes. How glad she must be that he was taking her away from all this. Taking her to the quiet of his own cottage, with only Robert and Susan about.

Robert was close beside him, nudging him. 'Look, Stephen.'

'What is it, Robert?'

'Look to the lough, see the round head of the seal?'

Durnan looked to where the old man's finger pointed. A seal was shaking his head, he was so close to the beach that his whiskers could nearly be counted.

'Stephen, would you not go to Portavogie next week and buy a couple of nets?' Robert asked pleadingly.

'Next week, Robert, I'll be married.'

'Yes, I know son, but the week after that, couldn't we go fishing?'

'We could, Robert.'

'Good, I'll keep minding you about buying the nets.'

The old man looked again and tried to whistle.

'What are you trying to do, Robert?'

'Whistle the seal to the beach. But I can't do it, Stephen. I've tried it often before. Sammy Killops could do it.'

'Do what?'

'Whistle a seal to the shore. They said it was by the power of the devil he was able to do it.'

'Do you believe in the devil, Robert?'

'I do. But I think he's not as black as he's painted. There's times, Stephen, when I think he must have many a laugh to himself.'

'Maybe you're right, Robert.'

The two of them stood watching the seal turn seawards. Then he dived and was gone.

CHAPTER TWENTY-NINE

WHEN he met her at the station, he said, 'Winnie, I've forgotten all about the ring.'

Peeling off her glove, she took the wedding ring from her finger and gave it to him.

'Keep this in your vest pocket, until the priest asks for it,' she said.

He took her arm as they climbed the steps of the grey Church of the Holy Innocents. Looking above its doors, he saw children reaching their little stone hands to a stone God. Inside the church she halted at the holy water font.

'I suppose we'd better go to the altar?' she said.

He nodded, and they walked up the long aisle. Near the altar rail a woman was mopping the floor. Crossing over, Durnan asked her if he could speak to the parish priest.

'Is it important?' she asked.

He told her it was, and she excused herself, disappearing through the vestry door.

'We'd better sit down until he comes,' Winnie said, moving into a seat.

He felt the ring in his vest pocket, and the nicked edge of the half-crown that Susan told him he would need. He turned the ring over between his finger and thumb. Years ago he felt Norton must have fingered this ring as he was doing now. Thinking about Norton, he went on his knees and whispered a few prayers for the repose of his soul.

He felt her nudging his arm. 'There's the priest,' she was whispering.

'You are the couple from Portaferry?' said the priest.

'We are, Father,' he replied.

'Let me see your letter. Haven't you one?'

Durnan reached into his pocket and handed his letter to the priest.

'Haven't you one, too?'

'Yes,' she said, taking the letter from her handbag.

The priest said, 'I'll read these in the sacristy. Meanwhile, while you are waiting, kneel down and ask God's blessing on your union.' The priest left them, and Durnan knelt on the cold marble knee stool of the altar. What could he pray for? He was about to be married, that was all. Prayer, to him, did not seem to matter. All this appeared unnecessary. His marriage would start when they were back in his cottage. She was beside him, her broad-brimmed hat hiding her face, and she was fingering her beads and whispering prayers.

'Where are your witnesses?'

Durnan looked up, seeing the priest, dressed in surplice and soutane, with a stole around his neck.

'We understood, Father, we'd get witnesses here,' Winnie said. The priest grunted impatiently, and, looking towards the cleaner, he cracked his fingers, beckoning her to him.

'Go and get the sexton. Tell him it's a wedding, and hurry,' the priest told her.

Durnan heard people moving behind him. It struck him that perhaps the Fenners might have come. Glancing round he saw it was three old women wearing shawls, and then he realized he hadn't told the Fenners what church, and he felt suddenly relieved, for he was beginning to sense humiliation in everything.

The cleaner appeared again, tucking her hair under her woollen cap, and talking silently to a small fat man. As the couple approached, the priest came down to the altar rail opening a little book that had red and green ribbons dangling from it.

'Stand up over here,' said the priest, calling Durnan and Winnie with a movement of his hand. The cleaner and the sexton stood behind them.

The priest muttered the service with a certain hesitancy, searching the book with the aid of the coloured ribbons.

Durnan was being married, and it all seemed so strange, almost laughable. The things now in his mind were the priest's hairy knuckles, and the ribbons that danced when the pages turned. Lowering his eyes, he saw the sexton's hands, his thumb-nail ridged and furrowed and coloured like flint. The cleaner's hands were dirty, their veins marked black with washing soda, and the sleeves of her knitted jumper straggling like worms down her square wrists. She opened her hand, and the colour of the palm reminded him of the translucent flesh of Joe Fish.

'Repeat after me . . .' the priest was saying.

Then the priest asked for the ring, and Winnie held out her finger while Durnan pushed it on. The ring seemed to slide down her finger, as if the red circle of flesh it had made for itself was a magnet.

Now they were married, and the fat sexton took them into the vestry where he produced the pen for them to sign their names. He hovered about, asking if the nib was all right, if the blotter was there, until Durnan gave him five shillings.

On the way out the cleaner met them midway in the aisle, and he gave her ten shillings, and all the time she stared at Winnie.

When they were outside, he said, 'Well, Winnie, it's all over.'

'Yes, it's all over,' she echoed.

'Shouldn't we have something to eat? We could go to the hotel where Mrs. Fenner . . .'

'I'm not hungry,' she said. 'But you have a meal if you like. I thought we might hurry home to your place. My things might arrive, and I'd like to be there to sort them. . . .'

She toyed with the broad brim, and he felt a sudden impulse to tear it off her head, just to see her face.

'All right, Winnie, we'll go home. Just as you wish.'

He asked a porter, as he passed through the waiting-room, when the next bus left.

'In ten minutes' time,' the porter said, hurrying away with his mop moving up and down in the bucket.

Durnan thought about the cleaner in the church. Dirty, she was, and the fat little sexton with the nose that was coloured like

172

boiled beetroot, and eyes in his head like the stops on the organ Fenner played.

There was a sordidness about it all, after the spiritual whiteness of Fenner's. It seemed like snow that had been firm and white and was now grey and slushy and ugly. But then, it was mostly Winnie's doing. She had wanted things quiet.

He was glad now that none of the Fenners had been present. It would have annoyed Mrs. Fenner to see them standing with the drunken sexton and the trollopy cleaner.

Good God, he almost trembled when he thought of Fenner's suggestion that he might come and play the organ for him. What would they have made of this morning's transaction? The Fenners lived in a different world from him, yet they had taught him that he might be able to make his world just a little like theirs.

And he was going home now, to do it. He would get a carpet for the room, and with the new furniture . . .

Winnie was saying, 'Hadn't we better get into the bus or we mightn't get a seat?'

He took her arm, but she walked a little away from him, still fingering her hat.

People were moving through the bus station, and once she was nearly ten yards away from him. But he knew she was a little nervous, and he felt it was harsh of him to be irritated with her.

She settled herself in the back seat of the bus, leaning her head against the window, like someone very tired and in need of sleep. Once or twice she yawned, and beat her hand against her mouth in a bored fashion.

He pointed out things of interest on the road home; the scattering of islands that dotted the lough, the tip of the peninsula from Bradshaw's Brae; the black swans at Mountstewart, the huge rock with Eternity painted on it, the ruins of Castleknock Monastery, where the monks were supposed to chant every All Souls' night.'

She kept nodding and saying, 'Uh Huh' in her far-away manner.

Tonight he would find out the meaning of this. Find out everything about her. Why she hadn't been happy with Norton. Tell her this was a new life. She was Mrs. Durnan now, and must forget that Mrs. Norton ever existed. Tell her she must banish her moods, break up the sadness or silence or whatever it was that seemed to be within her.

'What about food?' she asked, suddenly.

'We'll get some on the way home. There's a shop at the corner, Jane Whorry's, and she'll give us whatever we want. I think we'd best bring some bacon, and eggs, and tea and sugar and bread. There's a travelling grocery van calls twice a week at the cottage, so you'll find everything convenient.'

He hoped the harbourmaster wouldn't be about when he walked towards home. He didn't want to be drinking or have any fuss. They hurried along the narrow street.

'This is the shop, now,' he said. 'You'll know it when you've shopping to do.'

'You get the groceries and I'll wait until you come out,' she said. But she had wandered as far as the end of the street before he caught up on her.

When they got to the loanen, he pointed to the cottage.

'There must be somebody in it. There's smoke coming from the chimney,' she said.

'Yes, Robert and Susan King are there. Remember me telling you about them?'

'I don't remember you telling me.'

'But I did, Winnie, when we talked about my leaving your house . . .' But she was giving her attention to the walk up the loanen.

'Ach, have you arrived? Let me be the first to welcome you home,' Robert said, reaching out his hand. The old man almost bowed in his eagerness to reach her hand.

'I didn't expect the pair of you home so soon, otherwise the

174

kettle would have been plumping for tea. Well, you look a good sensible woman, and I'm sure you'll make Stephen a good wife.'

Durnan wished the old man would cease his talking. He watched a sudden coldness in Winnie's face.

'Come into the room and meet Susie. She's fair dying to get laying her eyes on you. And she's mad for a bit of talk.'

Ignoring the old man, she peeled off her gloves.

'There come a motor van with some stuff for you, a while ago, and I bid them put it in the room,' Robert said, looking at her, with his eyes closed in a smile. She gave him a quick look, pursing her lips.

'This is our room in here, Winnie,' Durnan said, sensing she wasn't pleased with Robert's easy manner.

Durnan told her about the new furniture, and who sent it, and he asked her if she'd like the new bed put up, or would she rather have the old one?

'Who slept in the old one?' she asked.

'My mother.'

'We'd better put up the new one. I'll air the blankets when we've had a cup of tea,' she said.

She hadn't made any move to take her coat and hat off. She toyed with the leather belt of the coat, tightening it impatiently.

'We'll need new curtains. Those are a disgrace.'

'Yes, Winnie, in a day or two. I'll take you into Lawson's. They have plenty of curtains.'

She was at the window, feeling the curtains, drawing them closer, shutting out the breadth of blue sky. Moving her fingers quickly in mid air, she muttered, 'Dust and dirt everywhere. Must be years since they were washed.'

'Yes, Winnie. My mother was an old woman, and old women sometimes aren't as clean as they might be. Besides, the window was very high for her to reach to.'

Robert entered the room. 'Aren't you coming down to meet

175

Susie? She's mad eager to shake your hand, and wish you well,' he said.

'I'll come when I'm ready,' she snapped.

Robert left smiling, heedless of the sting in her reply.

'Does he never knock when he enters a room?'

'He doesn't mean any harm, Winnie. He's a kindly soul, and Susan his wife is ill in bed. She hasn't spoken to a woman for a very long time, and likely she's lonely for a little of women's talk.'

She removed her coat, throwing her hat on the bed. She fastened the leather belt around her waist where her knitted jumper met her skirt. Coming close to her, he put his hands on her shoulders and tilting her back, kissed her. She moved her head away.

'No, no, Stephen; not just now, later. There are things to be seen to, and you haven't had any food yet.' Her tones were kinder, and he thought she had passed from the mood of a moment ago.

'What makes you so moody, Winnie? You spoke just now to Robert as if you suddenly hated him.'

'I understood we were to have the place to ourselves.'

'But, Winnie, I told you . . .'

'Now, don't let's start a whole discourse. Show me where the cooking things are, and I'll make a meal.'

Durnan took the frying pan from the wall. Robert told him he had been frying mackerel in it, and that he would take it outside and clean it for him.

When Robert took the pan outside, she asked, 'Do they use your cooking things too?'

He nodded and heard her grunt in her throat, as he went towards Susan's room.

'I want to meet your wife, Stephen, and shake her hand. Where is she? Fetch her here, man, till I tell you what I think of your choice,' Susan said.

'She'll come in and see you after we have a meal. You know

how it is, Susan, with all the fuss of the wedding, she's tired,' then lowering his voice, 'She's a wee bit odd, Susan, and you might think her queer.'

He stopped, and thought about what he had just said. He was making excuses for her, and her scarcely an hour in the house.

'A wee bit odd, did you say, Stephen?' Susan's voice was loud, and fearing it might be heard in the kitchen, he urged her to lie back in the bed, telling her she might catch cold, with no clothes about her shoulders.

'But you'll fetch her to see me?'

'I will, Susan.'

'Do, son, for I'm heartsore to hear the voice of a woman. It'll lift my heart, the bit of crack.'

Durnan left the room, and in the kitchen he heard Winnie ask Robert to move his chair from the fire.

Robert stood up, smiling. 'Am I in your road, daughter?' She made no answer, but kept turning the frying ham with a knife.

Durnan saw she had laid the table for two, and when she poured the tea, Robert glanced at her, then looked into the fire. Yet, as they ate, Robert tried to make conversation about the difference between Irish ham and English.

'Is there a sup of tea ready, Robert?' Susan was calling from the room. The old man pretended not to hear, but he fell silent, and started whistling under his breath.

Never had that happened before. Even in his mother's time, Durnan knew that anyone in the house during meal time was always given a share of what food was going. But maybe she was waiting until they themselves were finished. Then as she rose from the table and started clearing it, he said to Robert, 'Put some more tea in the teapot, and there's ham there if you feel like it.'

Winnie stopped, returning the bread to the table. Then she went into the room to unpack. Durnan dismantled the old bed and fitted up the new one. Soon now she would be in his arms, and yet deep down in his bowels he felt an uneasiness. He sensed an unsureness in her quiet. It dawned suddenly on him that if she had refused to sleep with him he wouldn't have been surprised. He himself hadn't been as talkative as he might, but then he couldn't go on making the conversation. Sometime she would have to start it.

He heard Robert talking in the room, and he wondered if the old man had been recalling the tea incident. Tiptoeing to the room, he listened, but Susan was only asking what the night was like, and Robert was telling her that the sky was star loaded, and there was a maiden's breath from the south.

CHAPTER THIRTY

WHEN she took the blankets from the fire, she said, 'I'm going to bed.'

Durnan remained at the fire, shuddering slightly as the coals dropped, sending a puff of grey ash to the hearth. He heard her move about the room, and first one shoe, then the other, fall to the floor. Susan's voice came from the room, telling Robert to watch how he got into bed as she was feeling worse than usual.

He raked the fire and lowered the lamp, and pushed the sand-bag against the door in case there should be rain during the night.

As he sat on the edge of the bed taking off his boots, he heard her sigh.

'How did the auction go, Winnie?'

'As well as could be expected.'

Silence. God, what else was there to talk about?

'Could anyone see in through those curtains?'

'No, Winnie, not a soul. It's quiet here. There wouldn't be a soul pass this house at night in years.'

'You're sure we wouldn't be better with a blind on the window?'

'No, Winnie. I tell you, no one ever comes here at night.

Even during the day, the postman only calls when he has occasion, and the grocery man the same. Robert meets the breadman at the loanen foot every morning. But if you like, I'll draw the curtains.'

'Pin them together, anyway,' she said.

He drew them together with pins, shutting out the night sky and the shining stars.

He sat on the bed again, removing his socks and putting on his pyjamas.

'Will I put the light out, Winnie?'

'No, let it be. Turn the flame lower if you like. I can't sleep unless there's a glimmer of light.'

Settling himself in bed, he turned and looked at her small face, almost hidden in the pillow. Reaching for her hand he caught it, and moved closer to her, thinking how frail she looked. Putting his arm around her waist, he turned her towards him. He stared at her thin red lips before he kissed her, feeling his own lips press against her teeth.

He lay back, pushing the bed clothes away from his warm chest, his eyes searching the dimly lit room. He wanted space and air, but the room window was covered, with only the gentle bellying of the curtains. The sickly light irritated him. He was nervous, with an itchy tingling in his head.

He breathed deeply. Her body had been lifeless. There was no urge, no warmth, no flame, just a lifeless submission, devoid of any passion. He held each breath, trying to smother his rapid heart beats. She was restless, turning this way and that.

'Are you content, Winnie?'

'Is anyone ever content?'

Must he thole these abstract and cold answers? God, his bridal night.

He must batten her down on something tonight, get satisfaction by all means.

'What makes you talk like that, Winnie? Are you sorry you married me?'

'You trouble yourself too much, Stephen. Did I say I was sorry I married you?'

'No, Winnie, but you're behaving as though you were.'

'Why, what have I done?'

'Well, you don't seem content about things. Tonight, at tea time, you never asked Robert if he'd take a cup, or Susan. . . .'

'I didn't come here to look after them. I came here as your wife.'

'I know, Winnie. But all wife and no woman. . . .'

'Why are they here anyway?'

Quietly, he told her, in detail, why the old couple were there.

'But she'd be better in the hospital,' she said, raising her head higher on the pillow.

'But you must try and see her way of it. Susan has roots in this place, Winnie. If she wasn't near the *Summer Breeze* and Robert and the tang of the sea in the air, she'd snuff out like a candle.'

Silence, broken only by a long sigh as she turned her head to the wall.

His bridal night.

'Tell me, Winnie, why were you not happy with Norton?'

'Norton is dead, and let him be. I never want to hear his name mentioned.' Her voice was fiery.

'But why, Winnie?'

An impatient wriggle of the head, and silence again.

His bridal night.

She was breathing heavily. Why should he have to ask her if she had been happy with Norton? If this lump that was within her was to break, it must break tonight. He must get answers to his questions. She wasn't going to be like his mother, put him off with silence or by telling him to let well enough alone and cease asking questions. There were things you had to know about. If harmony and understanding were the links that held them together, there must be some foundation. She just couldn't go about the house, moody and silent, wearing a mask of sourness. And surely to treat the old couple with a little sympathy wasn't asking too much from her.

His eyes wandered round the room, resting on the curtains. As they puffed with the breeze, he could see the dust on them like stubble. They were dirty. Like the bridesmaid and the groomsman they had this morning. Grey and foreboding, causing a sudden despair in his mind.

His bridal night.

And there should be laughter and gaiety, and song and dance, and a wild yearning, a nervousness of delight, and a great fullness of things. God, to compare it with Fenners. Here it was drab, an offshoot of hell.

His bridal night.

Yet this was only the starting point. Perhaps it was too early to judge. It might be a mood of his own, just a sudden dissatisfaction. In a week or so she might change. But he had just had her, and there was no response, no kindling of anything, like puffing a fire with a pair of bellows, and only the dull echo of the black coal in return.

His bridal night.

Had her lips, her hands, with their fine touch, and her eyes misled him? Was there truth in the saying that everyone in hospital fell in love with the woman who nursed him? She moved, coughing quietly, and sweeping her hair back.

'Are you too warm, Winnie?'

He had to repeat the question twice before she told him she wasn't.

'Your mind was far away that time, Winnie?'

'What's that?'

'I said, your mind was far away, Winnie.'

'Yes, yes, it was.'

'What were you thinking about, Winnie?'

'Nothing, nothing at all.'

'You were, Winnie. You were thinking about something. You're always thinking about something.'

'Surely I don't have to account for every thought in my head. . . .'

'No, Winnie, I don't mean it like that. It's just that, somehow, we seem to be strangers here.'

'We're not like strangers. You've just had me. What do you want me to say, or do?'

'Winnie. What is it that is far back in your mind? Did Norton make your life unbearable? Was he bad to you?'

'Why must you ask questions about Norton? Great God, can't you let me be?'

Her outburst told him he had pricked something inside her. Now was the time to go on and prick deeper.

'I'm only asking you a simple question, Winnie. Were you not happy with Norton?'

'If it eases your curiosity, I wasn't happy with Norton. I hated him, and I'm glad he's dead, and I hope he's in hell.'

She cried and pushed the bed clothes from her chest. Then she tore open the neck of her nightdress.

'Let me rest, can't you? Why all this questioning?'

This was how his mother had behaved. She, too, shook her head in tears, just as Winnie was doing now.

'Why are you crying, Winnie?' But she turned her head away from him, covering her small breasts.

He recalled the words of Mathews, the day he called to see Fenner. Mathews had said something about fancy curtains and silk cushions not making a home. Unless there was a warm-hearted woman you might as well shut the shanty. He tried to remember the other things Mathews had said, but her loud sighs made him aware that he had got no satisfaction from her.

She gathered the clothes about her shoulders. He lay quiet for a moment. Then he turned on his side, but he knew sleep was as far away as the stars. He heard her talking to herself, her lips smacking together, like someone tasting butter. He listened, moving his head to her, but he couldn't make out what she was saying. Later in the night she started talking silently again, only this time she beat the bed clothes with her hand, like someone in a temper.

'What's troubling you, Winnie?'

'Nothing, nothing. Not a thing. Are you never asleep yet?'

Her voice was tired, almost exhausted, as if she had been quarrelling with the strangeness that was within her.

'There's not a thing,' she said, and now her tone suggested that she had lost the quarrel. He felt sorry for her now, and he curled his arm round her waist.

'Look, love, if you talked about it, your mind would be easier.'

'If I talked about what? There's nothing the matter with my mind. Who said there was? Tell me, who said there was?'

'If it isn't your mind, Winnie, what is it?' He leaned closer, feeling her hair against his cheek.

'Look, my love. There are only the two of us here. We are husband and wife. This is our bridal night, and there's not a soul to hear what we say to each other. You needn't be afraid to tell me anything. I know the world, Winnie, and I know what happens to men sometimes. Did Norton cause you any pain? . . . Did he . . .?'

She sprang out of bed. 'Christ, can you not leave me alone? . . .'

'Winnie, is it because Robert and Susan are here that you're acting so queerly?'

'I'm not acting queerly. Is it too much to ask you to leave me alone?' Her lips were moving quickly, and there was a lace of saliva webbing from her mouth.

'No, Winnie, it isn't.' He repeated the words in a vague way, only dimly conscious that he was speaking at all. She turned the lamp-light higher, and stood looking into the flame.

'Better come back to bed, Winnie. Come, you'll catch cold . . . I won't ask any more questions.'

He thought about what she said, of her, saying she wasn't acting queerly. She was a liar. The worst kind of liar. Lying about her emotions. But he would force it all out of her. He would pester her . . . pester . . . until she told him. But then, to pester was to pain. He had pestered his mother and she hadn't told him a thing. Supposing Winnie were the same? He knew he couldn't go on pestering her, either she told him, or she had to clear away from him. His mother had torn one gap in his soul; his wife wasn't going to widen it.

His eyes were warm and his heart beat fast. From far away up the lough came the crying of gulls, and he knew they were diving for herring, staying away from their roosts on the high rocks to feed and play through the night. There was a stuffiness in the room. The grey curtains puffed gently. Getting out of bed he pulled the curtains apart, and stared out at the space and stars he loved.

He felt a tremor pass through his body as he looked at the majestic sweep of the starry Plough. Like a magnet it cleared his mind, studding its shadow on him, making him feel suddenly at rest.

Turning he saw she was looking at him, her eyes wide and shadowed. He came back to bed. Now he would sleep, for the starry outline was shining in his mind. Let her sigh, and mutter and beat the bed clothes; let her do what she liked, she couldn't now chase from his mind the silver calm of the starry Plough.

CHAPTER THIRTY-ONE

SHE was up before him, and had his breakfast covered on the hob. Robert was pouring water into the bath he had brought from the *Summer Breeze*. He asked the old man what he was for washing.

'A shimee of Susan's. I want to give it a rub through, before the rain comes, or I'd never get it dried at all.'

Durnan looked at Winnie as Robert went outside with the

bath, but she appeared in no way concerned. She sat toying with the poker, thrusting it into the fire and pulling it out again. If he had been a woman, he would have taken the bath from the old man and would have washed the garment. But if she felt that they shouldn't be there, there was no reason why she should help them. Yet, there were things that no woman stood by and watched a man doing, and washing a chemise was one of them.

'Is your breakfast all right?' she asked.

'Yes, Winnie. How do you feel this morning?'

'Touch of a headache. I didn't sleep well last night. Tell me, where does that path over the fields at the gable of the cottage lead to?'

'To the coastguard station.'

She helped him to more tea, and he said, 'I didn't sleep well myself.'

'Why didn't you?'

'You annoyed me, Winnie. My thoughts were heated and uneasy.'

Silence.

Then she said, 'I'll take a walk down that path. The air might clear my head.'

'Would you like me to come with you, Winnie?'

'No, Stephen, if you don't mind, I'd rather go alone.'

She pulled her coat loosely over her shoulders and left the kitchen.

He felt suddenly empty, frightened, and he almost stiffened in the chair. A rush of blood came into his neck, making his head tremble. She had left the kitchen with her coat hanging from her shoulders. It was a strange departure, leaving an echo of fear in his mind, an echo that sounded like the beginning of a death cry, like someone about to drown. He felt that she would never come back . . . Good God, was she insane?

He opened the door quickly and came to the gable. He saw her walk slowly, with the loose coat, like a monk in his habit, meditating. Her head was erect. Now and then she stooped to pick up something and put it in her mouth. He watched her until she descended the hill and he could see her body getting less until her head lost itself in the grass. Then he came inside to talk to Susan.

'Well, Susan, how do you feel this morning?'

'Not the best, Stephen son, not the best. But sure I'm never tired of talking about how old I am. And when you're old, and the heart isn't sound, there's always a fear on you.'

'My wife didn't come in to see you?'

'No, son, she didn't, and I'm vexed about it. There's no need for me to be, for she's not a drop's blood to me, nor is there any binding on her to shake my hand, but I'm vexed, just the same.'

'I suppose there isn't, Susan, but still . . .'

'I'm thinking maybe the doctor will let me back to the *Summer Breeze* again, if I ask him.'

'He won't let you back, Susan. You can make your mind easy on that point.'

'He must let me back, Stephen. Your wife doesn't want us here. I suppose she's right. There's no young bride wants two old fogies clocking in her nest.'

If Susan had met Winnie, he felt there would have been mockery in her words. The old woman imagined her as a young bride. The very words stung him, for they suggested love, gaiety, passion, youth, laughter. . . .

'Still, I think it might have been mannerly of her to have grasped my hand once,' Susan was saying.

'Yes, yes, Susan, she might.'

'She isn't natured like yourself, Stephen.'

'No, Susan, I suppose not. Still, we all can't be the same.'

'True words, son, true words. The world would be the better if we were. But if she's to your pleasing and pleasure, that's all that matters in the end. But Robert tells me that the smell of tar is away from the *Summer Breeze* . . .' She stopped, opened her mouth wide, and moved her head.

Her words now ended in her throat.

'You're talking too much, Susan. Take it easy, old girl.'

'I know, Stephen, but what's life without a wee bit of talk. I know it cuts my breath and taxes my heart, but sure, if I didn't talk I'd be dead.'

'Well, I'll leave you now, Susan, but you must forget about going back to the *Summer Breeze*.'

'But Robert says we must go back.'

'Have you talked to Robert about it?'

'It was himself that brought it up. He thinks your wife doesn't like him.'

'Does he like her, Susan?'

The old woman made to turn her face to the wall.

'Answer my question, Susan? Does Robert like her? Come on, Susan.'

'Stephen, son, I'm an old woman. Maybe the morrow or the day after I'll be facing God. I wouldn't like to face Him, son, with a lie on my old lips. So, I'd rather you wouldn't question me further about it.'

'He doesn't like her, Susan?'

She was crying, now, pulling her bony hand across her eyes.

'Say nothing to him, Stephen, if I tell you that he doesn't like her. Stephen, if you quarrelled with Robert . . . it would kill me sooner than my time. For when I go, as go I will, and soon, you're the only one here to keep an eye on him. That's why he's keen to get you going fishing with him, so as you'll be at home. . . .'

'Don't worry, Susan. I'll look after Robert. What did he say?'

'Few words passed his lips. "I'm not dying about Stephen's wife," was all he said.' The bed creaked as she moved her hand to touch his knee.

'I hope now, Stephen, I haven't talked out of turn?'

'No, Susan, you haven't. If Robert doesn't like her, he's entitled to say so. If he did like her, well, he'd be entitled to say he did, no matter what happened. . . .'

'But don't be angry with him, Stephen. He has a strange way with him has Robert. And he has a queerer way of judging women. Do you know why he married me?'

'No, Susan.'

'He married me because he said I laughed well.'

'You laughed well?'

'Yes, that's the kind of queer things he'd say. Once he told me, when we were younger, that there was a thrush's song in my laugh. People would think that silly, but I know him, Stephen, and I knew what he meant by it. He'd always tell you that you'd know a woman with love and kindness in her heart by the way she laughed; yes, Stephen, that's the kind of silly thing he'd say. . . .'

Durnan was silent, thinking about what Susan had just said.

'Now, Stephen, I've annoyed you and started you worrying. But for my sake, let you not question him about it. He's very fond of you, Stephen. He's a great old day dreamer. Before you went off to get married he said to me, it would be great if Stephen was our son.'

Her eyes were powerless against the tears that flooded them.

'You mustn't cry, Susan. Dry your eyes before Robert comes in.'

'You're right, son. It might set him wondering to see me crying. Would you open the window, Stephen? The room is very stuffy.'

He stood an empty medicine bottle under the bottom half of the window to keep it open. He could see Robert washing socks. He watched him poke his finger through a hole in the heel of one of them. On the hedge in front of him, Susan's chemise was spread; it was wide, like a strange vestment.

In the kitchen he lit a cigarette and stretched himself on the sofa. He tried to imagine the cottage without the old people. He heard himself speaking the words loudly, it almost seemed a voice was prompting him to speak them.

'They are gone and you are alone with Winnie.' The words

died, and an awful silence came, the awful silence he had known back in her own place. The deadness of everything. Gripping the back of the sofa he stiffened, almost afraid, as if the shadow of death was in the kitchen with him. He jumped to the floor as the door latch clicked, but it was Robert coming in.

'Would you mind, Stephen, if I held these socks to the fire to dry? I need them soon, for the cotton ones I'm wearing has my feet tortured.'

He bid the old man draw a chair to the fire, and taking one of the socks from him, held it close until the grey fog of damp came from it.

'Changed times, Stephen. A wheen of days ago I didn't have to ask your leave to do anything.'

'You don't need to ask even now, Robert.'

'They say, Stephen, that a wink's as good as a nod to a blind horse.'

'You don't like my wife, Robert, isn't that it?'

'It is, Stephen, though it isn't right for me to speak the words. I haven't to live with her, and you can tell me to mind my own affairs.'

The old man kept feeling the damp sock, and holding it closer to the fire.

'You'll not like me saying it, Stephen, but she's sullen.'

'Sullen?'

'Aye, sullen. I've told you what I think, and you can chide me for it.'

Robert turned away, bending his head to the sock that he kept turning before the flame.

Through the open door the breeze came in stronger, drawing small clouds of smoke from the fire, puffing them to the ceiling. The old man gathered his shoulders and complained about the draught. Before closing the door, Durnan looked down the field, but she was nowhere about.

'The gulls are diving madly, Robert.'

'Didn't I tell you the lough's lousy with herring?'

189

'The doctor's coming up the loanen, Robert.'

'Good, I'll go and tell Susan.'

Crossing to the room, Durnan sat on the bed. The word 'sullen' full in his mind, covered it with sudden pain.

Poor Norton, crouched in the wheelhouse of the *Glendry* and crying out, and the words of Mathews, 'She spoiled a good kindly creature.'

But she would not spoil him. Robert and Susan would live on in the cottage no matter what she did or said against them. Now was the time for him to put his foot down. He would pester her night after night until he broke up this strangeness that possessed her.

Robert was entering the room. 'Stephen, the doctor says we'll have to get a change of bed clothes.'

'All right, Robert, we'll see what can be done about it.'

'We have bed clothes of our own aboard the *Summer Breeze* but they are in need of cleaning too. I think I'll sit at the foot of the loanen and see if I can hail a passing laundry van.'

'Don't fuss yourself, Robert. I'll get you a change all right.'

'God should think well of you, Stephen. You are kindness itself.'

'Anyway, I'll get the clothes for you. It might be a good idea to see if you can get them to the laundry, for you'll need them again. If you ask the postman he'd get the laundry van to call.'

'I'll do it, Stephen; I'll do it.'

Opening the tin trunk, Durnan took out blankets and a quilt, and spread them over the chairs at the fire, to air them.

'What are you doing?'

He turned to the door. He hadn't heard her come in.

'I'm getting a change of bed clothes for Susan. The doctor has ordered it.'

Shrugging her shoulders, she trailed off her coat and entered the room. He followed her, watching her sit on the bed. He saw her lips were stained yellow at the corners of her mouth. She had been eating herbs.

190

'What were you eating, Winnie?'

She looked beyond him with her lips pursed.

'What were you eating, Winnie? Your mouth is yellow.'

She made no answer.

'What have you been eating, Winnie? Dandelion or buttercup?'

'I've been eating nothing.'

'Your lips are as yellow as the breast of a yorning.'

'Are they?' The expression on her face told him she was not interested in what he was talking about.

'They are. Tell me, Winnie, are you not content here?'

She dropped her head, flicking imaginary specks from her knees.

'We are man and wife, Winnie, and we can't go on with this awful whatever it is between us. We cannot live together like this.'

'Why did you marry me, then? I'm the same as I was when I was back home.'

He had no answer for her, and he came back to the kitchen and sat by the fire. He was conscious of sitting alone while his wife was in the room. But what was there to talk about? They were married and there seemed a dreadful finality about it.

From the room came sounds of her talking. Going over quietly, he listened, but he could make nothing of the low murmur. He cleared his throat loudly, to let her hear he was in the kitchen, but the talking went on, and again she was beating the bed clothes with her fist.

He came outside, leaning against the gable of the house. Below him he could see Robert throwing crumbs on the deck for the one-legged gull. The lough was blue and still, and the fields that stretched away from Strangford on the other side looked cold and sleepy and lifeless. Why had she been eating herbs? Was she suffering some great pain? He knew that people in rural parts believed greatly in herbs as a cure for disease. A strange sound came to his mind, and looking towards

191

the ash tree he saw a magpie, its tail bobbing up and down. It sounded as though it was laughing, and he remembered the old rhyme. One for sorrow . . . The bird flew away, and he moved closer to the ash tree. How strange it was that he carried the image of this tree about with him. The nail was there in its trunk, the six-inch nail he had hammered in to make a clothes line for his mother. His finger and thumb were young then and chubby. Now they were hard and horny from work, and he had slid the ring on with this same finger and thumb.

Christ, what did it all mean? Had God left his soul unfinished? What was this emptiness? What was this craving? What was this devil that led him? Would he have to stay with her? Go back to sea? But she would always be there. He could leave her, but where could he go? He must always come back to this cottage. He wasn't one that could uproot and replant. He could ramble away, as Jane Whorry had said, but his mind was twisted round the ash tree just as the ivy was round its thick trunk.

Down on the road he saw a policeman dismount his bicycle at the loanen. The policeman was coming up. He walked to meet him.

'You are Mr. Durnan?' the policeman asked.

'Yes.'

'A short time ago a phone message came through from Barholm. There's a body washed ashore there and the authorities think it might be someone from the *Glendry*. So they want you to have a looksee, just to know if you can identify it.'

'Yes, I'll do that. When do they want me?'

'The inquest is tomorrow at noon. Could you manage that?'

'Yes, I'll get the ten-thirty bus.'

The policeman pushed his cap back, produced cigarettes and they talked about the sinking of the ship. And when he was gone Durnan realized that this was his chance to see Mathews again and ask him about Winnie.

CHAPTER THIRTY-TWO

IN the morning he told Robert that while in Barholm he would look about and see if he could buy one or two nets. But the old man was not so enthusiastic now about the fishing, and he wished him 'good buying' in half-hearted tones.

Winnie prepared the breakfast, and was now sweeping the hearth. She had not spoken since he told her about going back to Barholm for the inquest. She had lain awake, sighing, muttering and beating the clothes. This morning her eyes were shadowed, and her hair was uncombed.

Leaving the house, he called back to her good morning and she answered quietly in her disinterested tone.

He was nervous, wondering what Matthews could tell him about her. If she was insane he could get her put away. He felt there must be madness in her, but then why should she eat the herbs?

Passing the harbourmaster's brother's house, he heard loud laughter. He was glad no one had seen him passing, otherwise he might have to tell them about the wedding.

Winnie would never change. He knew, too, that she'd never make for him the home he longed for. That was evident last night when she beat the bed clothes; it frightened him. Last night, too, he knew he wanted rid of her. But even if she was proved to be insane, he'd still be tied to her.

In the bus, he wondered whether Mathews or his wife would be the better person to talk to. Mathews, of course.

In Barholm he called at the police barracks and the sergeant ordered tea, while they waited for the arrival of the coroner. During the tea the sergeant described the body, and Durnan knew it was that of the mate.

The doctor came and shook hands with Durnan.

'You had a narrow escape yourself,' the doctor said.

'Yes, I suppose I had.'

'You suppose so? Not that I'm taking any credit for it, but

you were in a bad state that night I was summoned to Mrs. Norton's to see you.'

The doctor might be able to tell him about Winnie. Now was his chance, but a policeman came in to say that the coroner was here, and the sergeant took Durnan out to the coroner's car.

He would try and work it on the way back that he'd be in the doctor's car. The sergeant said the body was in a barn about two miles from the village. Then the coroner started telling the sergeant about a poisoning case he had attended yesterday.

They pulled up at a grey barn, and the sergeant unlocked the gate. The body was on a staved door and was covered with a grey army blanket.

Durnan bent over it.

'It's badly mutilated,' the sergeant said.

'Yes, it's the mate all right. I don't know where he came from, but it's the mate all right.'

'You're positive?' the coroner asked.

'Yes, absolutely.'

When the coroner satisfied himself that death was due to drowning they left the barn. The doctor shook hands with the coroner, saying he was going in the opposite direction as he had a call to make.

Durnan asked the sergeant to let him off near Mathews's house. 'I know where it is, and I'll let you know when to stop.'

Durnan found Mathews at home and, suggesting a drink, Mathews took him to a small pub beyond the quay.

'They keep stuff there that a man can drink and still retain his self-respect,' he said.

He ordered a light drink for himself and a double whisky for Mathews. He wanted to loosen Mathews's tongue.

'You'll hardly trouble the sea for a while?' Mathews said.

'Not for a while. But I was thinking of buying a couple of herring nets. Anyone here willing to sell a couple?'

'I think Adam M'Master would oblige you. Anyway it's no harm to make inquiries.'

'What about another drink?'

'Jazses, I'll be on my ear if I sink another double,' Mathews said, baring his teeth.

'Not at all. Have another one?'

'Well, whatever you say. I never refuse a good thing.'

Mathews added water to the second drink, holding the tumbler to his small eye.

'What about Mrs. Norton?' Durnan asked, as Mathews had finished the drink.

'Left the town, bag and baggage, and a bloody good riddance if you ask me. Sold everything by public auction, with terms, cash on the nail. And nobody knows where the hell she's gone to, and, what's more, damn the one cares a tinker's damn, and that's not much. Do you know what a tinker's damn is?'

'I don't.'

'It's the clippings of tin.' Mathews was laughing loudly, with his hand over his glass eye. He pointed to it and said, 'Terrible, I have to hold this bugger in every time I take a hearty laugh . . . She broke a good man.'

'Yes, you told me that before.'

'Did I now? •Well, I'm telling it to you again.' He bared his teeth, and continued, 'She's mad, that's her trouble. But foxy enough, mark you, not to get put away under lock and key.'

Durnan fixed his eyes on Mathews. He said, 'During the time I stayed with her, I thought she ate dandelions.'

'Ate them? She'd stuff them into herself like a bear eating cakes. There's folks in this town would tell you that cancer's her trouble, for she was aye stuffing her gut with herbs and other things that you'd find growing in a grass bank. The school childer used to gather them for her and she'd give them a sweetie or a polite thank you. She used to tell them it was for a pet linnet she had. Damnation to the linnet she had, or ever had. For Norton, God rest his soul, told me there wasn't that much kindness in her whole body.'

Durnan ordered another drink. Mathews took out his glass

eye, and from an envelope that he took from his vest pocket he fished out a cover. He put the cover over the space and pushed the glass eye into the envelope. 'It would drop out when I get a drink in me and am excited. I don't want to break it, for I'm going to a British Legion do, the morrow night, and I want to be decent looking,' he said, reaching for the glass.

'Was she born here?' Durnan asked.

Mathews bared his teeth again. The cover gave his face a ferocious expression.

'She wasn't born in this town, if that's what you mean. She was born on the island of Tamarsheeland, about six miles up that lough that's flowing fornenst us. Her father was a Belgian. He owned a ketch called the *La Belle Marie*, and she sunk beyond the bar. She was done and the arse fell out of her beyond St. John's point. Then he settled on Tamarsheeland and went in for rearing sheep. Not much of an occupation for a sailor, if he was one, but I hae me doots, as the Scotchman said. She had four brothers and they all took to the sea.'

'But how did Norton meet her?'

'She came down the lough to attend the technical school, and got lodgings in a house that Norton used to frequent. She was wild when she come here first. Used to take buck leaps to herself, like a young horse. She was only two months in the house when Norton married her. But marry in haste, repent at leisure. I courted my woman for seven years. . . .'

'Yet she was very kind to me during the time I was in her house,' Durnan said.

'She couldn't but be otherwise,' Mathews almost shouted.

'The day that the other young fellow and you were brought here, the doctor went straight to her house and told her to get a bed ready. That's why she took you in, because the doctor ordered it. And if she had played any of her tricks, Dr. Grant's the very boy to give her a showing up. She knows what side her bread's buttered on when Dr. Grant's about. He's the most powerful man in this town and the next seven to it . . . But she isn't worth the breath we've wasted. Let me get you another drink.'

'No, I don't want any more. Let's go and see if we can buy the nets.'

'Right you are. I'll take you straight to Adam M'Master.'

M'Master was a small man, with a huge nose and no teeth. When Durnan bought the nets, M'Master told him he would get them delivered for him.

'Now you'll come to my place for something to eat,' Mathews said.

But he told Mathews he had to hurry back, and Mathews told him never to be a stranger in Barholm as long as his house was there.

He had got nothing definite from Mathews. Still, he thought, there must be truth in one thing or the other. Either there was a touch of madness, or a touch of cancer. He knew that country people had a way of finding out things.

Again, Winnie came from a small island, where the people were few, with no doctors, or medicine shops, and where herbs were eaten as a cure for most ills. He knew that old habits and superstitions lived in these remote parts. He made up his mind to tell her what Mathews had said. If what Mathews had said wasn't true, her denial might give him some clue.

Susan was calling from the kitchen when he got back. She was wanting to know if there was any sign of Robert, as he had crossed the fields to talk to the Canon about his baptism.

'No, Susan, there's neither sight nor sign of him, yet.'

'Maybe he'll be late. Likely the Canon will be asking him about the prayers and telling him how to be a Catholic.'

'There's nobody here at all, Susan?'

'Your wife went out early, and I haven't heard her since. Would you shut the window, son? The draught is strong and cutting.'

He closed the window. Then he gathered the clothes about the old woman's shoulders.

'She hasn't been in to see you yet, Susan?'

'No, son. The doctor was here today, and warned me against spending my strength through talking too much. But he won't let me back to the *Summer Breeze*.'

'Yes, Susan, I knew. . . .'

'I see you're in no mood for talk. I can see it in your face. Your face is pale. You're not sickly, are you?'

'No, no, Susan; I'm all right.' But he was restless, and came back to the kitchen. He sat staring at the fire, seeing the smoke force itself through the coal, and curl madly up the chimney. The silence was burning in his ears again, the awful silence he knew back in her home. Footsteps on the gravel made him turn, and the door opened and she came in.

'You've got back,' she said quietly, walking to the room. He saw she had four dandelions in her hand.

'Yes, I've got back,' he called after her.

'Have you had anything to eat?' There was a weariness in her voice.

He felt he wanted to shout at her. But what could he shout? His mind was fogged. He got up and entered the room. Now he knew what he wanted to shout. He wanted to scream it at the top of his voice. To yell at her that she was mad, and tell her to clear away from his sight. You're mad, you bitch. You fooled me, get away from me. . . .

She was bent over the pillows, pushing the dandelions under them. He called her name quietly, and she looked round at him. He closed the room door, and pulling the pillow to the floor he pointed to the drooping and crumpled dandelions.

'What are these yellow flowers doing here, Winnie?'

'What harm are they doing you?'

'No harm. I just want to know what they are doing here?'

No answer was forming on her face. Her lips were set and a disinterested expression in her eyes. She looked away from him, to the window.

'Winnie, once and for all, this has got to stop.'

'What has got to stop?' she was suddenly attentive.

'This must stop, and it must stop tonight.'

She leaned her head back with a slow defiance.

'I was in Barholm today, Winnie. I had a talk with Mathews, and the conversation drifted to you.'

'You had little to do with your time,' she said.

'Perhaps I had. But Mathews told me two things.'

'What were they?' Patches of red flooded her cheeks and her head shook, almost jumped.

'He told me two things . . . one was you were bad with cancer, the other . . . well, I don't like to say it . . .' He felt suddenly beaten. Why couldn't he have said it?

'Tell me what he said. I want no honeyed words from you. Tell me what he said.' Her voice rose to a scream and anger darkened her eyes.

'He said you were mad.' Now he had spat the words at her. She made for the door, but he stepped back, preventing her from getting near it.

'Yes, Winnie, that's what he told me. You are going to answer me. I married you. I can't tell why. I just can't . . . If it's cancer, we must see a doctor . . . but if it's madness you must get away from here. . . .'

She moved back towards the window. She was like an animal. Her face seemed to get smaller and pointed, her cheek bones shot out making a curious hollow in her cheeks. Her eyes widened, and were shiny, like the eyes of a rat at night. There were no words forming in them, and they seemed at that moment to reflect her trouble. In an instant he knew Mathews was right. It was madness.

'Are you going to answer me, Winnie?'

She stamped her heel on the floor. 'I'll go back to Barholm, and tear the eyes out of that blind liar.'

'No, Winnie, you won't. Let us sit by the bed and talk it over. Make the most of a bad bargain. Christ, what else is there we can do? I'm a sensible fellow, Winnie. Surely there's a way out that will be best for both of us. Now, love, let's take things calmly. Why do you eat dandelions? Did you do it on Tamarsheeland for any particular purpose?'

'I wasn't eating dandelions.'

'Look, Winnie, God above me, I'm not blind. You have them there, look, four of them on the bed. Why do you eat them? If it's cancer, do you eat them to relieve your pain?'

She sprang from the window, but he caught her hand as she tried to open the door. Her face was close to him, and he could see the film of green that stained her teeth and gums. Curling her arms behind her back, he looked into her eyes as he forced her towards him.

'Is it as Mathews said? Is it madness, Winnie?'

She tried to force herself from his grip. He tightened his hold. Then he felt the sharp point of her shoe stinging his shin. But he caught her again, and she fell to her knees. Now she was scoring his hands with her teeth, as a rat might gnaw a turnip.

He threw her from him, and she got to her feet quickly, making for the small dressing-table. Jesus, she had picked up the razor that lay in the cracked soap dish. With his arms outstretched, he watched her swing the razor in the air as she came towards him. He reached out to catch her arm, but her hand came down quickly and the razor cut into his chin, and blood spurted from it to her face. He felt his eyes close for an instant, then a sharp pain burned in his face, and twisting her wrist she turned, and her back fell against him. Then he curled his fingers around her neck. Crushing his teeth together, he cried out, 'You witch, you wicked witch . . . A witch, that's what you are . . .' He felt his arms tremble with effort as his hands curled tighter on her neck. Then she ceased kicking, and he let her fall in a heap at his feet. . . .

He nearly fell over her body as he staggered to the dressing-table to look at the gash in his chin. On the mantelpiece some envelopes lay. Tearing the flap from one of them, he wet it and covered the wound. Then he sat on the bed, trembling. What had happened? She had screamed and the scream seemed to be in the room with him. God, what was it? Had Susan heard it? It seemed to be there filling the room in a strange way. He looked at his hands, they were warm and sticky with the blood. The paper fell from his chin, and he tore another envelope. He wanted some flour but he was afraid to go to the kitchen in case Susan had heard the scream. But Robert would soon be back and he must see to the wound. He tiptoed to the kitchen, and got the flour. Susan was calling out, 'Is that you back, Robert?'

But he made no answer as he tiptoed into the room again, and started to fill the split in his chin with the flour. His legs felt weak and his hands trembled. He wanted to fling himself on the bed, but he knew he must stop the flow of blood. He opened the window, and the cry of a wood pigeon suddenly soothed him. Then he looked at the coloured sill, at the drops of blood losing their redness as they flattened themselves into black blobs on its cream top.

For ten minutes he forced the flour into the cut. Then he tore another flap from an envelope, and this time the blood had ceased.

CHAPTER THIRTY-THREE

TURNING slowly, Durnan looked down at where she lay. She was on her side, with her legs gathered, her heels almost touching her hips. Her hair shivered along the floor as the draught coming from underneath the door caught it. Lifting her on to the bed, he stared at her bosom. He wasn't sure whether she was breathing or not. His eyes were warm and misty, and as he blinked to clear them they seemed to get worse. Her skirt bulged where it met her jumper. Then he pulled the skirt off. Her underskirt was silky and it rose where her bosom puffed, clinging to her flesh like a cushion cover, just as smooth and as lifeless. She was dead. A voice within him whispered the words through his brain. In a dazed way he took the small mirror from the wall and held it close to her mouth. It was opened a little, and he saw her teeth with their wash of green, and the pin heads of dandelion in their spaces, reflected in the glass. He saw the dark flesh around her eyes, wrinkled and coloured like a fig. He took the glass away and examined it, but its silver clear surface was unfogged.

She would trouble him no more. But the echo of her scream still tingled in the room. Had Susan heard it? He looked at her still body. The scream had come up her throat, a loud yell, that had carried with it the last breath of her body, the last beat of her heart . . . but she was dead now, and she would scream no more. Even the drooping dandelions beside her head spoke of the silence.

He came into the kitchen and crossed to Susan's room. The old woman had her hands outside the bed clothes, fingering her beads.

'Is there sight or sign of Robert, yet?'

'No, Susan. But don't worry yourself. He'll come back, all right.'

'Did you cut yourself while shaving, Stephen? There's a trickle of dried blood under your chin.'

'Yes, Susan, I cut myself; the razor was too pointed.'

'I do often wonder how Robert manages, and his hand so shaky,' she said.

'Did you hear anything, Susan?'

She looked at him, and shook her head.

'I heard nothing but the scream of the gulls. But it's queer, son, what happens when you're old. I do be lying here, maybe in a doze for five minutes and when I waken, I think I have slept the round of the clock. And when I'm awake and Robert not here, every minute seems like eternity.'

'I'll go outside, Susan, and see if Robert's coming.' He left

202

the room. And in the kitchen he dipped his hand in the water bucket and washed the dried ribbon of blood from under his chin. He was glad Susan hadn't heard the scream. If she had he wasn't sure now whether she would mention it.

From the open doorway he looked down at the lough flowing as swiftly as its current-pocked face would let it. The evening heaviness of the fields made the atmosphere thick with a broody silence, as if everything was asleep on the land. Again the wild pigeon cried out its doleful lament, seeming to praise the gloomy silence. Here in this spot he felt remote from everything. He felt suddenly confident and relaxed with a sweet tiredness in his body. She was dead. The woman he married in the dismal church. He hated to think of her as his wife. Dead, he whispered the word softly. He had choked her. Again he whispered the word 'choked' softly, It wasn't an ugly word, and then a sudden pain stabbed into his bowels, filling him with a terrific warmth, when the word murder gripped his brain.

He had murdered her. Murdered her. These quiet fields would be searched, the silent cottage turned inside out, the hedges combed, every footprint examined, Susan and Robert questioned and re-questioned, until these tall men from the city found their clue . . . that was what murder meant. . . .

But tonight he would take her body to the lough. Wait until it was dark and then . . . Now he was almost breathless, and his heart thumped.

Was it conscience? What was conscience? He leaned against the wall, breathing deeply, to clear his mind. He had felt all right until the word murder curled round his brain. He must purge the word out of his head, and think of her as being dead, and still in the room. He could purge it away. The air soothed him, and he brought his hand to his chin, feeling the wrinkled flap of the envelope on his chin. He must keep his mind clear. He was all right. Everything about him, he knew. The lough and the robin on the twig opposite and the cormorant diving beyond the stern of the *Summer Breeze*, and the spider feeling its way up the wall, and tonight he would lift her in his arms and throw her into the lough, and Robert was coming round the gable.

'Well, Stephen, taking a breather?' the old man asked.

'Yes, Robert.'

'Well, next week I'm gonna be baptized, Stephen.'

In the kitchen, Robert busied himself with making tea, calling to Susan what the Canon had said to him.

Durnan had a sudden urge to go to the beach to find out where he would throw her body. An uneasiness was gnawing somewhere at the back of his mind. He felt that Robert might make his way to the room. No, it was better to wait until dark. He knew Robert would never question her absence. Another couple of hours and it would be dark, and the tide would be full. He could take Robert's punt and row out to the middle of the lough. Yet Robert might ask questions about the punt. It would be better to go to beach, just underneath the hill that jutted out above the high-water mark. If there were any questions asked, who was to say that she hadn't fallen from the top of the hill? Yes, that would be better. Wade out and lay her in the water, like laying a wreath on a grave. In another two hours Robert would be in bed. Her body might drift out to sea, down with the tide. Maybe tangle itself in the rocky fingers of the lighthouse at the bar. If that happened that was the last of her: but if her body was washed ashore, what then . . . ? His uneasiness left him as he stared down at the lough, aware of the sleepy silence of the surrounding land. If her body was found, there would be plenty to give evidence. Robert could say that she was 'sullen' and Susan had never seen her. Yes. There was the story. Susan lying ill, and never once did she lay eyes on her. Susan saying too, that she was 'odd', and Mathews, too, baring his teeth and spitting out his litany of her madness, and the neighbours of Barholm shaking their heads knowingly.

He heard Robert crossing the kitchen, and turning, saw him make for the room.

'Where are you going, Robert?'

'Into your room, Stephen, to get the jersey I gave you. I'll need it next week and me going to be baptized. I'd like to see if there was maybe a neck button to be sewn on it.'

Durnan wondered if the old man had noticed his abruptness. He said, 'I'll get the jersey for you, Robert.'

'You must pardon me, Stephen. But I keep forgetting you are married. . . .'

'It's all right, Robert. I'll get the jersey for you.'

He was glad now he hadn't left the kitchen. Robert would have seen her in the bed, and it was best for his own plans that the old man didn't see her.

He took the jersey from the drawer and threw it to Robert, shouting jovially, 'Here you are old sport, catch.'

Robert thanked him and took the jersey down to Susan.

Durnan came into the room again, and looked at her still body. In such a short time the make-up of death was upon her. Her flesh was cold, her lower lip slightly blackened, and trying to force itself under her top teeth. Her neck, where his hands had crushed it was becoming brown, like the colour of a codfish fresh from the sea. Her stockings were wrinkled and loose on her legs, making him feel her flesh was shrinking.

He put his hand on her head, feeling it all over with his flat palm. It bulged at the back, reminding him of the stern of a ship, not massive, but shaped like one. Her hair was flecked with dandruff, like fine sugar. It was a small head, and the hair grew firmly out of her mousey grey skull. Inside this head what was wrong? Something in this small skull, no bigger than the coconut she talked of when telling him about Norton. What was it? In the mass of something that was inside this little round thing, there must be a tiny part of it in rebellion. God, could it not have come out? Such a small head. . . .

Or was it down in her bosom. Was it cancer that burned within her? Cancer, with its mad heat, poker hot, piercing her bowels with its black finger of pain. Stabbing her, until she shivered and beat the bed clothes with her closed hands. He touched her bosom. There was still a trace of heat, but it was going, and he was unsure whether it was the warmth of his own hand that misled him. Her bosom was small. She was dead. Her spirit or soul had gone. Was it with God? Could she see him now, as he touched her? He became afraid, and he suddenly thought of the hymn he had heard when he went to church with the Fenners. 'Et Exspecto Resurrectionem Mortuorum . . .'

Now he wanted to cry out. In that moment he believed in God. He wanted to cry out, like Fenner, for Jesus to have mercy on him. He trembled. If he was out of the room he might be all right. It was looking at her body that was doing it. Her dead body twisting itself inside him. He must get out. His eyes watered and the back of his head tightened.

Again he opened the front door. The moon was gathering her brilliance from the fading evening. Its rising brightness made him impatient. He must get her body away from the house. He was breaking down. He tried to clear his mind, asking himself was it fear? No, it wasn't fear. He had crushed the life out of her . . . Christ, was he mad himself? He was cold, right down his back, and there was icy sweat oozing from his forehead and his hands.

For a long time he sat over the fire; the heat burning into his face soothed his mind. Then he came to the door again. The lough reflected the bright moon, causing a grey clearness. Looking up at the sky he saw it was close and even with no clouds to kill, even for a moment, the brilliant moon.

Everything was quiet, except the sighing of the now ebbing tide. The old couple in the room spoke in low contented murmurings, like the purring of cats. He must get it over. Take her body underneath the hill and wade into the water with it.

Wrapping her body in a grey blanket he left the house, tiptoeing across the kitchen. He was excited and warm, and his heart seemed to beat in his ears. Pausing at the end of the loanen he listened, but all he heard was the cry of the wood pigeon.

Her body was heavy, and her hair shook itself out of the blanket with the movements of his arms. As he stumbled down the beach the blanket became loose and he stood on the end of it, making a loud noise on the gravel as he tried to keep from falling. Again he paused, hearing nothing but the reassuring cry of the pigeon.

Sweat was running down his cheeks, and a long tear of it tickled his back. He was close to the hill, and only a few yards away from the water. He felt a stone in his shoe, pressing against the ball of his foot, making him nearly cry out.

Now the water was flooding his shoes, chilling his body. His trousers swelled as it curled above his knees. The water was over his knees, creeping to his thighs. Bending easily he laid her body in the water. It sank quietly. Her shoe buckle flashed for an instant, like the belly of a small fish.

He gathered the blanket to his chest, in a ball, and stood listening. Bubbles tapped the surface. The moon got brighter, lighting the dark balloon the water was making in her skirt. It was getting smaller until it looked like a little hump no bigger than a clam shell. Her hair was last to disappear, like a sudden sigh the water seemed to suck it down in triumph. Now all he heard was the drip, drip, of the wet blanket.

He hurried up the beach. The one-legged gull flew from the bowsprit of the *Summer Breeze*, crying loudly. He stopped, angry with the gull for shattering the silence. In front of him the hedges seemed to move like humans. He must control himself, get back to the cottage and remove his wet trousers.

He steadied himself, waiting till all was quiet again. She was in the water, and there was no need for him to get frightened. If anyone saw him on the beach, what would it matter? He hadn't to explain why he was there.

Throwing his head back he walked boldly, stopping before he entered the loanen to look left and right on the road.

When he reached the cottage he paused and looked down at the lough. He wasn't sure now where he had thrown her. His eyes were warm and all he could see was black shadows on the water. He hurried through the kitchen into the bedroom to change his trousers. Taking his wet pants he wrung them into the flower pot at the window. Then he heated the smoothing iron and pressed them until they were warm and dry.

As he sat by the fire, thinking, he knew he must go into the room to the old couple and ask them if they had seen anything of Winnie. Winnie . . . he spoke her name aloud. He felt that she shouldn't have a name. She was just that woman . . . . She was in the black part of his soul, the part that stored his bastardy. He must forget about her. She was away . . . away in the sea for ever.

CHAPTER THIRTY-FOUR

DURNAN knew he must piece his story together. He knew, too, his story must be simple. Like the sinking of the *Glendry*, he must have half a dozen words to repeat. 'She went out after I left to attend the inquest at Barholm and that's all I know about it. . . .'

He must have a story something like this, simple and convincing. But he must see the old couple first. The lamp-light in the room was low when he entered. Robert sat up in the bed, reaching out to turn the flame higher.

'Is it yourself, Stephen?' Robert asked.

'Yes, Robert. Is Susan asleep?'

'Deed and I'm not, Stephen. Divil a wink's in my eyes, good or bad,' she said, thrusting out her withered hand in a gesture of weariness.

Durnan sat on the bed. He said, 'My wife hasn't come in yet.'

'Boy's O,' Robert said, 'and mind you it's getting late on.'

'She wouldn't have gone to the town for groceries, and maybe took the wrong turning, you know, to the chapel?' Susan asked.

'I don't think so, Susan.'

'She wasn't about much all day. Unless she came back from her walk when I was over at the Canon's,' Robert said.

'What time did she leave at, Robert?'

'Well, I was washing one or two things when she left. It was just about noon, for the postman came up the loanen with some Oxo's I bid him get for Susan.'

'And you haven't seen her since?'

'No, Stephen, I have not,' Robert said emphatically.

'What about you, Susan, did you not hear her in the kitchen?'

'I did not, Stephen, son. You know when my ear is against the pillow I can hear nothing. And sure I doze and waken, and waken and doze, until there's times I think I'm not in the land of the living at all, but between the two.'

'She has a great fancy for walking alone in the field that stretches to the coastguard station,' Robert said.

'Well, isn't that her own business? People do have odd ways with them sometimes, but sure they be as God made them, and that's the truth,' Susan said.

'That's true,' Robert agreed.

'People do be odder than others,' Susan went on. 'But as I say, it's their own way of going about.'

Durnan sat quiet, moving his fingers to cool the intense heat that burned in them. He was watching the old couple. How little they knew. Robert telling the truth, and poor old Susan trying to be noble about everything. But he had got from them what he wanted, their simple testimony of his own simple tale. Robert had said how fond she was of walking alone and Susan had talked about her being odd.

He bid them good night, and Susan told him not to worry, that his wife would be home all right.

He poured water from the kettle into the fire, putting it out. Then he went to bed. He lay listening to the murmur of the tide. Now and then a gull cried out and a curlew whistled impatiently. He blew out the light, and lay back, spreading his warm legs on the cold sheet.

She was in the water, her body moving with the waltz of the tide. Or perhaps it was caught in some nook in the rocks. The uneasiness was still in his mind, and his fingers were warm. It seemed to him the stiffness in them would never leave, as if they would be perpetually curved from the shape of her neck. He moved them quickly, then cooled them by touching the top of the bed. But they tingled with heat again, and he kicked the clothes from him, tearing his pyjama jacket open.

Would it be better if her body was never found? Would it? It might be . . . but then that meant endless talk to police, and search parties. He knew how crafty these people could be in asking questions, and they might easily tire of hearing his simple tale. Much better if they found her body. There would be an inquest, with no evidence to show how she had met her death. And the general conclusion that she must have fallen into the sea. His case was watertight. Not a flaw. Unless someone had seen him dumping her body in the sea. But that was remote. He knew none of the villagers ever came this way at night. There were no courting couples, for the simple reason there were no sheltered banks about the place where they could lie and love each other. No, there was no fear of his ever being accused of murdering her.

But the gnawing was in his mind. Stabbing now and then, almost making him stagger and gasp. He heard a noise and raised his head from the pillow listening. It was a mouse, and he knew Robert had flattened a tin over the hole in the floor, and the mouse was gnawing another hole. He lifted his boot and flung it into the corner where the mouse worked. Then there was quiet.

He must get this feeling out of his mind. What was it that a murderer feared? Was it that his crime might be discovered? Was it the constant fear that events moved slowly and slowly until they threw the net over the murderer's head? Was that the great fear? He was suddenly excited, conscious again of the stiffness in his curving fingers. Was there no confidence in knowing that his crime would never be discovered? If he could face the world and say, 'Damn you, she's dead. You may hold as many inquests as you like. You may call in your famous crime doctors, to measure this and analyse that, you may question me until you are blue in the face, but there's nothing more to it than she went for a walk and didn't come back, and her body was found on the beach.'

Surely there must be strength in satisfaction like this. The strength of confidence. Christ Almighty, life owed him a break, or if not life, God did. There was no gnawing in his mind, no craving emptiness when he saved three lives, now that he thought about **it**.

People talked about keeping good deeds quiet. He knew what they meant about good deeds, giving someone an old suit of clothes that they didn't need themselves, or lending somebody a five pound note. He knew the merchant in Barholm when he gave him the money considered that a good deed.

There were others who gave away thousands of pounds and got high honours from the king.

These good deeds cost them little. His three good deeds might have cost him his life each time. He could easily have drowned when saving Norton the first time, it might have happened when he was saving Fenner, or when he dived into the sea at Truro to save the cook from the Danish tanker.

This was a weapon to fight the uneasiness that was inside him. It was a weapon of good. If there was evil in his mind there was good also, and they must balance like a well-stowed ship. God could look down from His heaven and tell him that he had killed that which he couldn't create. He had also saved that which he couldn't create.

So, now, it wouldn't worry him. His only concern was that if they found her body and there was an inquest, as there must be, he must be calm about it all. Tell them quietly that she went out after he left the house and he never saw her alive again.

He would wait for a day or two, then if her body wasn't found

211

before that, he'd go to the police and report her missing. But supposing she was washed in near the *Summer Breeze* and he should be the first to find her? If that happened, what then? No, it mustn't happen. Even if it did, he must know nothing about it. He must keep himself completely aloof from it all.

He must always be surprised about everything. He relaxed his body, and from a distant corner of his mind the voices of the choir sang again. 'Et Exspecto Resurrectionem Mortuorum. . . .'

He was weeping, feeling the tears run down his cheek. He had murdered her . . . choked the life from her frail body . . . but she provoked him . . . Again the gnawing of the mouse made him lift his head from the pillow. A tear curled into the corner of his mouth, and he licked it, feeling its salty taste. Lifting up the quilt he dried his eyes. Then he lit a cigarette.

Was he a sentimental fool? Was it this thing called conscience that was starting to torment him? But why should evil be the only thing to torture him? If it left this awful emptiness, surely good must leave something too?

The cigarette soothed him, and he rested his head against the top of the bed. It must be, he felt, a matter of concentration. Forcing himself to think of the good and not of the evil, he covered himself again, his mind taken up with the loud noises of the hungry mouse. Then for a moment he wondered if it mightn't be a rat, the sounds were so loud. In his mind he saw the pointed snout of the animal tearing at the timber, and it suggested her face as she had attacked him this afternoon. Then he was circling her throat and she was screaming. He shook his head, and the bed creaked. The mouse ceased working and all was quiet again. He tried to force his mind to think of the future. The nets would arrive, and Robert and he could go fishing in the lough. He would call with the harbourmaster and suggest to him that one of his nieces might come out at night and stay with Susan while they were at the fishing ground. He knew Sandy would be pleased to do it for Robert. He would go back to Fenner's again, and spend another week among the freshness and whiteness of things there. He would keep the old couple in the cottage, move Susan into this room, so that everything would be spick and span for the doctor and the priest. He would encourage Robert to fish, night after night, make the old man take things easy, doing most of the work himself. From this on he would do good, good as he knew it and felt it.

CHAPTER THIRTY-FIVE

IN the morning Durnan looked down at the lough, but the curtain of grey fog hid everything. It shut out the water, the sky, the fields, seeming to wrap them up in a great silence. This fog strengthened his confidence, making him feel it was there to blot everything out. In a soothing way it suggested to him that good was on his side, taking his part, and he felt that her body would be found, but that this fog would delay its finding until the brown marks of his fingers on her neck had disappeared.

This fog would impede everything. No search party could succeed. He knew these fogs that webbed the lough and the land. This fog could get into your eyes and your ears frightening you, making you hold your hands in front of you like buffers on a railway coach. It was this fog that made the locals say, 'Well, it's here, and damn the thing we can do until it lifts.'

But he must do something now, go to the police and report her missing. He must go there and tell his simple story, 'My wife went out and didn't come back.'

He heard Robert behind him.

'Thick as an army blanket,' the old man was saying.

'That's right, Robert.'

'It'll take it a day or two to lift. I pity Susie's breathing. She had a bad night of it.'

'I'm going to the village, Robert, and I'll fetch her some brandy.'

'God bless you, Stephen, for your kindness.'

'Do you know why I am going to the village?'

'No, Stephen.'

'I'm going in to the police. My wife hasn't been home all night. I'm just wondering if anything could have happened. . . .'

'You are doing the right thing, Stephen. She looked a queer person, Stephen, if you don't mind my saying it. So I think you're doing the right thing. But I'm making a bite of breakfast and you won't leave until you've shared it. Will you?'

'I won't, Robert.'

God, how simple things were going to be for him. As he ate his breakfast he mapped out his plan for the morning. See the sergeant of police, then call on the harbourmaster. He would tell the harbourmaster too, tell him to keep his eye opened about the quay in case her body would be washed ashore there.

He knew everyone about would accept him as being innocent.

He was Stephen Durnan, the oddity, the queer fellow. Stephen Durnan, the bastard who didn't know who his father was. Stephen Durnan the harmless soul. He was in the good books of the harbourmaster, and this small wheezy man was the uncrowned king of the village. If he spoke good of you, you were accepted.

He left the house. He would go to the beach and walk along the water's edge to the village, but the fog was dense and once or twice he was ankle deep in water. He came to the road again, a wild delight within him, was it the devil was cloaking things for him, or was it God? He hurried on kicking the weeds that grew on the grass bank. He heard himself crying out loudly, 'My wife went out and didn't come back. . . .'

He stopped outside the harbourmaster's house, but the little man wasn't in, he had gone to the quay. Durnan decided to go to the barracks. He told Sina he would be back shortly and she replied if the harbourmaster came back she would keep him.

In the barracks the sergeant wrote down in a notebook, and

repeated, 'So that is all you know, your wife went out yesterday morning and didn't come back?'

'Yes, Sergeant.'

'Was she given much to going out on her own?'

'She was, Sergeant. She had a habit of walking over the fields beyond the house.'

'Did you not think it strange, when she didn't come last night?'

The sergeant, he felt, was getting foxy; policemen were queer for asking awkward questions. But he remained cool as he answered:

'You see, Sergeant, we're such a short time married, that I didn't think for a minute that she wouldn't come back.'

'She wouldn't have gone to her own place, back home, I mean?'

'I hardly think so, Sergeant. She had no home there. She sold out everything before we were married.'

'I think we'll check on it, just to make sure.'

'If you like, Sergeant. And I'll get back and get someone to help me search the field beyond the house. It'll be difficult now with the fog.'

'What makes you think she might be about the fields?'

'I discovered she was just a little bit odd, Sergeant.' He felt the sergeant's hand on his shoulder, 'Well, don't worry unduly about it. Don't think the worst, she'll turn up all right.'

'Thank you, Sergeant. If you need me at all, or if you have any news, you have my address.'

'As I say don't worry, she'll turn up all right. But I'll check in her home town. If you could look in here in about an hour's time, I might have some news for you.'

Again he thanked the sergeant, and left the barracks. What could the sergeant ever know? What could that man with his puffy red face and little black moustache ever know? He would phone and phone, and then have to say 'I am sorry, Mr. Durnan, but there is no trace of your wife anywhere . . .' And then they'd find her maybe in the sea, and they would think she had fallen in or else she had drowned herself.

He found the harbourmaster at the quay.

'God, is it yourself, Stephen? This bastard of a fog is gonna kill me if it doesn't soon shift.'

He shook the little man's hand and suggested a drink.

In the pub they sipped brandy and he told the harbourmaster all.

'Heavens, man, you kept your wedding quiet, I must say. . . .'

'Well, I didn't want any fuss or botheration. . . .'

'I know, I know,' the little man said. 'But it's serious that she hasn't come back. The only thing you can do is wait. We'll have another drink, anyway.'

There was a silence; suddenly the little man said, 'I suppose you wouldn't be in the mood for talking shop?'

'What do you mean?'

'If I could get you another job would you be interested? This isn't an ordinary job, but a worth-while one, and you'd be at home every night.'

'What's the job?'

'Brandon, the big Belfast building contractor, you know him that keeps the yacht here. . . .'

'I do.'

'Well, he's building a big cathedral in Belfast. It's a granite job, and all the granite is to come from the Jackdaw Island in the lough. He's bought a boat to take it from the island to here for transport to Belfast. He wants a good man to take charge of the boat, seven quid a week he'll pay him, and he won't have to touch, handle or finger the cargo, just pilot the boat from here to the island and back again, two trips a day, and home to your bed every night. You're the man for the job and I'll get it for you if you bid me.'

'I'd love the job.'

'It's yours,' said the little man as he went towards the counter to order another drink.

216

Again there was a silence, then the harbourmaster said, 'Have you had any breakfast?'

'I had, yes.'

'Well dammit, another egg and a slice of ham wouldn't do you any harm. Come along to Sina's. . . .'

The harbourmaster was pulling him from his seat. Before they reached the street, the little man said, 'Don't talk to me as we are walking. I have to keep my mouth covered with the fog.'

They walked quietly, the harbourmaster burying his covered mouth in to his chest, just like a sleeping hen. At the slip they heard a man shouting. Durnan cocked his head, and he heard footsteps coming towards him. When the figure came close, Durnan saw a man and a little boy. He knew the man as Tom Byers. The little boy was crying. The man was shouting he had seen a body.

The harbourmaster thumbed him into the house.

'Well, what's the matter, Tom? You know I can't talk with that bloody fog.'

'I was out there, thought I'd hug the shore and see if there was anything in the lobster pots. There's a drowned woman beyond the *Summer Breeze.*'

'Why didn't you haul her on board?' the harbourmaster asked.

'I was going to. But the wean here was in hysterics when he saw her. Look at him, he's trembling. Sina, would you get him a glass of hot milk or something? I couldn't hold him in the boat. I thought he'd jump out of her with fright.'

The child slid to the floor, green saliva curling from the corner of his mouth.

'Christ, I'd better get the doctor for him,' the man said.

'Now, there's no need to flurry,' the harbourmaster said. 'Sina, there, has reared a goodly brood of her own, and she knows how to handle children.'

Sina lifted the child to the sofa, 'He'll be all right,' she said. 'He'll be fine when he sips a hot drink.'

'Tell us your tale. Where is the drowned woman?' asked the harbourmaster.

'Slightly south of the *Summer Breeze*. Beyond your cottage, Stephen,' the man said.

'Would you go down with him, Stephen, and get her ashore?' the harbourmaster said.

'I'm damned if I'm stirring out of here, if all the women in the bloody village were drowned. I'm not budging until I'm sure my wean is all right,' the man said excitedly.

Durnan breathed heavily. In spite of the few brandies he had had he was aware that his brain was clouded. He must not say anything. The only words he wanted to say were, 'My wife went out and didn't come back,' but he must watch and not speak them now. He would wait, wait to see what the harbourmaster would do.

Sina was forcing hot milk into the child. The child opened his eyes.

'What age is he?' she asked.

'Twelve, he'll be, come Our Lady's Day,' the man answered.

'He's coming round all right,' she said. 'Let him rest on the couch for an hour or so, and I'll wrap a warm blanket about him.'

'Did you mark where the body was?' the harbourmaster asked.

'How could I do that?'

'Couldn't you have dropped a lobster pot, with a bouncing cork on it?'

'And the wean there tearing mad with fright about the boat, until I thought he'd jump overboard with the fear,' the man said.

'I'd go down there and search myself, but the fog would kill my chest,' the harbourmaster said. Then he turned to Durnan. 'What woman could it be, Stephen?'

'Could you see her dress at all?' Durnan heard himself ask. But the man was bent over the child, coaxing it to speak.

'I'll go to the barracks and report it,' the harbourmaster said. 'And you, Stephen, maybe you'd pull down in Tom's boat and

218

see if you can pick her up. I'll get the police out in the harbour motor boat. Will you do that?'

'I will.'

When the harbourmaster left the house the man stood up as Durnan was about to leave.

'You'll find her slightly south of the *Summer Breeze*. That's the only markings I can give you, for the fog is thick. She's near the shore, very near it.'

'Is your punt at the slip?'

'Yes, the black yawl with the yellow band.'

When Durnan pulled away from the slip he rested himself. Thinking about what he was going to do. The fog was suffocating. An awful thought struck him, suggesting that he should hurry down to the *Summer Breeze*, search for the body, and, if he found it, take it to the middle of the lough. He let the thought burn itself out. Then another suggested, it would be better if her body were found. For they could prove nothing, not a single thing. 'My wife went out and didn't come back.'

He started rowing again. The boat was touching the bottom and he knew he was close to the beach. Now he could see the water's edge. The distance was short and whilst he followed the water's edge he couldn't miss the *Summer Breeze*.

He looked over at the stream spreading itself in the lough and he knew he was below the brown banks. One hundred yards and he'd be directly under the *Summer Breeze*. He rested his oars again, and started thinking. What was he going to do? Drag her body further out, or pick it up and take it home, or take it to the *Summer Breeze* for the inquest? And if they should see the marks on her neck, and see them they would? He must risk that. He must find her. Get it cleared up that she drowned herself.

He heard voices, and the chugging of a motor boat. He pulled the punt closer to the shore. He knew he must sing out to the motor boat, if he remained quiet they would suspect him. He called out, and a voice answered him. He sang out again, he was directly below the *Summer Breeze*, and he recognized the voice in answer as Tom Byers.

Durnan listened and he heard Byers tell them in the boat, they must cruise about here, as this was the spot.

He felt his fingers touching his chin, feeling the long thin line of scab where she had gashed him with the razor. Then he realized he was quiet, that he must call out again. He was trembling, trembling with the sudden urge to find her body and take it to the middle of the lough, into the heart of the hurrying tide. He shouted, and the answer came back. 'We're cruising round here, you keep to the water's edge.' He heard himself shout, 'Aye, Aye.' Then the slow coughing of the motor boat stopped, and he heard the oars being pushed over the side.

Standing up, he urged the punt by pushing the oar into the gravel. He knew where he was now. Just below his own cottage, the green sleech that carpeted the stones told him so. Her body must be somewhere here. God, there it was. Lying face upwards between two large stones. He stared for a moment at the swollen stomach. The feet were in the water. The hair was hidden and a lacey web of seaweed covered the face. From the motor boat came the sounds of the oars and anxious voices.

He was about to sing out he had found her. But a great coldness flooded his bowels. They would say he knew where to search for her. In this fog that was grey as lead they might think it strange that he should row to the exact spot. Christ, killing a person was a terrible thing. All the small things that added up. There was still time; time to take her further out. He brought the punt closer, and as he bent to lift her into it he shouted out, 'No sign of anything yet. No sign at all,' and the voices in the other boat answered, 'Same here, same here. Nothing to report.'

How heavy her body was. Strange, that as she lay face downwards in the punt, the water that bulged in her stomach was oozing from her mouth in a wrinkled ribbon. If the motor boat came closer they could see her. Taking the two lobster pots from the bow he put them flat on her body. Then he saw a child's coat, taking it he covered her face. As he did so a stump of a red pencil rolled from the coat, down to her mouth. Now he turned the punt loughwards. Feeling his way out, stabbing the oar until its point failed to feel the bottom. Out and out he rowed. The voices from the motor boat shouting, 'You're going too far, keep nearer the shore.' But he didn't answer, he rowed and rowed, nine feet, ten feet, fifteen feet, now into twenty feet of water, where the water was snail-tracked with the tides; now over the side with her gently, and row beachwards again, singing out, 'No sign of anything, no sign at all. . . .'

She was away now, away in the tides, never to be found. She was his charge. She was the obstruction in his life, let them row and search, row and search, she was away now for ever.

The fog darkened, and it became colder. Several boats had arrived, and the place was alive with voices, all calling out the same chant, 'No sign, nothing to report.' Then night came, and they beached the boats below the *Summer Breeze*, and went back to the village.

Durnan was alone, and he felt he wanted to follow the others to the village. He walked quickly, trying to overtake the person whose heavy sea boots echoed on the road.

CHAPTER THIRTY-SIX

IN Sina's he found the harbourmaster, supping porridge. 'Did they get the body?' the little man asked.

'No. Do you know, I think it's my wife?'

'God bless us this night,' Sina almost shouted.

'Was she such as would lay hands on her own life?' the little man asked.

'What is it you're asking him?' the bewildered Sina said.

'She was an oddity, I discovered that soon after I married her,' Durnan said.

There was a sudden quiet. Durnan sensed in it that the others did not want to talk any more about the thing.

The harbourmaster cleaned his mouth, belched and took his chair to the fire.

'You are still keen on the new job, Stephen?'

'Yes, when can I start?'

'The boat is due here next week. I'd say in about a fortnight's time.'

'Good, I'm looking forward to it.'

'You'll be worried from this on about your wife?'

'Yes.'

'Take it from an old stager, Stephen, tears shed over death are quickly dried.'

'You're a heathen,' Sina shouted at the harbourmaster.

'He doesn't mean it that way, Sina,' Durnan said.

'You know well I don't. It's just that life's taught me a thing or two, that's all.'

The little man stood up. 'I'll look at the quay, and see if they've made fast the motor boat. I daresay they'll need it at dawn again, for they'll continue the search until they find the body.' At the door, he said, 'Dammit, do you know, I think the fog's lifting. You'll be here when I get back, Stephen?'

'Of course he will,' Sina answered. When he was gone, Sina said, 'I'll make you something to eat, Stephen.'

He thanked her. Then he let his head fall back on the sofa. He would go to Fenner's. Tell Mrs. Fenner what happened and stay there in the great whiteness of things for a while. Winnie was away now for ever. There was proof that Tom Byers had seen her body. The other sailors went searching for it. They could do nothing to him. Forget about it all. When it troubled him he must think about the three lives he had saved. Balance, that was it. Good and evil.

Three girls came into the kitchen. They greeted him, and one said to Sina, 'Hurry, Mother, with the tea, there's a choir practice.'

The girls excused themselves, going upstairs. He could hear

talk among themselves about the music, and one of them started humming, so that the others might get the music right.

It was the hymn he had heard Fenner's choir singing. The girl's voice was clear and she seemed to love the words that came so softly from her. 'Et Exspecto Resurrectionem Mortuorum....'

He was crying. Crying with his hands covering his face. God was charging him with being a murderer. Charging his mother with being an adulteress. Charging his father with being an adulterer. Falling to the floor on his knees, he felt his fingers curl around the table. Fenner's voice was in his ears calling out on Jesus. Then he saw Christ, the Christ he knew from the pictures in his school book. Christ in a flowing white robe that hid his feet. Christ had a whip in His hand and He was lashing out, stinging Durnan's ankles. His mother was there, crawling after this Christ, begging for mercy, and he could see his father crouching, his felt hat against his chest. He could see Winnie, see his hands about her neck, and her swollen stomach. Then he saw her sprawling in the water like a frog. Then all went black and his eyes were burning into red bulbs, a huge port light was coming to meet him. Then he fell limp on the floor. He couldn't hear Sina calling out to her daughters to go to the corner and fetch the men, as Stephen Durnan was acting like a madman.